The Kid
Who Batted
1.000

Also by Troon McAllister

The Green

The Foursome

The Kid
Who Batted
1.000

Troon McAllister

DOUBLEDAY

New York   London   Toronto   Sydney   Auckland

PUBLISHED BY DOUBLEDAY
a division of Random House, Inc.
1540 Broadway, New York, New York 10036

DOUBLEDAY and the portrayal of an anchor with a dolphin are
trademarks of Doubleday, a division of Random House, Inc.

Library of Congress Cataloging-in-Publication Data
McAllister, Troon
The kid who batted 1.000 / Troon McAllister.—1st ed.
p. cm.
1. Baseball players—Fiction. I. Title: Kid who batted one
thousand. II. Title

PS3557.R8 K53 2002
813'.54—dc21

2001052948
ISBN 0-385-50337-7

PRINTED IN THE UNITED STATES OF AMERICA

May 2002

First Edition

Designed by Cassandra J. Pappas

1   3   5   7   9   10   8   6   4   2

Any resemblance between the characters in this book and real people is pretty amazing when you stop to think about it.

For Bob Allison and Frank Ernest Hill,
who wrote the original

THE TEAMS OF MAJOR LEAGUE BASEBALL

AMERICAN LEAGUE

West	Central	East
Anaheim Angels	Chicago White Sox	Baltimore Orioles
Oakland Athletics	Cleveland Indians	Boston Red Sox
Seattle Mariners	**Des Moines Majestyks**	New York Yankees
Texas Rangers	Detroit Tigers	Tampa Bay Devil Rays
	Kansas City Royals	Toronto Blue Jays

NATIONAL LEAGUE

West	Central	East
Arizona Diamondbacks	Chicago Cubs	Atlanta Braves
Colorado Rockies	Cincinnati Reds	Florida Marlins
Los Angeles Dodgers	Houston Astros	Montreal Expos
San Diego Padres	Milwaukee Brewers	New York Mets
San Francisco Giants	Pittsburgh Pirates	Philadelphia Phillies
	St. Louis Cardinals	

THE DES MOINES MAJESTYKS

Owner	Holden Canfield
Manager	Zuke Johansen
Starting pitchers	Wade Cogburn Zacky Ghirardelli Bobby Madison
Relief pitchers	Bryce Thomason Rafael Fuentes
Catcher	Cavvy Papazian
First base	Federico Guittierez
Second base	Chi Chi los Parados
Shortstop	Donny Marshall
Third base	Darryl Bombeck
Left field	Juan-Tanamera "Bueno" Aires
Center field	Bill Blyvelt
	John "The Deacon" Amos
Right field	Vince Salvanella
Designated hitters	Grover DuBois Marvin Kowalski
Bench coach	Sal Spinale
Pitching coach	Jimmy Hazeltine
Batting coach	Lefty Peterson
First base coach	Bink Iverson
Third base coach	Dave Morgan
Equipment manager	Geoffrey "Pudgy" Slagenbach

Aside from this sentence,
every word of this story is true.

The Kid
Who Batted
1.000

One

Des Moines, Iowa—April 23

T WAS AN ACHINGLY BEAUTIFUL DAY, the sky so blue you wanted to mount it in a ring and wear it on your finger. The air was tuned to such a fine temperature you weren't even aware of it, and you could practically taste the sunlight syruping itself onto the empty seats. A phantom breeze swirled through the infield as though it had just knocked one out of the park and was taking a triumphant victory lap around the bases, shaking hands with the ghosts of storied giants as it eddied its way home. It was a dead-perfect day for baseball.

Down in the locker room, Zuke Johansen wanted to crawl into a hole and die.

Even the distant but sharp crack of a bat slammed solidly into a ball, a sound ordinarily as melodious to Johansen as a Gregorian chant to a monk, struck him today as intrusive and, even worse, entirely beside the point, the Des Moines Majestyks having dropped into a cellar so deep that heartless wags wondered in print how they could've gotten there unless they'd started playing before the season had actually begun. The good citizens of Minnesota, who'd loudly bemoaned the loss of the Twins when the team had moved to Des Moines and changed its name, quietly stopped complaining. The team's dispiritedness had taken such firm hold that every loss, rather than serve as a rallying call for the players to reach down within themselves and work harder, became only further affirmation that it was no use even trying. One reporter wrote that he'd spotted second baseman Chi Chi los Parados in line at the mezzanine hot-dog stand. In uniform. During the top of the third inning.

Team owner Holden (né "Homer") Canfield, a former software geek who'd struck it big with some Internet start-up and thereby achieved dangerous delusions of adequacy, had sunk every dime of the club's money purchasing the athletic gifts of Argentinean-born basketball star Juan-Tanamera "Bueno" Aires, one of the most beloved sports figures on the planet, if not the most beloved figure, period. Within two days of having dragged the rest of his sorry team to its second consecutive NBA championship, he'd announced that he was bored and looking for a new challenge.

"How about baseball?" Canfield had asked the star's agent, and soon afterwards critics began filling their columns and talk shows with the kind of derision not seen since a U.S. vice president had misspelled a word, something which, astonishingly, none of those reporters and television talking heads had ever done in their entire lives.

As it turned out, "Bueno" had quickly developed into a ballplayer of jaw-dropping skill, even to the extent that commentators who should have known better began daring to wonder whether he might eventually go down in history as the best who ever lived.

Bueno at the plate was like Reggie Miller at the foul line or Secretariat at the starting gate. A columnist for *Sports Illustrated* had written that "trying to throw a fastball past Aires was like trying to sneak sunrise past a rooster." When he was in left field, any ball unlucky enough to find itself occupying the same zip code as the transplanted gaucho was as good as caught, and when the situation called for it he could burn it into home plate with such stunning power and accuracy that there was no need for it to first get to the shortstop, who would mutter *"Incoming!"* to the equally superfluous third baseman and hope that veteran catcher Cavvy Papazian had enough time to steel himself for the impact.

Juan-Tanamera's glove was where fly balls went to die, and it was said that three-quarters of the earth was covered by water and the rest by Bueno, so he wasn't the problem on this team. The problem was that, having spent everything to acquire him, Canfield didn't have enough money left to fill out the roster with similarly skilled players.

Initially, it seemed as if Bueno might be able to carry the rest of them by whacking balls into big gaps in the outfield or out of the park altogether, after which Zuke Johansen would cross his fingers and hope that his other players might manage not to blow the lead the gaucho had given them. But once the opposing teams realized that, batting-wise, Bueno was a lone anomaly on the Majestyks ball club, few opposing hurlers wanted to pitch *to* him so they pitched *around* him, purposely throwing balls far to the side so he couldn't hit them, declining to give him anything hittable, hoping he'd swing at junk but perfectly delighted to let him walk since it wasn't too bloody likely that anybody batting after him was ever going to bring him home.

Which was why the Majestyks won the first four games of the season and lost all but one of the next fifteen: It had simply taken exactly four games for the rest of the league to figure it out. And while the fans in and around Des Moines might have been quite happy to watch Bueno play even though the team kept on losing, there wasn't a whole lot of thrill in watching him get walked nearly every time he came up to bat.

True, at first there was the occasional pitcher who, if he could work up a big enough lead over the Majestyks, took Bueno on *mano a mano*. But the Majestyks really weren't at all a bad defensive club. Since they didn't usually allow the other side to *get* big leads, opposing pitchers stopped trying to get Bueno out altogether and just kept walking him as a matter of course, and so the likelihood of seeing him blast one out of the park fell to near-zero.

The fans, as they say, began staying away in droves.

"MISTER JOHANSEN?" said an absurdly timid voice.

Johansen squeezed his eyes shut without turning around. "What is it, Pudgy?"

"Well, I'm awful sorry to disturb you, I know you're busy, but, uh . . ."

"It's okay. What's up?"

"Well, like I said, I sure didn't mean to—"

"Pudgy," Johansen said as he opened his eyes and turned around, in order that he might fully behold the perpetually terrified and obsequious face of equipment manager Geoffrey Slagenbach, "tell me what you want or I'll kill you where you stand."

"Yessir. Thank you. It seems that, um, there's this gentleman? Upstairs? Who wants to see you? Says he knows you?"

"Does he have a name?"

"Huh? Oh, 'course he does, Mr. Johansen. Sorry. It's, uh, Henry Schmidt, sir."

Johansen began rubbing the ruined shoulder that had ended a career that at one time had been filled with as bright a promise as any in the modern era of the game. "No shit?"

"No, *Schmidt*. I heard it very clearly, and, uh . . ."

Slagenbach jumped aside quickly as Johansen, more than willing to knock him into the whirlpool bath if he didn't get out of the way, strode past him.

AS HE EMERGED from the dark and dingy tunnel onto the field, Johansen reflexively paused for a moment, as he had all his life, to let the brilliantly lit panorama lance its way into his brain. There were few things that uplifted him as much as the sight of blue sky, bright green grass, a huge and imposing scoreboard and even the riotous profusion of garishly colored advertisements that made up an out-door sports arena.

But he felt no joy today as he took in the interior of the Mahoney Fertilizer Stadium, a not-bad venue affectionately referred to by teams around the league, and in private by local commentators, as the Shit Hole.

"Jeez, Zuke, you look like crap."

Johansen turned his head toward the sound of the familiar shout and sighted Henry Schmidt behind the batting cage. "Better'n I feel," he called back as he started forward.

Fact was, Johansen looked pretty good and felt pretty good, at least physically, notwithstanding his shoulder. He was tall—nearly six-foot-three—and rail thin, and walked with a very slight stoop, but that had nothing to do with any specific physical detriment, because he'd walked that way since he was twelve years old, when something in his upper spine hadn't quite gotten around to keeping up with the surrounding parts that had shot up virtually overnight. His salt-and-pepper hair had begun to thin a little, which somewhat enhanced the patrician angle of his nose and comported well with his nearly nonexistent eyebrows.

Schmidt, a former big-league scout now scratching out a living representing marginal ballplayers since an unfortunate incident whose details were lost in the clouds and murk of unpleasant memory, was sweating even in the perfect, early season temperature of the American Midwest. It wasn't just the heavy suit, tie and fedora he always wore, it was because he was fat, in that unself-conscious way that some South Sea Islanders were fat. Proud of it, in fact, since he thought it connoted prosperity and success to his clients.

They shook hands but without warmth, then Schmidt pointed with his elbow toward the bench, his left hand being otherwise occupied with a foot-long Mahoney Dog dripping the bright yellow and orange of mustard and a gloppy onion concoction onto the sand, where they immediately coagulated into dirty brown clumps. "So what's with Pampas Boy?" he asked as he took a bite, indicating Bueno Aires sitting disconsolately with a bat in his hands.

"Man's bored," Johansen answered. "What do you expect from a guy, he gets walked every goddamned time he comes to the plate?"

"Who'd a thunk it?" Schmidt responded sympathetically, gesturing with the Mahoney Dog and thereby increasing the aforementioned drippage. "That kinda talent getting shut down like that, never gets a chance to strut his stuff at bat? Who'd a thunk it."

"Not Holden Canfield, that's for goddamned sure. All's I woulda needed, just one or two more guys can get on base once in a while." Johansen stopped talking, wondering why he, with two years of college under his belt, always automatically fell into talking like a hick whenever Schmidt was around. He looked out at the batting-practice pitcher throwing easy ones from behind the small fence that protected him from line drives headed squarely for his head.

"Yep." Schmidt nodded in understanding as he took another bite.

Johansen couldn't even figure out why he was having this pleasant little chat with Henry Schmidt in the first place. Maybe because there was no polite way out of it. Then again, who said he had to be polite to him in the first place?

Schmidt turned around and scanned the empty bleachers behind home plate until his eyes came to rest on a field-level seat. "See that fella over there?" he said around another mouthful of Mahoney Dog.

Johansen tried to follow Schmidt's gaze, but all he saw was a skinny kid with his nose buried in a book. "Nuh uh. Just some kid."

"That's the guy."

"What guy? Who is he?"

"Far as you're concerned, Zuke, he's Jesus Christ."

"Jesus Christ."

"Uh huh. Your personal savior."

Johansen turned back toward Schmidt and folded his arms across his chest. "Henry, you see anybody standing in front of you looks like he's in the mood for any'a your particular brand of bullshit today?"

Schmidt grinned. "Zuke, my man, gonna come a day when you'll rue those words, when you remember how disrespectful you behaved to the bearer of your salvation."

"Have another dog, Henry," Johansen said as he dropped his arms and began walking toward home plate. "On me. And wash it down with something harder than a Mahoney-goddamned-Cola."

"Zuke!"

Johansen stopped and turned. "Come on, Henry . . . I'm busy here."

"With what, Zuke?" Schmidt came toward him as he spoke, gesturing at the field with his left hand. "What're you gonna do, tell me: whip this sterling corral of high-class talent into a real ball club?"

"Damned good buncha fielders," Johansen said without much conviction.

"*Fielders?*" Schmidt echoed incredulously. "How the hell do you put runs on the freakin' board with *gloves!*"

"Hey!" Johansen held his hands out and pumped them, palms down. "Keep it low, will ya?"

"What, I'm gonna hurt their feelings?"

"Henry, what the hell do you want from—" Johansen stopped and slapped a hand over his ear as Schmidt stuck two fingers in his mouth and let out a piercing whistle, then gestured at the skinny guy in the stands.

"I'm listening to the game on my transistor yesterday in Chicago," Schmidt said as he turned back to Johansen, wiping his fingers on a paper napkin so soaked with mustard and onions it only made his fingers worse. "I hail this cab and I get in and I say to the cabbie, 'Majestyks have three men on base,' and the cabbie says to me, he says, 'Oh, yeah? Which base?'"

"Very funny. So what exactly do you—"

"Let the kid take a turn at bat, Zuke."

Johansen watched as the boy closed his book, stood up, took one step toward the aisle and promptly went down, landing on a folding seat that popped open and broke his fall.

Johansen closed his eyes, the sight of a book flying through the air still persisting in his vision. "That guy? The one who could probably trip over the *foul* line?"

"Kid's nervous. Don't worry about it. Hey Marvin, shake a leg, will ya!"

"Sorry, Mister Schmidt!" came the slightly nasal reply.

Marvin? "His name is Marvin?"

"Marvin Kowalski, yeah. You're gonna love him, trust me."

The last time I trusted you . . . Johansen drove the thought from his head before it could fully develop.

Kowalski made his way tentatively down the aisle, then clambered inelegantly over the low wall that separated the players from overzealous fans, although not from things they occasionally threw. He managed to land standing up this time, then looked around and began walking forward as Johansen sized him up.

He was about six feet tall but couldn't have hit 160 pounds. As he drew closer, Johansen could see that he had a pleasant face, with even but undistinguished features and sandy hair that had never seen anything fancier than a two-dollar haircut. He wore an ordinary plaid shirt, ordinary corduroys and a pair of Reebok walking shoes that looked almost new.

Johansen saw all of that in about two seconds but then found himself arrested by the kid's eyes. Their color was nothing special, sort of a slate blue, but it was their quality of hyperawareness, although Johansen wouldn't have known to call it that, which was so startling. Kowalski seemed to see everything, not missing any details, as though his brain was making an archival record of what his eyes were scanning. When he stopped looking around and settled his gaze on Johansen, the grizzled manager felt as though he'd been staked to an examining table and stripped bare under klieg lights.

"Marvin Kowalski. Pleased to meet you."

Johansen accepted the proffered hand—"Likewise"—and decided based on the kid's grip, posture and gait that the reason he'd tripped back in the stands was because he was nervous, not a klutz.

"So let him hit a few," Schmidt said.

"Henry—"

"Whadda you got to lose, tell me?"

"I won't waste your time, sir," Kowalski said, obviously not feeling that he needed a lot of care and feeding from Schmidt. "Ten minutes and I'm out of there. I got things to do myself."

"Things to do!" Schmidt laughed and pointed toward Kowalski. "Kid's a real card, in't he?"

"Regular riot. Okay . . ." Johansen curled his tongue and whistled loudly to get Donny Marshall's attention.

"W'sup?" Marshall called out from inside the batting cage.

"Take a break!" Johansen ordered. "Kid, get a helmet, and gloves if you need 'em."

"Don't need a helmet *or* gloves."

"Yeah," Schmidt affirmed. "He doesn't need a—"

"Wear a helmet or hit the road." Johansen walked around the cage and out toward the pitcher. "No idea who this guy is, Jimmy," he said when he got within a few feet. "Throw him a few, we'll see what's what."

Kowalski stepped to the on-deck circle swinging a bat. Nothing hard, just some lazy arcs to loosen up his muscles. Johansen didn't see anything particularly special about the motion, and in fact he saw a lot that was wrong. For one thing, Kowalski wasn't fully extending his arms, but rather holding them too close to his body, a guaranteed pull to left field for a right-handed batter, if he could even reach the outfield with that constrained a swing.

For another, it was almost entirely an arm-swing. He wasn't getting his hips or legs into it at all, and therefore had no way to generate any kind of power.

"Ready?"

"Yessir," Kowalski replied, and began walking toward home plate.

Pitching coach Jimmy Hazeltine kneaded the baseball in his hand. After Kowalski took a few final warm-up swings and set the bat on his shoulder, Hazeltine leaned back and threw the ball with little preamble, an easy toss down the middle.

Kowalski didn't move a muscle, just stood there as the ball *whumped* into the net behind the plate. Like most teams, the Majestyks didn't use a catcher during batting practice.

Kowalski took another practice swing, then waited again. Hazeltine picked a ball out of the cart stationed behind the mound and plopped another softy in and, once again, Kowalski made no move to go after it.

"Ain't gonna get any better than that, kid," Hazeltine called out as he reached down for another ball. "Easy down the middle."

Hazeltine threw once more, and once more Kowalski did nothing.

"Fabulous, Henry," Johansen said. "Really, I'm getting goose bumps here."

Schmidt took a few steps toward the batting cage and held out his hands questioningly. Kowalski took the bat off his shoulder, set the tip down in the dirt and leaned on the handle. "He's grooving junk, Mr. Schmidt."

The agent nodded and turned to Johansen. "Hazeltine's lobbing marshmallows right down the middle."

"Course he is; give the kid something easy to hit. What, you want Nolan Ryan to burn a few rockets at him?"

"Put a pitcher in there."

"Oh f'Chrissakes, Henry! I don't have—"

"Goddamnit, Zuke, what the hell else've your guys got to do with their time! You're five and fourteen so don't let's make it sound like you got a lotta fine-tuning to do, so will you for shit's sake put a freakin' pitcher in there!"

"Henry . . ."

"When have I ever led you wrong, Zuke?"

Johansen looked at him incredulously.

"Okay, not counting that."

Johansen took a deep breath, then let it out slowly. It was true; Schmidt had never let him down, if you didn't count that one time.

He looked over toward the sidelines and called out to one of his pitchers. "Cogburn!"

Wade Cogburn looked up. "It's pronounced *Co*-burn, goddamnit. Told you a million fuggin' times. *Co*-burn!" He'd hired a publicist to help with his image so he could land some product endorsements. It was the same flak formerly used by Hamilton "It's pronounced *Jerdan*" Jordan.

"Right. C'mere, whatever-the-fuck your name is." Johansen

jerked a thumb toward Hazeltine, who shrugged and walked off the pitcher's mound.

"Cogburn?" Schmidt said.

"Yeah. Why?"

The agent gulped audibly. "Well, I mean jeez, Zuke. Bit of overkill, don't you think? Cogburn, Christ . . ."

"Was your idea, Henry," Johansen said as the pitcher walked up. "Wade, pitch to that beanpole at the plate."

"Yer kiddin'."

"Do I look like I'm kidding?"

"You want me to throw him real stuff?"

Johansen looked at Schmidt, who shrugged by way of a positive, albeit hesitant, response. By that time catcher Cavvy Papazian had wandered by to see what was going on.

Cogburn chuckled stupidly, a kind of cross between a chortle and a snort that sounded like *h'nrk h'nrk*, and headed for the mound, tossing a baseball up and down as he walked.

When he got there, Kowalski was still standing away from the plate, still leaning on the bat, making no move to step up and hit.

"Now what?" Johansen asked.

"Need somebody to call balls and strikes," Kowalski said calmly.

"Oh for Pete's—"

"Three strikes and I'm out of your life forever, Mr. Johansen."

"Let Papazian catch," Schmidt said.

"No problem, Zuke," Papazian said. "I'll do it."

"Would that be quite alright with you, slugger?" Johansen asked Kowalski.

"You bet."

Johansen exhaled loudly and waved Papazian to the plate just to get this over with.

"Whaddaya say?" the catcher mumbled as he took up a casual half-squat.

"Not much." Kowalski picked the bat back up and took some more practice swings, then set himself up at the plate. "You?"

"Same. How you want 'em?"

"Whatever he's got."

Papazian shrugged and held up his glove. Cogburn reared back and threw a breaking ball that dove down and away.

The kid didn't move a muscle.

Papazian leaped to his feet, threw off his mask and spun around like a flamenco dancer, pointing to Johansen and yelling, "Ball one!" to the great amusement of his teammates around the infield.

"Fuckin' wisenheimer," Johansen growled, and Papazian threw the ball back to Cogburn.

The pitcher wound up again and tried another breaking ball, this time inside.

"Ball two," Schmidt called out needlessly, making a note in a little pad he'd pulled out of his shirt pocket as Kowalski did nothing and Papazian nodded his agreement with the call.

Cogburn then launched one straight down the middle, no sidespin on the ball at all, and it headed for the center of Papazian's upheld glove.

Kowalski swung, his arms tucked in just as they had for his practice swings, and connected with a mild knocking sound. The ball dribbled foul down the third base line.

"Strike one!" Cogburn shouted.

He threw three more pitches—a slider, a vicious curve and another slider—all called as balls. Kowalski might as well have been made of stone for all the reaction he showed, even to one high pitch that came within inches of his hands.

Sensing Cogburn's brewing frustration, Papazian went into his full game-squat and pointed straight down with his index finger, pumping it slightly in the universal "fastball, and put a little extra on it" sign, receiving a slight and knowing smile in return. Cogburn straightened up, took a breath, then reared back twice as far as he had been doing. As he uncoiled forward, his body looked like fifteen kids in a game of Snap the Whip all rolled into one, a single long arc of pure power with his right hand at the very tail end of the chain. The entire piece of choreography was designed to use every muscle in Cogburn's body to propel himself forward so fast that the trailing right hand would be slingshotted toward home plate as it struggled to catch up with the rest of him. At that exact moment he let loose the ball, giving it one last nudge with the tips of its fingers to get that last measure of momentum that separates fastballs from *fastballs*.

Cogburn could throw heat as well as anybody in the game, and while there was a rather significant probability that it might not go quite where he intended, it moved so fast that batters had virtually no time in which to make a decision about whether to swing. If it looked from his release like it was basically coming in the right vicinity, you either prayed and swung away or played the odds and let it go by, hoping for a called ball.

Kowalski swung and splattered the ball over the third base line again.

"Strike two," Papazian said.

"Hah!" Cogburn nodded in satisfaction. "One more and you're back to Bumfuck, Idaho!"

"Iowa," Kowalski said calmly.

"Whut?"

"I'm from Iowa."

"Roger." Cogburn hauled off and burned another fastball in, low and outside, and Kowalski let it go. That was followed by three more curves, all balls, and then Papazian called for another fastball, and Cogburn grunted with the effort and launched a screamer and Kowalski stood there and watched it.

"Strike!" Cogburn yelled, and threw his hands into the air. "Yer outta here, Skippy!"

Kowalski shook his head slowly back and forth.

"What the—?" Cogburn had started walking off the mound but stopped in his tracks.

"Cavvy . . . ?" Johansen asked.

Papazian pulled off his mask. "It was a ball, Zuke."

"Back to the mound!" Johansen called out to Cogburn.

"What the hell are you talkin' about! That was a goddamned—"

"Doesn't matter. Keep throwing."

Cogburn scowled for a few seconds just to assert himself, then returned as ordered. He threw half a dozen more pitches, four of them balls, the other two hit foul down the third base line.

"Okay, Henry," Johansen said as Cogburn exhaled loudly and put his hand on his hip to take a break. "What the hell is going on here?"

"What do you mean? You're watching a guy show you somethin' here."

"Showin' me what? He hasn't had a single hit!"

Royally pissed off now, Cogburn threw five more fastballs, three of them called balls, the other two hit foul again.

He shook his arm and grimaced just as pitching coach Jimmy Hazeltine returned. "What the hell's *Cog*-burn doing out there!" he demanded.

"*Co*-burn!" Cogburn insisted.

"Pitching," Johansen told him. "The hell's it look like?"

Cogburn launched another one, this time under Hazeltine's keen eye. As he came forward and released an inside slider, Hazeltine saw him grimace and also saw him fail to extend fully. "Holy Christ . . . Zuke, are you out of your fucking mind? He's supposed to pitch Tuesday!"

"I know that!"

"Well look at him!" Hazeltine pointed toward the mound, where Cogburn had his back to them and was shaking his arm repeatedly. "Suppoza be restin' up after Seattle and he's toast, fer cryin' out loud! We'll be lucky if the sonofabitch pitches anymore this *month!*"

Johansen could see that his pitching coach was right. Cogburn's head was hanging down despondently and he was rubbing his right shoulder as he hitched it up and down to try to relieve some of the strain that had built up. "Where're we at, Henry?" he said as Hazeltine ran out to the mound to check on his prize stallion.

Schmidt looked at his pad. "Count is thirty-five and two," he reported. "Kid got to first base eight times already."

Johansen felt something electric running up and down his spine. "How long can he keep this up?"

Schmidt smiled as he sensed realization beginning to dawn in the venerable manager. "Forever."

"I don't get it."

"What's not to get? He sees a ball heading out of the zone, he lets it by for a ball. He sees a strike, he hits it foul. He's either gonna get to first on four balls or the pitcher's gonna throw a whole game at once and run outta gas trying to get him out."

"How come he hasn't had a single hit?"

"On accounta he can't hit worth a shit. All's he can do, he can yank 'em foul."

Hazeltine had reached the mound and was already walking Cogburn off, glaring at Johansen and Schmidt in the process.

"I don't get it," Johansen said again.

Schmidt put his pad away and waved Kowalski out of the batter's box, then folded his hands across his ample belly. "What it is, the kid sees fast."

"The hell does that mean, he sees fast?"

Schmidt lifted a shoulder and let it drop. "Beats me. Kinda like he sees things in slow motion. Sort of. Only not really. He notices everything, and it doesn't take him long. He can tell what a pitch is going to do in plenty of time to decide whether to let it go or take a whack at it."

Johansen wasn't buying it. "Wade over there, the guy can throw over a hundred miles an hour. That means it's out of his hands and in the catcher's glove in less than half a second. Now are you telling me that this kid, this Kowalski, are you telling me he can—"

"What the hell difference does it make what I tell you, Zuke? You seen for yourself."

That was true. He'd watched fifty-two big-league pitches, thirty-five of them out of the strike zone that Kowalski had let go by, seventeen of them strikes that he'd fouled harmlessly away. "He can do that every time?"

"Far's I know."

It took about ten seconds for the possibilities to array themselves in Johansen's mind, another five for him to map out a strategy and a few more to ask Schmidt, "What do you want for him?" Johansen, of course, had no authority to negotiate for a player, which was the general manager's job, but there was nothing that said he couldn't gather a little information.

"What's your offer?"

And here we go. "You know I can't speak for . . ."

"Yeah, yeah, and I can't speak for the kid on accounta I'm not his agent. So?"

"You're not?"

"Not what?"

"Not his agent?"

"Nope."

"Then—"

"I'm just a friend. What's your offer?"

"You're the kid's friend?"

"No, yours. What's your offer?"

"My guess, front office'll start him off at union minimum, day-to-day contract, see how it goes."

It was, of course, a totally ridiculous proposal that barely merited mention even as a starting point for the real negotiations yet to come, which would be the GM's problem, not Johansen's. There wasn't even such a thing as a day-to-day contract in baseball.

"Done," Schmidt replied as he held out his hand.

It took a moment for all the syllables of that complex word to sink in. "Whaddaya mean, *done*?"

"Just what I said. Look, Zuke, I owe you one, you know that. You got me out of a jam, and, uh—" He thought it best to leave the rest unspoken "—I always said I'd do you a solid in return someday. So? This is it."

Schmidt braced himself for a storm of protest, the beleaguered manager insisting that no such return favor was necessary, he couldn't commit on behalf of the team, et cetera ad nauseum.

"Sounds good to me," Johansen responded, taking Schmidt's hand.

Two

MARVIN KOWALSKI SPENT his first week on the team polishing the bench with his butt, not yet having taken the field in a game. Given his lack of big-league experience—or even minor-league experience, for that matter—Johansen had kept him on the bench during the previous week's out-of-town stand in order that his debut could be at the Majestyks' home field, however small a measure of comfort that might provide.

Bench coach Sal Spinale took some time to acquaint him with the finer points of the game. Baseball was far and away the most complicated sport in the world, with a set of rules which, while officially occupying only 103 pages, would fill a volume the size of the Manhattan phone book for a full explanation covering all possible situations. Foreigners visiting to these shores were constantly amazed that American seven-year-olds could cope with so intricate an endeavor and could even recite the seven different ways a batter could reach first base without ever hitting the ball.

"And then there's the *ground* rules," Spinale had told him when they were in Anaheim, "which differ from ballpark to ballpark. Take Edison Field here. A ball strikin' any forward-facing green-padded dugout or photographer pit railing, well, that there's considered a live ball. But a ball going in, through or over any dugout photographer pit is just plain dead. Now when it's dead, if it was pitched, you get one base, but if it was thrown, that's two bases. A ball strikin' them guy wires holdin' up the backstop, that there's also considered dead, and if it was batted it stays dead, but if it was pitched, that's one base, and if it was thrown, that's two again. S'ppose you hit one fair, and it gets stuck under one a'them tarps out in the field. It's dead and you get two bases. Now if it gets stuck under a field pad . . ."

Spinale knew his stuff, no doubt about it, but having something complicated explained to you by the Majestyks bench coach was like learning the theory of flight by observing a pigeon who'd just been run over by a truck.

Kowalski hadn't complained about sitting out, and he hadn't sulked. For one thing, it had taken him nearly two days just to get over having been issued his Majestyks uniform. Geoffrey Slagenbach had nearly lost a hand when he'd reached toward Kowalski to try to take the shirt back after Spinale commented that it seemed a tad big in the chest. Speculation had been that the kid had slept in the damned thing the whole time they were on the road.

No, he hadn't complained one bit about not playing. On the contrary, his absorption in the out-of-town games he'd witnessed from the dugout had been total. Like most of the other players, he'd taken to sitting on the ledge behind the seats with his feet on the seatback. The dugout was one of the worst places in the park from which to see the game. Sitting down, you were at eye level with the field. Perched on the ledge, though, it wasn't too bad.

As well as he thought he knew the game, there were little things that surprised him, such as a few days before when the national anthem had been concluded in Baltimore and the home plate ump had pointed to the pitcher to start the game. "Hey," he'd said to Jimmy

Hazeltine, "I thought he was supposed to yell 'Play ball!'" Hazeltine told him they never said that. Maybe "Play!" on occasion, but usually nothing, or they just pointed at the pitcher, as they did at various times throughout the game whenever there was an interruption to the normal flow.

Kowalski seemed to care little for what was happening beyond the infield, though, concentrating instead on the pitcher versus batter duels that constituted the heart of the game. He even seemed to talk to himself, and at the end of every three outs he went back to his ever-present textbook, raising his head once again only when the next pitch was about to be thrown.

Maybe that would end today. Maybe today Kowalski would get his turn, batting in place of the pitcher who, according to the American League designated hitter rule, would be spared the horrible embarrassment of having to bat and make a fool of himself in the process, as all the pitchers in the National League ended up doing except for the rare few who could actually get a base hit once in a while, a feat comparable to a stevedore dancing the lead in *Swan Lake*.

Johansen, like many in the game who were not just hired hands but true aficionados, detested the DH position, considering it an abomination in a sport that, heretofore, had not separated offensive from defensive players. For well over a century every fielder got a turn at bat and every batter had a position to play, until the AL decided in 1973 that what the fans were paying to see was hitters, not fielders, and they weren't going to see a hitter when the pitcher hefted the bat, notwithstanding the fact the Babe himself had been a pitcher.

It was only one of a handful of changes that had swung the pendulum in favor of hitters in the years following the late sixties, when pitchers had been so dominant that fans were falling asleep in the stands. But many felt that tampering with long tradition ought to be done carefully, especially in baseball, where many owners of ball clubs felt that they were owners of the game as well, rather than merely its caretakers.

Geoffrey Slagenbach appeared, lugging a huge canvas bag he'd just retrieved from the umpire-in-chief, which he opened and up-ended near the dugout. Kowalski's eyes widened at the sight of dozens of brand-new but slightly soiled baseballs tumbling out. "Holy cow! What're all of those for?"

"For the game, whadja think?"

"One game? There must be over a hundred balls there!"

"Hundred and fifty."

"I don't get it. Why so many?"

"I figure on about eighty a game," Slagenbach explained unhelpfully, "so I bring extras."

"No, I mean . . . eighty a game? You must be kidding!"

"Average. So I bring extras."

"Pudgy, what I'm asking—"

Cavvy Papazian reached down and picked up one of the balls with surprising tenderness, letting it nestle in his palm. "Fifteen or twenty are gonna get scuffed up and taken out of the game by the ump," he said. "We'll keep those for batting practice. Another sixty or so are gonna get whacked foul into the stands, free souvenirs for the fans, not to mention two, maybe three home runs. It all adds up."

Kowalski shook his head in wonder. "How come they're all dirty?"

"Ain't just dirt." Papazian held the ball up with his fingertips. "It's mud, special from the Delaware River. Umps rub 'em up before the game t'take the shine off."

Chi Chi los Parados had stepped back toward the sideline and was looking over the beverages arrayed on a long folding table. "Hey, Spinale," he yelled toward the dugout. "Why's it you never tell the clubhouse guy to buy no grape Gatorade?"

" 'Cuz every time I do," explained Spinale, "you guys drink it all up."

"GOOD MORNING, baseball fans. This is Skeeter Phalango for KDSM-Des Moines reporting to you live from Mahoney Stadium in

Capitol Heights, where we're privileged to bring to you an exclusive KDSM interview with Majestyks manager Zuke Johansen. How ya doin' a'day, Zuke?"

Phalango declined to point out the results of the team's recent out-of-town stint. He wasn't Woodward or Bernstein, and his job wasn't to nail his interview subjects on hard issues. He was a local reporter for a station that valued its symbiotic relationship with the hometown team. Of mutual benefit to both organizations was the maximization of revenue from fans, and there was little to be gained by getting into irrelevant ancillary matters, such as why the Majestyks had just lost both their road games.

"Just fine, Skeeter, thanks."

"Folks, as you all probably know already . . ."

"Then why the fuck's he telling 'em again, fer cryin' out—"

"Shaddap, Sal!" Cavvy Papazian jabbed bench coach Sal Spinale in the ribs. They were watching the on-field interview from the dugout.

". . . was one of the most promising pitchers in the big leagues some years back when a terrible tragedy . . ."

"Not again," pitching coach Jimmy Hazeltine said as he jumped down the dugout steps to join Spinale and Papazian.

". . . were in a restaurant, isn't that right, Zuke, when you spotted three—"

"It was a bar."

"Say what?"

"It was a bar, not a restaurant." It looked to his three watching players like Johansen would have been happy to tear off Skeeter Phalango's head and use it for batting practice.

"Uh, right. Well anyway, so these three tough guys—"

"And like you said, Skeeter, it's an old story. Now here's a new story for you, if you take a look right over there at Bryce Thomason. He's been working hard all winter and we feel—"

"You ever watch a hot young pitcher like that and regret what you might have become, Zuke? I mean, it's gotta be tough just—"

"You think I regret being a manager, Skeeter?"

"Well, it seems—"

"You think leading a team and developing the roster is something to be ashamed of?"

Phalango tried to grin and laugh it off. "Course not, Zuke. Only—"

"Then have a look at Thomason, watch his stuff. This is a great young man who hasn't even begun to . . ."

"Go save him," Spinale said to Hazeltine, "but don't look straight into the camera."

"Why not?" the pitching coach asked, as he immediately leaped back out of the dugout.

"It's your bad side."

Spinale himself was forbidden by the front office from ever talking to the press, and not just because he was a bit funny looking— with a low center of gravity, leathery face, prominent ears and thickness everywhere, he bore a striking resemblance to a fire hydrant. Nearly fifty years before, moonlighting from the minors as a cub reporter for a now-defunct sports weekly, Spinale had cleverly managed to work his way to Don Larsen's side minutes after the pitcher had thrown the only perfect game—27 batters up, 27 batters down—in World Series history, and only the fourth perfect game in the entire modern era. Spinale stuck a microphone in Larsen's face and uttered a question that had since become immortal: "Mr. Larsen, was that the best game you ever pitched?"

Incredibly, Spinale's command of logic and the language had gone downhill from there. When Mark McGwire broke Roger Maris's all-time home run record in 1999, Spinale sent the Maris family a telegram that read, "I knew Roger's record would stand until it was broken." (When Barry Bonds then broke McGwire's record in 2001, rumors that Spinale had exclaimed "Somebody broke Roger's record *again*?" were entirely speculative.) And when asked by a surprised reporter why he had shown up at a memorial service for an obscure ballplayer killed in an automobile accident, Spinale had replied, "Always go to other people's funerals; otherwise they won't come to yours." It was just as well that nobody but two of his friends had heard his muttered speculation as to the dead man's final words: "Hold my beer and watch this!"

The bench coach was the closest thing baseball had to an assistant manager, and was generally an older and wiser veteran whose job it ostensibly was to discuss strategic options as the game progressed. With two men on and two outs in the bottom of the eighth, do we put a right-handed reliever against a right-handed power hitter who's one-for-three tonight and likes to hit to the opposite field where the fence in this ballpark is only 316 away, but the wind's out of the southeast and he's also a pretty good bunter, so do we play the fielders in or out?

Nobody had ever quite figured out what the front office had in mind when Sal Spinale was brought on board to fill this role, but he loved the game more than life itself, and hadn't even seen anything amiss when on-air announcer Phil Rizzuto, following a news bulletin announcing the death of Pope Paul VI in 1978, said "Well, that kind of puts a damper on another Yankees win."

Phalango watched the monitor and when he saw Johansen's face filling it rather than his own, motioned frantically to his cameraman to pan over to Hazeltine. "With us also this morning is the Majestyks pitching coach," Phalango said brightly. He asked a question and, when he was sure Hazeltine was firmly into a long answer, turned to Johansen off-camera and off-mic.

"Chrissakes, Zuke . . . gimme a fuckin' break here, will ya?"

"Give *me* a fucking break, Skeeter! Whaddaya always gotta go bringing that shit up for?"

"It's what people want to hear!"

"Fine, then *you* tell them, and leave me the hell out of it!"

"You're a hero to them, for God's sake! How come every time I try to give you a little coverage you shove it down my throat?"

"Cover the goddamned team, not me! Jesus, Skeeter, I told you that a million times already!"

"Well, help me out here, Zuke. Gotta get back on track, you're making me look like a schmuck, and Hazeltine's got a great face for radio. I mean, shit, how many good sports reporters you think there are in the world?"

"One less than you think, Skeeter."

"Fuck you, too. C'mon, gimme some—"

"No more'a this—"

"Yeah, whatever." The wide smile clicked back on. "Quite a resounding vote of confidence from your pitching coach there, Zuke."

"Can't blame him for being excited, Skeeter. There's only one thing that can make this team lose its concentration—"

"Yeah," Spinale muttered back in the dugout. "The umpire yelling *Play!*"

"—and that's forgetting the fundamentals."

"Let's take a quick Mahoney Fertilizer break for some . . ."

Phalango finished and dropped the microphone to his side, then ran a hand through his hair. "I brought it up, now I gotta finish it."

"Do whatever you want, but I'm done here."

"In five, Skeeter," the cameraman called out, holding up that number of fingers. "Four, three, two . . ."

"We'll speak with Bryce Thomason in a few minutes, folks. But as I started to say before, Zuke Johansen's pitching career was cut tragically short . . ."

It had become a legend already, how Zuke Johansen's rotator cuff had been torn during a barroom altercation in which he'd bravely braced three young punks who were harassing a woman who'd stopped in to ask directions. He'd gotten more ink about what he *might* have become than most other players had ever gotten about what they actually had. Johansen himself, with what was taken as extraordinary modesty, refused to talk about it, which only enhanced the legend.

The previous owner of the Majestyks had offered him a ten-year contract to manage the club, something widely regarded as a sympathy gesture, but Johansen had proven brilliant at the task, taking the team to its first World Series two years into his contract. Even though they lost in five games, what he'd managed to do with what was generally considered a sub-par pool of talent had been an immense achievement.

As that pennant race marched on, the owner had sold a huge number of multiyear season seats, and eventually figured out that he could make a profit even if his team never won another game. Accordingly, he'd lost nearly every one of his best players to free agency as he refused to meet salary demands, and the team had tanked miserably. As Zuke had put it in a weak moment when asked about the downturn in his performance as manager, "It's a poor workman blames his tools, but these tools are the shits."

That's when ex-geek Homer "Holden" Canfield had put together a well-funded consortium and bought the team at a fire-sale price, then proceeded to blow the entire player budget on Juan-Tanamera Aires.

"We're back in three," the cameraman informed Phalango.

"Okay, I'm done with your favorite bit, Zuke," the reporter said to Johansen. "Need one more shot. What's with this new kid on the roster, Kowalski . . . worth bringing up?"

Johansen shook his head dismissively. "Nah. Just a future journeyman DH to round out the roster."

Phalango narrowed his eyes and looked suspicious: Since when do you "round out the roster" with a designated hitter? "When'd he come up?"

"Last week." Johansen didn't bother to mention that Kowalski hadn't come up from the minor leagues, he'd come up from high school. Leaning in close, as if to spare the feelings of the new man in case he should overhear, Johansen said, "I'm not holding out much hope. Don't waste your time here, Skeeter. May not even play him today."

Phalango turned slightly and eyed Kowalski out of the corner of his eye. The kid was swinging a bat, somewhat awkwardly and self-consciously. "Tell me this is, like, a favor to an in-law or something." When Johansen smiled and shrugged noncommittally, Phalango said, "You're a soft touch, Zuke."

Once his gear had been packed up and his sound man sent away,

Phalango sidled up to Spinale. "Off the record, Sal: What's the deal on this Kowalski?"

Spinale shrugged. "I think we're bitin' off a whole new can'a worms here."

"SUMBITCH IS KILLIN' US," batting coach Lefty Peterson spat.

The *sumbitch* in this case was Sandy Williams, star hurler of the Cleveland Indians, and his method of execution was pinpoint precision that had thus far kept the Majestyks to three hits, three walks (all of them on Juan-Tanamera Aires, to whom Williams refused to serve up anything in the strike zone) and exactly zero runs. The only good news was that the Majestyks were holding their own defensively and the score halfway through the seventh inning was only 2-0.

"Looks fresh, too," bench coach Sal Spinale observed as Williams burned in another fastball strike. "We're not gonna hit shit off this guy."

"Somebody want to tell me something I don't already know?" Johansen snarled. He watched morosely as the notoriously slow Williams ground the ball into his glove, adjusted his jock, pulled at the brim of his cap, took a sign from his catcher, shook it off, adjusted his jock again, ground the ball in his glove some more and took another sign. "Swear to God, the guy's a human rain delay."

The human rain delay threw a ninety-eight-mile-per-hour fastball that Majestyks batter Darryl Bombeck barely saw before uselessly bringing his bat around.

Johansen started to drop his head, but a movement in the dugout caught his eye. He turned to see designated hitter Grover DuBois stand up and stretch in preparation for taking up position in the on-deck circle. DuBois had been sitting next to Kowalski, but the kid hadn't seemed to notice him standing. As usual, Kowalski's eyes were glued to the pitcher and, as usual, he was mumbling to himself. It occurred to Johansen that, as intently as Kowalski was studying Williams, DuBois didn't even seem to be noticing that there was a pitcher worth watching prior to his turn at bat.

"Kowalski!" Johansen heard somebody shout, and then realized it was he himself doing the shouting.

The kid jerked his head upright and attempted to ascertain the source of the sound. "Me?" he asked the air.

"Yeah, you." Johansen waved DuBois back down and waggled his finger at Kowalski. "C'mere."

Kowalski scrambled to his feet so fast the forgotten book in his lap dropped to the floor, face down so that the front and back covers both splayed into view. *Introduction to Rotational Mechanics,* Johansen read upside down. "You ready?"

Kowalski blinked. "Ready for what?"

Behind him, Chi Chi los Parados snorted gleefully. "To paint'a dugout, wha' else?" he sang out, causing laughter among players who hadn't done much laughing so far this game.

"You mean, to play?" Kowalski asked, puzzlement evident in his voice, and the level of the laughter increased.

"Yeah, Kowalski," Johansen sighed. "Are you ready to play?"

As he hesitated, Spinale spat a wad of chew at his shoes. "Don't kiss a gift horse in the mouth, kid."

Kowalski grew calm and stood up straighter, and the laughter behind him subsided somewhat. He looked out at Williams rearing back to fire off another cannon shot, then back at Johansen. "You bet."

Johansen looked back toward the field, where Darryl Bombeck had just thrown his bat into the sky in disgust at the ump's call of a strike. "If that comes down," the ump barked at him, "you're outta here!"

And so he was. Bombeck headed for the showers, which was probably the only way he was going to avoid a "K" going onto the official scorecard to indicate a strikeout.

"Go," Johansen said to Kowalski as Donny Marshall headed for the plate, then motioned for Spinale to notify the plate umpire of the change in lineup.

Kowalski walked up the dugout steps and over to the on-deck circle in the full glare of an Iowa sun and thirty thousand angry Majestyks fans.

•   •   •

KOWALSKI PUT three bats together and swung them around to loosen up, never taking his eyes off Sandy Williams as the confident pitcher blew a curveball past Marshall's ineffective swing, then another, then a fastball thrown so wide the catcher had to dive for it.

To some it may have looked like a wild pitch, but Marshall saw it for the arrogant nose-thumbing it was, a taunting invitation from Williams to swing at any old piece of shit he might throw, for all the good it was going to do. He let it go for a ball.

Marshall finally connected with a slider, but not cleanly, and the ball skipped its way toward an easy pickup by the shortstop and a lazy throw to first for the second out of the inning.

Kowalski didn't seem to notice as his name was announced, although it was a good bet he wondered briefly if anybody noticed his uniform number. The higher the number they gave you, the worse chance they thought you had of staying on the team. Higher than 60 was generally considered certain death. Kowalski wore 88. (He'd asked for 42, not realizing that every major-league team had retired it in 1997 in honor of Jackie Robinson.)

He threw two of the bats away and walked—gingerly, it seemed to onlookers—toward home plate. Williams had his hands on his hips and a deliberately exaggerated look of confusion on his face, as if to say, "Who the hell do you think you are to walk out on a ball field with the likes of me?" It was a standard intimidate-the-rookie look, and Kowalski had been prepared for it.

What he wasn't prepared for was the ump making a circling motion with his hand. Confused, he slowed his steps, then realized he was being told to walk around the back of the ump and catcher rather than across the plate to take up his position. Funny how he'd never noticed batters doing that before. He wondered, did left-handed hitters coming from third base side dugouts do the same?

His mind caromed around of its own accord, bouncing off a hundred irrelevant thoughts he couldn't seem to keep at bay. Even as he stepped into the box and felt the soft ground give slightly under his cleats, he thought about how in baseball even the dirt was special. The base paths and warning tracks, the "skin," were a mixture of silt, clay and sand quarried locally by a hundred-year-old construction company that had begged for the privilege of supplying twenty-two tons of it per season at no charge. A different company formulated the "top dressing," a one-eighth-inch layer that combined calcined clay to retain moisture and vitrified clay for the deep reddish-brown hue that contrasted so pleasingly with the Kentucky bluegrass covering the rest of the field.

Kowalski's distraction, however, was short-lived.

"What the fuck kinda piece'a shit gate-crasher we got here?" Cleveland catcher Jook O'Shaughnessy said, ostensibly to the umpire but really to Kowalski. "Where you from, the Make-A-Wish Foundation? This your big dream before you die?"

The umpire didn't admonish O'Shaughnessy for his verbal harassment, and wouldn't so long as he didn't overdo it. There was a special connection between catchers and home plate umps, probably because nobody else understood what it was like to work behind the plate. If a catcher got good and rocked by a ball tipped foul right into his mask, why, that might be a good time for the ump to take out his little whisk broom and brush off the perfectly clean plate, taking a little extra time to get that bit of dirt off the corner that nobody else could see, finishing up at just about the time the catcher caught his breath and pulled himself together. And if that tipped foul were to slam into the ump instead, well, that would be a perfect opportunity for the catcher to trot on out to the mound and have a little conference with his pitcher, who wasn't in any trouble at all, thank you very much.

Kowalski, on the other hand, had no such implied bond with either of them, and felt himself get a little thrown by the catcher's taunts, not because of the specific phraseology, but because it was happening at all. Contrary to popular belief, there was actually very little of that kind of razzing in baseball, so what it said to Kowalski was that O'Shaughnessy didn't respect him as a fellow professional. "No," he said casually, "my really *big* dream is to hit .223, but you can pretty much do that even if you're already dead." Now the catcher could spend a few pitches wondering if it was just pure coincidence or did this rookie smart-mouth actually know that O'Shaughnessy's batting average was exactly .223?

Kowalski could practically hear O'Shaughnessy's right index finger flick straight down and pump a few times—*Show this asshole some heat!*—and it was confirmed when Williams acknowledged the sign with a half-grin and reared back into his windup. Even though Kowalski was prepared, the sound of the mortar shell *whooshing* over the plate was frightening, and it was all he could do to hold himself rock-steady and let it go by.

The umpire made no big motion, just looked down at his hand counter and rotated a dial: Ball one.

Kowalski knew it meant nothing to the pitcher. How many players had ever swung at the very first pitch their first time up in the Bigs? He steeled himself for another monster fastball and wasn't disappointed.

This one was going to be in the strike zone, about six inches northwest of dead center. Betraying little strain, Kowalski brought the bat around with perfect timing and swatted it into the ground and down the third base line where it crossed into foul territory before reaching the bag. He saw the umpire flick his counter to denote the strike. The count was now 1-and-1.

Williams nodded knowingly: *The rookie's not afraid to swing. Well alrighty then, swing at this.* He threw again, this time a vicious slider that appeared at first to be heading for the center of the strike zone but veered sharply away with less than fifteen feet to go. Again Kowalski stood still and let it go by: 2-and-1.

"You believe the *shit* he puts on 'at ball?" O'Shaughnessy said in mock awe. "Goddamned wonder it don't leave the park altogether. Sakes alive . . ."

This time Kowalski ignored him and concentrated only on Williams, who threw another monster fastball down the middle. Kowalski swung and sent it high and into the left field stands, foul again for his second strike: 2-and-2.

O'Shaughnessy called for a curveball but Williams shook him off and threw another fastball right down the middle. Kowalski swung and hit it foul.

Williams, getting a little irked now, again shook off O'Shaughnessy's signs and again threw a fastball, only to see it hit foul once again.

This time O'Shaughnessy insisted on some other pitches, and let Williams know he wasn't fooling around. Kowalski let a breaking ball down and away go by, and now Williams was facing a full count. One more pitch outside the strike zone not swung at, and Kowalski would be on first base.

A nervous fluttering sound began drifting down from the stands. Had anyone on the field bothered to try to sort it out, they would have realized it was the sound of several thousand spectators uttering variations of "What the hell . . . ?" Williams started a curveball aimed squarely at Kowalski, hoping the rookie would flinch when he saw it coming, but as the ball began moving toward the strike zone the kid swung and knocked it foul. Williams tried it again, assuming the batter wouldn't expect the same pitch twice. Foul again.

The pitcher clenched his teeth until his gums hurt, then waited for a fastball sign from O'Shaughnessy, wasting no time once he got it. He aimed it at an outside corner but still inside the zone, hoping the ump would recognize it as such when it blew past the batter. Kowalski hit it foul. Williams threw another fastball, harder this time, toward the opposite corner. Kowalski hit it foul. Williams banged a fist onto his knee in exasperation, and tried not to listen to the noise from the crowd, which now began to sound like open amusement.

"Get a gun on him, Pudgy," Spinale said from the dugout. Geoffrey Slagenbach picked up the radar gun, ran up the dugout steps and aimed it carefully. Williams threw another fastball and the grunt of his effort was audible even at this distance. Slagenbach looked at the readout and blinked, then held it out for Spinale to see as he went back down into the dugout. The bench coach's eyes grew wide as he read the three—not two—digits.

Even as the ball ran down the third base line, O'Shaughnessy stood up and called for time, then jogged out to the mound to confer with his pitcher, who was cursing and jerking his head around in frustration. Back at the plate, Kowalski stepped back calmly and took a few easy swings to stay loose.

Pulling up to the mound, O'Shaughnessy put what looked to the crowd like a comforting hand on Williams' shoulder, but said, "What the fuck're you throwing inside the zone for?"

"That piece'a shit?" Williams pointed toward the plate with his gloved hand. "I can strike the fucker out!"

O'Shaughnessy turned his head toward left field and sneaked a covert glance at the batter, who was looking around the field and scratching his chest in feigned boredom. "I don't know what the hell is going on here," he said, turning back, "but take something off the ball and let him get a bat on it. Don' look like this string bean can get it outta the infield."

By that time the shortstop had pulled up. "Jook's right. Fuck the 'K' and let's get this over with."

Williams nodded miserably and O'Shaughnessy headed back to the plate as the shortstop signaled the infielders as to what was happening. The catcher twirled his finger inquisitively toward the Cleveland manager—*You want 'em in?*—got the nod, then turned and motioned for the outfielders to move in closer.

Once everyone was in position Williams threw a half-speed pitch just outside, the kind most batters in the league could put into the centerfield stands. Kowalski knocked it foul down the third base line. Williams threw a slow one inside. Foul again. And again.

Now *O'Shaughnessy* was getting steamed. He called for a fastball, then another.

"What's his count, Jimmy?" Johansen called out without taking his eyes off the field.

Pitching coach Jimmy Hazeltine, who'd been tracking how many pitches Williams threw, looked down at the mechanical counter in his hand. "Seventy-seven," he announced. "The book says he's good for a hunnerd 'n' twenty, maybe twenty-five."

"And the kid just used sixteen of 'em," Johansen mused out loud. "Get the gun on him again, Pudgy."

Slagenbach hopped out of the dugout again, pointed the radar gun toward the field just as Williams launched another fastball, then turned it around and showed the display to Hazeltine.

"He's losing it," the pitching coach said to Johansen after scanning the digital readout.

The manager nodded and watched his batter knock two more fastballs foul. By now the fans were on high alert that something was going on, and they began to cheer each time Kowalski put one out of play. Some started counting the fouls out loud, but there was no agreement on how many there'd been before they'd started paying attention, so everybody shouted out different numbers and they soon stopped.

Out on the mound Williams hitched his shoulder up and down a few times, then took a deep breath and almost fell over with the effort of his next pitch. It hit O'Shaughnessy's glove so hard the catcher had to put a hand on the ground to steady himself. As the sound of the impact shot up toward the stands, Kowalski threw his bat off to the side and began loping toward first base.

Williams glared as he waited for the umpire to call him back and signal a third strike. He still hadn't caught on by the time Kowalski reached first, and finally did so only as he realized that the crowd was roaring as if a game-winning grand slam had just flown into the stands.

Up in the press box a sports reporter for the *Register* sniffled once or twice. "Weird," he said, half to himself.

The KDSM statistician sitting nearby shrugged. "Willie Mays started off in the majors o-for-24 until he finally hit one onto the roof."

The reporter narrowed his eyes slightly but didn't otherwise move. "Not what I meant."

Down in the Majestyks dugout Johansen was grinning even as Spinale slapped his back and several of the players, who had subconsciously gotten up and drawn close to the wire mesh screen to watch, began drifting back to the bench, shaking their heads in wonder.

"Bueno gonna move him to second!" somebody exclaimed as Juan-Tanamera Aires strode to the plate. Dutifully, O'Shaughnessy stood up and held his arm out to the side, and Williams complied, throwing wide purely for the formality of it, intentionally walking Aires.

But even as he did so, it was obvious that Williams had nothing left. While Aires took his customary jog to first, the Cleveland manager signaled for a relief pitcher and walked out to the mound, where Williams started pleading his case.

"I can throw to this guy."

The manager tersely cut off the reflexive protest from his pitcher. "Straight to the whirlpool." He grabbed Williams' arm and saw the pitcher try to suppress a wince. "G'wan, kid," he added gently. "You've had it."

"I still got some—"

"Chrissake, Sandy, you couldn't throw a *tantrum!* Now give it a rest!"

A thoroughly dejected Williams hung his head, massaged his sore arm and tried to figure out what had just happened.

In the Majestyks dugout, Geoffrey Slagenbach made a mental note to bump the count of balls he ordered up for home games.

Three

SLAGENBACH ASKED KOWALSKI to sign some balls. Robert Leffingwell, owner of Mahoney Fertilizer, was up in the bleachers. He'd put up most of the money for the stadium just so Des Moines would have a team, but hardly anyone knew him. He called his company "Mahoney" so he could maintain his privacy. Leffingwell wouldn't allow advertising for cigarettes, alcohol, fast food, leaf blowers or dot-com companies inside his stadium, but he wasn't at all humorless, having personally authorized a billboard in right field that read "Mac's Auto Radiator Repair: Best Place to Take a Leak." And, despite the presence of luxurious skyboxes that would make movie-star patrons of the L.A. Lakers jealous, Leffingwell himself was sitting in the bleachers, alongside three or four dozen lucky kids who got tickets he kept out until just before game time, just like he did at every home game. A bunch of those kids—the ones with the best grades in school—would be getting balls with player autographs today.

Leffingwell also lobbied heavily to keep ticket prices reasonable.

As Sal Spinale observed, "We lose money on every ticket, but if we have a good season he can make it up in volume."

Kowalski's debut game had left the fans in head-scratching confusion, but at that point his performance was seen as some kind of perverse anomaly rather than part of a planned, recurring strategy.

The Majestyks had lost anyway. With Kowalski on second and Juan-Tanamera Aires on first, Billy Blyvelt had hit a high fly deep to right field. If caught, that was the end of the inning, but there was no reason for Kowalski not to hightail it to third with everything he had as soon as he heard the sound of bat striking ball, on the off-chance that the fielders couldn't make a play on it.

But Kowalski had started off too tentatively, and only when he heard Aires screaming on his way to second did it occur to him to dig toes and make a mad dash for it even as the third base coach waved frantically for him to for God's sake get a move on.

As it turned out, the ball was caught in right field to end the inning, but that wasn't the point.

"Point is—" Spinale had begun.

"Kid should've been off like a rocket," Johansen had concluded for him. It seemed that so much attention had been focused on getting Kowalski on base that not enough had been expended on exactly what he was going to do once he got there. "Doesn't have to be a Wills or a Robinson, but let's start working on some basics."

Spinale had walked away, muttering unintelligibly, but Johansen could have guessed what he was saying: *What's more basic than running like hell on two outs?*

Kowalski had morosely entered the dugout a few seconds later and walked up to Johansen. "I'm sorry, skipper. Should've been off like a shot."

"What happened?"

Kowalski had shrugged and taken a look around. "Game sure looks easier from here."

Had he been nervous? Johansen narrowed his eyes and regarded Kowalski carefully; the kid hadn't looked nervous. "What were you watching out there?"

"Watching?"

"You weren't looking at the plate."

"I was looking at the pitcher."

"That's not where the play was going to be."

"I know, but . . ." He cut himself off just as he seemed, unwisely, about to try to explain himself. "Won't happen again, Zuke."

Down in the training room Spinale kicked a chair across the room. "Losing hurts worse than winning feels good," he said to Wade Cogburn.

"Yeah," the pitcher replied, "but you can only show you're a good sport when you lose."

TWO DAYS LATER, Sal Spinale stared at Marvin Kowalski as Kowalski stared out of the dugout at the pitcher, "Steely" Dan Andresen of the Detroit Tigers. As intently as Spinale could stare, it was nothing compared to the fierce concentration with which Kowalski riveted his eyes on the mound. Another difference was that Sal didn't talk to himself while he stared, while Kowalski mouthed a few words with every pitch thrown.

"Why's he do that?" the bench coach said to Johansen.

"Do what?"

"Talk to himself alla time."

"Beats me."

"Gotta be a reason."

"Maybe it's the chip the CIA planted in his brain. How the hell do I know, Sal, and why the hell should I care?"

"S'weird, is all."

"Why don't you just ask the guy?"

"No way! You kiddin' me or what, here? Too weird."

Johansen cast a sideways glance at Kowalski, who was sitting with his palms pressed prayerfully together, fingertips just touching his chin. The ever-present book lay open in his lap as he swayed back and forth very slightly, never taking his eyes off the opposing pitcher. Johansen saw his lips move briefly just before the sound of a ball slapping into the catcher's glove reached the dugout. "Looks like one'a those autistic kids, sits and rocks all day and doesn't say anything. Not even reading his book."

They heard another ball striking leather, then turned to see the umpire make an exaggerated chopping motion toward the ground as center fielder Billy Blyvelt slammed the bat into the dirt and walked off the plate, out on three strikes in a row. They could just picture the smarmy Detroit play-by-play announcer mouthing his obnoxious trademark line—"Good morning, good afternoon and *goooood night!*"—into the microphone that hugged the side of his face like a Nerf condom.

Kowalski had abandoned his vigilant contemplation of the pitcher and had his head down in the book.

"You figure, what," Spinale said, "he's putting spells on the guy?"

"If he is," Johansen replied, "his aim is off and he's spooking our batters instead."

"Yeah!" Spinale nodded vigorously. "Maybe you should stop him, Zuke!"

Johansen looked at his bench coach to see if he was serious, and, sadly, found nothing of humor or sarcasm in the man's ruddy face. "Don't we give you enough to do around here, Sal?"

Johansen hadn't played Kowalski in a week, electing instead to get some fundamentals ground into him. Surprisingly, it turned out that the kid's knowledge of the game was fairly solid, and his observation after his debut showing—*Game sure looks easier from here*—explained a good deal. It *was* easier from the stands or the dugout or the announcing booth, where people watching knew at all times precisely what the correct thing to do was under a wide variety of circumstances and were vocal in their criticisms of any overpaid player who failed to follow suit.

Out on the field it wasn't quite that easy. Especially for a rookie who, student of the game though he might be, simply wasn't used to the pressure, the lights, the noise and movement from the stands, and especially the intimidation of the opposing players. Not until he was actually at the plate had it occurred to Kowalski for the first time that baseball was essentially about nine guys against one or, at the most, four, if the bases happened to be loaded.

"What we ought to do," Spinale said during the fifth inning, "we ought to send him down. Let him get slapped around where it don't do no harm."

It wasn't an unreasonable suggestion, letting Kowalski get some experience in the minors. "Thing is," Johansen countered, "we need him now. There's no time. And besides, when he's at the plate, he looks like a guy who's been in the Bigs for ten years."

"But between the plate and first base he's like a reverse Superman," Cavvy Papazian said, having overheard most of the conversation. "Guy goes into a phone booth and comes out Clark Kent."

"Still has his uses," Johansen insisted, ending the discussion and returning his attention to the progress, or lack thereof, in the 0-0 game.

Three innings later, Juan-Tanamera walked, Papazian hit a clean single to right and Bombeck made it to first on an error by the shortstop.

Bases loaded, bottom of the eighth. Designated hitter Grover DuBois was up, having grounded out, struck out and popped out in his three previous at-bats.

Johansen turned and started to yell something, but Marvin Kowalski was already on his feet, batting helmet in hand. Johansen nodded and Kowalski hopped out of the dugout as DuBois, already on his way to the on-deck circle, shrugged and went back to his seat.

"Steely" Dan Andresen smiled, a Grim Reaper kind of sardonic grin meant to communicate malice and doom more than good humor. But Kowalski had been watching him, studying him for eight innings, and was not at all cowed by the blatant attempt at bullying.

Andresen started off with a howitzer of a fastball, right down the middle, which Kowalski, much to Johansen's consternation, let go by for a called strike. Andresen threw the same pitch again, and again Kowalski let it go by.

"What the . . . !" Spinale started to sputter. "He *never* lets a strike go by!"

Johansen nodded but stayed silent. Andresen threw another fast-ball, and this time Kowalski hit it foul. At 0-and-2 Andresen was ahead of this batter and had plenty of room to maneuver, so he threw yet another fastball. Foul again, and still 0-and-2. A change-up and two breaking balls . . . same thing. A slider, two more curveballs and another fastball. All hit foul.

Then Andresen, clearly getting steamed, muttered, "Hit *this* one, muthafucker!" and threw one so far outside the zone his catcher had to spring out of the box to snag it. Kowalski let it go by for a ball. The next one was well inside, and he had to take a half step back to keep from getting hit. Two balls and two strikes.

As the frustrated pitcher took a moment to try to regroup, down in the dugout Johansen smiled to himself and mentally tipped his hat to Kowalski, who had the situation figured perfectly.

There was no doubt in the kid's mind that he would eventually get a walk and bring in a run, making the score 1-0 in favor of the Majestyks, with a chance to score again this inning. But Detroit would have one more turn at bat and could conceivably come back with a couple of runs. After that the Majestyks would have one more chance, and what Kowalski was doing was making sure that, when that happened, Steely Dan Andresen, who'd held the team to just two hits in eight innings, was either dog-tired or out of the game.

Johansen's assessment was confirmed when Kowalski went after two obviously wide pitches, either one of which he could have let go and simply taken his base. Andresen grew angrier and threw two more blazing fastballs, both of which Kowalski swatted foul.

The catcher signaled for time and headed out toward the mound. As the exasperated pitcher, jaw grimly set, ground the ball into his glove waiting for him, Kowalski turned and looked at the dugout, directly at Johansen. *Enough?*

Johansen jerked a thumb over his shoulder and Kowalski nodded his understanding. He turned toward the left field stands and took a few easy swings to stay loose, aware that he was the only player on the field who seemed completely unconcerned as to what was developing, also aware of the bewildering effect it was probably having on the opposition. Trying not to overdo it, he was in position when the catcher returned, forgoing the usual *Are you guys ready yet?* psyche-out routine that most batters would have employed to further rattle a pitcher in trouble.

The next pitch was an ordinary fastball inside the zone and he hit it foul. Then Andresen threw a curve, starting it toward the inside edge, probably intending it to drift in and cross the center of the plate. But it had gotten away from the tiring pitcher and broke much more sharply than that. Kowalski didn't swing, didn't even back away from it, just stood still as a statue, keeping his eye on the pitcher, as if he didn't even have to follow the ball to know it was outside the zone. Full count, 3-and-2.

Andresen threw a breaking ball to the outside corner. Had balls and strikes been called by a machine, Kowalski would have let it go, but the ump was human and there was no way to know for sure how he'd read one that close, so the only safe bet was to hit it foul. *He's getting me to reach,* Kowalski thought, *hoping I'll accidentally put it in fair territory.*

Andresen threw the next one toward the same spot, only wider, playing with the envelope to see what he could get away with. This time Kowalski let it go, taking the bat off his shoulder and tossing it away almost as the ball was hitting the catcher's glove, to signal to the ump that even the hot-dog vendor up in nosebleed heaven could see it was half a mile outside the strike zone.

Over on third Juan-Tanamera Aires gave a similar performance, clapping his hands and loping easily for home as Kowalski headed for first. The Majestyks had the lead, 1-0.

"Son'bitch bastard's gonna brain me now," los Parados said to Johansen from the on-deck circle, yelling so he could be heard over the wild cheering from the crowd. Sure enough, Andresen, enraged but still in control as the count went to 1-and-2, threw his next pitch at the second baseman's head, taking enough off of it to keep it from being lethal, but leaving enough to make it intimidating.

Los Parados, prepared for the beanball, spun away and ducked, then took first on the third-strike wild pitch as the ball got away from the catcher, advancing the runners and bringing Papazian home to make the score 2-0. Once safely ensconced on base, los Parados grinned and touched two fingers to his cap as a *Thank you* salute to Andresen, who started forward to rip his throat out but was restrained by the Detroit manager, who'd come out to the mound to replace him.

The reliever ended the inning, Majestyks pitcher Bobby Madison allowed only one run in the ninth, and the game was over, the crowd reacting like it had been the seventh game of the World Series.

"You did good!" Johansen shouted to Kowalski over the hubbub. Kowalski would get credit for an RBI, a run batted in, because he'd walked with the bases loaded, even though he would have no official at-bats in the game.

"Yeah, beautiful walk!" Spinale yelled, unaware of what, in any other situation, would have been a ridiculous sentiment.

"Wasn't the walk I was talking about," Johansen said so only Kowalski could hear it.

The kid grinned conspiratorially. "Kinda pissed off Andresen, didn't I?"

"Yeah, almos' got me killed, joo foggin' moron," los Parados said, wrapping his arm around Kowalski's neck from behind and giving him a squeeze.

"Sacrifices you make for the good of the team," Kowalski choked out from within the tight embrace.

Los Parados let go and turned Kowalski around by the shoulders. "Next time you up agains' him, he gonna be gunnin' for *you*, kid . . . get me?"

They walked together with Juan-Tanamera Aires toward the locker room. In the connecting tunnels underneath the stadium some fans were milling about, undoubtedly at Robert Leffingwell's invitation, since there was normally no way fans could get in there. A boy of about twelve ran up to Kowalski and held out a piece of paper.

Kowalski took it but it was blank, so he turned it over. Still blank. "I don't get it. What—"

"Wan' you autograph, azzhole," los Parados whispered to him as Bueno snickered.

Caught off-guard, Kowalski tuned back to the boy and saw that he was also holding out a pen. He took it and began writing his name, forming each letter carefully. M-A-R . . .

Aires and los Parados both stopped their own signing to look.

Kowalski had his tongue sticking out of the side of his mouth as he concentrated. V-I-N . . . He then shifted position to get himself prepared for the next part. K-O-W . . .

Aires shook his head and signed eight more by the time Kowalski got to S-K-I, smiled and proudly handed the pen back. The kid whirled and left without saying thanks, and another one held out a pad of paper and a pen. Kowalski got himself set and began again. M-A-R . . .

"Hey, kid . . ."

Kowalski looked over at los Parados, who was using one pen and stabbing at pieces of paper with some kind of scrawl that seemed to require about three-quarters of a second per autograph. "Firs' of all, use you own pen," he said. "Saves time, takin' it, givin' it back."

The kids swarming around Kowalski were growing impatient, flapping their pieces of paper and scowling. V-I-N . . .

"Make son' kin'a mark dey kin recannize," Aires called over, " 'n' scrash'out da rest." He held up a piece of paper. On it Kowalski could see a large "A" and then a tail that looked like a spermatozoa's.

The boy Kowalski was signing for stamped his foot and glared at him, and the rest boosted the intensity of their own indications of displeasure at the delay. Kowalski made a bold "K" and then squiggled the pen to the right, which seemed to please the boy, who grabbed the pen and scurried away to get a signature from Aires. Kowalski took the next pen and did the "K"-plus-squiggle, then did it again and again until he had some kind of rhythm going.

"Okay, thas' it!" he heard los Parados announce, followed by a chorus of disappointed groans from his little audience. As his teammate parted the crowd and walked through it, Kowalski's own flock began turning away as well.

"Hang on," he said, continuing to sign, as did Aires. In seconds his group was joined by the other one, all of them pushing and jostling, trying to get his signature before he, too, announced he had to go. But he and Aires stayed until the last piece of paper was signed.

Later, on the way out of the locker room after they were showered and dressed, Johansen nodded in approval when Spinale related what had happened.

"One of them asked me to sign two," Kowalski said when they were out in the tunnel. "What do you do then?"

"You sign them," Johansen answered, loud enough for los Parados to hear twenty steps ahead of them. "Those kids pay your salary."

They heard some muffled cursing coming from the locker room.

"What the . . ." Spinale stopped walking, frowned, then grabbed Kowalski by the arm. "Kowalski, did you schmeer da guy?"

Kowalski stared at him. "Did I what?"

"Did you schmeer da guy!" Spinale insisted.

"I don't . . . *what*? What do you mean, did I—"

"Ah, shit," Spinale growled as he pushed past the confused rookie, headed back to the locker room and swung open the door.

"Whass goin' on?" a familiar voice said, and Kowalski turned around to see Aires just as he was emerging from the door Spinale had opened.

"Kid didn't schmeer the guy," Johansen explained, pointing toward the locker room.

Kowalski turned once again, just in time to see Spinale slip some bills into the clubhouse man's hand, nudge his chin toward Kowalski and shrug, as if by way of helpless explanation. The attendant nodded forgivingly, tucked the bills in his back pocket, and touched two fingers to his cap as Spinale strode back into the tunnel, throwing a noisy *harrumph* at Kowalski as he passed.

"Jeez, kid," Johansen scolded as they resumed walking. "You *gotta* schmeer the guy!"

Four

CHI CHI'S RIGHT," Spinale said with authority. "Hate to admit the overblown so-and-so is right, but he's right."

Kowalski had been lulled into semi-somnolence by the soothing *clickety-clack* of the train wheels on the rails. There was nothing else to do anyway while Donny Marshall agonized over whether to fold or raise. "Right about what?" he said groggily.

"'Bout Andresen," Federico Guittierez chimed in. "'Bout how he's gonna take your head off the next time you're battin' against him."

Kowalski opened his eyes fully. "Why? What'd I do?"

"Make him look like a' azzhole," los Parados said. "Donny, joo gonna f'Chrissake' chit or get off the pot!"

"I'm thinkin'!" the shortstop said as he stared intently at his cards, as if they might change if he looked at them long enough.

"Ever hear'a Bob Gibson?" Spinale asked.

"Oh, no' this again," los Parados groaned.

"Shaddap, Chi Chi," Cavvy Papazian said. "S'good story."

"Are you kidding?" Kowalski said. "Gibson practically changed the game."

In the late sixties, baseball was so dominated by pitchers that fans, who favored crowd-pleasing homers over aficionado-satisfying pitching duels, started getting restless and looking for other things to do than watch low-scoring baseball games. The nadir of this uncomfortable situation was Gibson's 1968 ERA of 1.12, which meant that, on the average, he gave up barely one run per nine innings pitched. For people who appreciated the nuances of stellar pitching, and who were aware that the last time a pitcher had an ERA like that was 1914, it was the most exciting development in years. For the less knowledgeable, it was like watching a lawn-growing contest.

In an effort to lure fans back, major-league baseball decided to even the odds a little and give the batters a break, by making such changes as lowering the pitcher's mound from fifteen inches to ten and, in the American League a few years later, instituting the designated hitter. The result over time was an offensive explosion, or more correctly a backfire, that tipped the balance so heavily in the other direction that there was now talk of doing something to restore equilibrium.

"Yeah, well he damned near changed a guy named Pete LaCock," Spinale chortled.

"Donny, go'damnit!" los Parados said through clenched teeth.

"Uhh-ightaready!" Marshall picked up several bills and threw them into the middle of the fold-down table. "Raise!"

Guittierez threw in his hand, but Kowalski and los Parados, sighing simultaneously, both called the raise, evincing no surprise when Marshall gulped, his bluff having failed to force them out.

"Two pair," los Parados announced, laying them down.

"Trips," Kowalski said, laying down three nines.

"Shit!" Marshall said, showing his single pair. He looked around for a way to vent his irritation. "What the heck're we doing on a train, anyway!"

"Saving dough." Now with a chance to get their attention, Spinale jumped in before the next deal could disrupt his story. "It's

LaCock's very first time up in the Bigs, right? Bottom of the ninth, his team is down 3-2, and he swings at the first pitch Gibson throws. Gets a base hit, drives in two guys and wins the game."

"Heck of a debut," Kowalski had to admit.

"*Fuck* his debut, listen'a me. The guy, this LaCock, he rounds first and he's so happy he starts jumpin' up and down, high-fivin' his teammates and generally behaving like someone who just won the game, which he did, and after all the slappin' and shit the manager says to him, he says, 'Pete,' he says, 'Pete, you shouldna oughta done that.' And this new kid, he says, 'Done what?' and the manager says, 'Take the Cadillac Trot like that, not while Gibson's standin' there with his thumb up his ass.' "

"So the next time he comes up to bat—" Papazian began.

"Hey, who's tellin' the story here? So anyways, three weeks later they're in St. Louis and Pete's up third and *whammo!* Gibby hits him with the first pitch. Hits him again a few innings later. Next time they meet he hits him three times *in one game*. Went on for years, until, finally, it's Gibson's last big-league game. I mean it's *Bob Gibson Day* at the stadium, f'Chrissakes. His mother's there, they give him a motor home, all kinds'a shit. Then they play, and at the top'a the ninth it's a 6-6 tie. Chicago's got the bases loaded, two outs, and who comes up to bat?"

"LaCock!"

"Yep. Pinch-hitting, no less, and the guy whacks a grand slam off Gibby, right into the upper deck. Dances his round-tripper like a friggin' Rockette. Meanwhile, the ball bounces off the mezzanine and rolls back onto the field. One'a the infielders picks it up and tosses it to Gibson, and as Pete's goin' down into the dugout, Gibby launches it right at his head."

"In the dugout?"

"Yeah. Missed him, though. And that's the last time Gibson ever threw. He retired on the spot."

"Heck of a story," Kowalski agreed.

Papazian dropped his head and tried to stifle a laugh.

Spinale looked at his cards, milking the moment, then said matter-of-factly, "Couple years later Gibson hit Pete in an Old Timers game."

As Kowalski, Marshall and Guittierez exploded in laughter and disbelief, Papazian assured them that every word was true. They also told him about the time Pittsburgh's Frank Traveras beat out a two-strike bunt, and on his next at-bat Gibson hit him with a fastball. Not too unusual except, as Papazian pointed out gleefully, it was in a spring-training game.

"A good night against Gibson," he observed, "was going 0-for-4 and not getting hit in the head."

With only twenty minutes until the train pulled into Boston, they packed up the cards, stowed the fold-down table and began gathering up their belongings.

"Hope iss windy," Aires said.

"How come?" Kowalski asked.

"Wind helps batters in Fenway," Guittierez explained. "They built this new press box in the eighties, makes the wind swirl around and blows foul balls back into fair territory."

"Luckiest damned pitcher I ever seen, Gibson," Spinale mused as he reached into the overhead bin. "Guy always pitched on days the other team didn't score any runs."

Boston—May 3

Johansen turned toward his bench to see Federico Guittierez get up and start stretching in anticipation of coming to bat. A few feet away, Marvin Kowalski sat in his usual half-tranced examination of the pitcher, left-hander Brett Taylor of the Boston Red Sox.

Johansen lifted his chin beckoningly, and Guittierez walked toward him. "You hang with Kowalski a little, don'tcha, Freddy? Play poker 'n'all?"

Guittierez shrugged and lifted his arms above his head, pressing his palms against the low ceiling. "Much as anybody, which in't much. Why?"

Johansen inclined his head toward the bench. "How he sits like that when a guy's pitching. Talks to himself."

"Yeah." Guittierez smiled and pushed his hips to the left and then to the right, using the ceiling to balance himself. "But only when our guys're up. What you figure, he prayin'?"

"Don't know. Why don't you go on over there and sit next to him, see if you can hear what the hell's he's saying."

Guittierez shrugged again and sauntered back to the bench as casually as he could, dropping down next to Kowalski without trying to look obvious. The kid blinked during the half-second Guittierez blocked his view of the field, but otherwise indicated no awareness of his presence.

Guittierez looked from the mound to Kowalski and back again. As Taylor reared back, Guittierez heard Kowalski mumble something, but he couldn't make out the words. Over on first base, Cavvy Papazian took a long lead, crabbed back toward the bag, took it long again, sidled back, all to try to addle the pitcher into wondering if a steal was in the works. Papazian was one of the few catchers in the league—in history, for that matter—whose knees weren't so corroded that he couldn't run. He could, and Taylor knew it.

Taking the sign from his catcher, Taylor nodded slightly and then stood stock still, trying to see first base from the corner of his eye without turning his head. Kowalski mumbled and then Taylor twisted awkwardly and threw to first, the ball arriving a fraction of a second after Papazian dove and got his fingertips onto the bag.

Guittierez saw Kowalski smile, barely, and tap his fingertips together as though applauding. Looking past the kid's face, Guittierez saw Johansen lift his shoulders inquiringly.

As Papazian stood up, keeping one hand on the bag and only letting go when he was able to get his foot onto it, Guittierez leaned over to tie his shoe, which he hoped Kowalski didn't notice hadn't been untied in the first place, but Kowalski didn't seem to be noticing anything that was going on inside the dugout, intent as he was on the action out on the field. As Guittierez straightened up, he coughed and shifted so he was as close to the kid as was possible without actually sitting in his lap.

Once more Taylor eyed first base after taking his sign, then leaned back and went into his pitch.

"High 'n' outside."

Guittierez turned at the sound of Kowalski's barely perceptible voice just as he heard wood swishing uselessly through thin air and the ball hitting the catcher's glove. He knew just from the sounds that Majestyks right fielder Vince Salvanella had swung at the pitch and missed.

"Slider wide."

Salvanella straightened up and relaxed as the catcher stretched to grab the ball from outside the strike zone.

"Fastball."

Taylor grunted audibly with the effort of throwing a fastball, which Salvanella swung at but barely managed to connect with, sending it springing back up into the safety screen behind him for a foul.

"Breaking ball, low and inside."

Salvanella let it by for another ball.

"Fastball."

"Change-up."

"Breaking, up and away."

Guittierez frantically scanned the field to try to figure out how Kowalski was finding out what pitches the catcher was calling for. Papazian at first base was far too busy trying to steal second to be stealing signs and relaying them, which couldn't really be done from first base anyway because the catcher's right knee blocked his signal hand. Somebody in the center field stands with binoculars and a radio?

"Changeup."

"Sinker."

But Kowalski had no earpiece to receive messages, and what would be the point of relaying stolen signals to a guy sitting in the dugout anyway?

"Curveball."

Salvanella swung and missed. Sure as hell *he* wasn't getting the word on what pitches were coming.

"Straight and hard!"

The fastball tore by and slapped into the catcher's glove before Salvanella seemed even to have noticed that it had been thrown. "*Sdddrrraagghhhh!*" the ump yelled, and Salvanella walked off in disgust.

By now Guittierez had abandoned any pretense of inattention and was staring at Kowalski open-mouthed. The kid snapped out of his demi-trance and reached down for his book, but was startled and nearly dropped it when he noticed Guittierez's gaping maw about six inches from his face. "What's the matter with you, Freddy?" He put a finger under the outfielder's chin and pushed his jaw shut.

Guittierez, eyes wide and slightly frightened, pulled back, gulped and looked around before leaning in toward Kowalski once again. "Whadda fock you doin'!"

Kowalski frowned in confusion. "I'm not doing anything."

Guittierez peered at him as if he were a frog lying spread-eagled on a dissecting table. "You just called evvy goddamn' pitch the son'bitch t'rew!"

"Yeah? So?"

"*So?* Wadda hell you mean, *so?* How the hell you can read signs from a catcher, you can' even see his fingers fron' here!"

"I'm not reading his signs."

"Then how you know what pitches Taylor gonna t'row!"

"Jeez, Freddy—all I'm doing is watching him."

Guittierez stared, blinked a few times, and creased up his brow in futile concentration. "The pitcher? You watch the pitcher and know 'zackly what he's gon' t'row?" Guittierez shook his head in wonder. "Who does shi' like that!"

Kowalski's own confusion deepened. "I thought all you guys did, at least to some extent. Only difference is, I also watch the pitcher when I'm not the one hitting."

Guittierez grabbed the top of his cap and dragged it off his head. "Marvin, wadju *talkin'* about!"

Kowalski, still frowning, pointed out toward the mound. "Well, what are you looking at when he's winding up?"

Guittierez tilted his head to the side. "I'm lookin' adda pitcher. Wadju *think* I'm lookin' at!"

"But that's all I'm doing. What are you *watching*?"

"Watching *him*. Watching his release point. Come on, *niño*!"

"Why?"

"Why? Whadda you, *loco*? I ain' lookin' at him, how'm I 'spoza know when he t'rows!"

"That's it? You're just looking at him to know when he throws?"

"Marvin, wadda fog you talkin' about!"

Kowalski stared at him a moment, as if to see if his leg was being pulled, then he turned his attention back to the mound, where Taylor was hitching up his shoulders and craning his neck around to stay loose as Majestyks shortstop Donny Marshall took his time swinging a weighted bat and getting to the plate. When he was in position, Taylor took the sign from his catcher and started his pitch. With a runner on base, he didn't use a full windup, which would give the runner too much time to steal, but instead pitched "from the stretch," an abbreviated motion that kept the runner from taking too generous a lead.

"Low and inside."

"Goddamnit!" Guittierez exclaimed as the ball sank and was caught close to Marshall's ankle, Kowalski shaking his head in disapproval because Marshall had swung at the crummy pitch for a strike. "How in the—"

"Watch the pitcher!" Kowalski commanded. "Gonna break right!"

Marshall swung at the slow curve, but the ball's eccentric trajectory made him connect early and he sent it foul down the third base line.

"Marvin . . ." Guittierez growled.

"Watch the pitcher, Freddy!" Kowalski pointed to his own left arm. "Every time he lets it drop away behind his back like that, he's throwing a curve. Heat!"

Taylor let rip a blazing fastball.

"Hear that little grunt?"

"Little? He damned neared screamed his—"

"Not when he throws, Freddy. When he first leans back, on account of he's not very flexible and it's a struggle for him to get enough stretch. Knuckler, watch his head!"

It was a sign of Taylor's mounting confidence, even impudence, that he threw an almost insulting junk-ball pitch like the knuckleball, a technique generally favored by pitchers who were no longer capable of laying down "real" pitches like fastballs and sliders. The absurdly slow ball meandered its way in crazily. Marshall swung and missed it completely.

"What *about* his head?"

"He flips it to the left and back again," Kowalski replied. "Like it was some kinda joke." Which a knuckleball was to a pitcher like Taylor.

Guittierez watched as Taylor once again wound up. "Fastball?" he said as the pitcher emitted a slight squeal.

"But wide!" Kowalski answered quickly, as Marshall let the awkward fastball go by. "When his left leg is tucked in too tight."

They watched a few more go by, Guittierez calling a few of them correctly. "Never heard Sandy Williams grunt," he said after a while, referring to the star pitcher of the Cleveland Indians.

"He doesn't," Kowalski explained. "He squints."

"But—"

"Every pitcher is different, Freddy. You've got to watch each one on his own. They're even different on different days, and some of them, like Taylor here, their . . . uh, you know . . . those little things that give them away change as the game goes on and they get tired, or they're behind, or they see a relief pitcher warming up in the bullpen." Kowalski pounded the side of his head, then called out to los Parados. "Chi Chi! What the heck is it cardplayers call it when somebody gives you a clue about his hand but doesn't know he's doing it?"

Los Parados looked at him uncomprehendingly but Spinale had

started nodding halfway through the question. "It's called a *tell*," he said.

"A tell! That's it!"

"A tell?" Guittierez echoed.

"Yeah. A tell is the giveaway. It's a little sign that tells you what you need to know. It's how I always take money from you when we're playing poker."

"Bullshit!"

Kowalski grinned mischievously and turned toward him. "Your whole body is like a billboard, Freddy. Every time you draw one card and fill in a straight, you sniffle three times, put your cards down, then you pick them up and look at them again, like you want to make sure you really have it, then you sniffle three times again and say, 'Whose fockin' bet, go'damnit!'"

"Bullshit!" Guittierez said again, but with less conviction this time.

"And when you're bluffing?" Kowalski touched the little finger on the outfielder's left hand. "This little guy taps on the table about ten times a second. Kind of amazing what you can see if you look."

A loud round of cheers arose from the stands. Kowalski and Guittierez turned to see Marshall toss the bat away and take his base on balls. "I'm on deck," Guittierez said.

"Rip one, Freddy."

Guittierez rose and arched his back. "You know waz coming, why the hell come you don' get a hit every time you're at bat?"

"Because I can't hit. Never had a chance to learn. I can get on base every time I'm up *without* hitting, so who'd want me to trade a double one out of ten times for first base ten out of ten?"

"So why's it you can—"

"Hit it foul?" Kowalski gestured toward the left field stands. "Foul covers a lot of territory, Freddy. Nowhere near as hard to hit it foul."

Five

B Y MARVIN KOWALSKI'S THIRD WEEK with the Des
Moines club, his teammates were becoming more aware
of the pitchers. Like Ted Williams relentlessly grilling the
top of the order on what had been thrown to them, Majestyks batters hammered on Kowalski for any bit of information he could glean
on their behalf. A sharp-eyed statistician might have noticed that
most of their hits came after the first three innings, when they'd had
a chance to size up and read the pitcher. Of course, as the season
wore on and they became familiar with the opposing hurlers, they
were able to read them earlier and earlier in the game.

As valuable as Kowalski had become, Zuke Johansen had a strong
sense that talent was being wasted. The kid could hardly run—if
he'd ever have to sprint to first to beat out a throw, he'd be as good
as gone; but since he never hit a fair ball it was a moot point. Once
he got on, though, his options were few in number, and therefore his
utility as a designated hitter was limited to only a few situations. If
there were already men on base, he could move them around and in-

crease the likelihood of an RBI or two by a subsequent batter. He himself wasn't much good for a run once he got to base unless someone walked or put one into the stands and brought him home that way.

"Can't we teach him to hit something other than foul balls?" Johansen complained to batting coach Lefty Peterson. "He's coordinated as hell and he'd know exactly what pitches he'd have a chance of hitting."

"Teach him to hit what?"

"I don't know . . . sacrifice flies for when we got a guy on third."

"If we had guys on base, he could move them around with walks."

"Only if there's already somebody on first. What I'm saying, suppose we had a guy on second or third. Deep enough fly, we might get a run out of it. Or maybe with a little practice he could put one through an infield hole."

Peterson scratched at his chin and thought about it. "He *has* been putting them out pretty good past third base, I gotta admit."

"Puts 'em where he wants to."

"That I don't know about. Like he says, foul covers a lot of territory. You put a fifty-foot putt within two feet of the hole and that looks pretty good, too, but two feet from the hole covers—lemme see here—thirteen square feet."

"Still, it can't hurt to work with him a little, Lefty."

Peterson leaned way back in the ancient chair and put his feet up on the desk. "Unless it rattles his confidence in the one thing he already does know how to do. But—" he held up his hands and let them drop "—let's give it a shot."

The Bronx—May 13

The one pitcher Kowalski couldn't read was Mars Lee of the New York Yankees.

Lee had an ERA of 2.10 and, for some reason nobody could figure, more batters got to first because of the catcher failing to get a glove on third-strike pitches than they did on hits or walks. Rumors of spitballs and psychokinetic powers spun around the league in an effort to explain why his pitches were as hard for catchers to catch as for hitters to hit.

Spinale signaled for some of the Majestyks to come in from the field where they'd been playing "pepper" to loosen up, one guy swatting short grounders to the others until somebody missed and had to take up the bat and try to get somebody else out. Most ballparks had big signs in the outfield saying NO PEPPER! but, as Chi Chi los Parados had once put it so succinctly, "Whadda they gon' do if we play pepper . . . take our bats and balls and send us home?"

So they were happily engaged in that great pregame tradition when Spinale called them in and instructed them to take a few seemingly innocuous runs around the bases, making sure to innocently trample the dirt along the infield foul lines and stomp down the loose sand in front of home plate.

Kowalski sneaked a peek around the dugout wall and into the faces of the first Yankees fans he'd ever seen close-up, then quickly pulled his head back and sat there, wide-eyed, staring straight ahead.

Wade Cogburn smiled knowingly. "Kinda like wakin' up in a Turkish prison, ain't it?"

"WHASSA TELL, MARVIN?" Freddy Guittierez demanded excitedly, pointing at Mars Lee out on the mound. "This overgrown son'bitch been blowin' down hitters like corn in a hurricane." He smiled conspiratorially. "Gividda me, kid . . . whassa sign?"

Kowalski shook his head slowly. "Hasn't got one."

Guittierez's smile froze in place. "Wadju mean, he hasn't go' one? You been watchin' him two innings already. Come on!"

Kowalski's eyes bore in on Mars Lee as the big guy burned one in over the plate and Donny Marshall took a mighty swing, missing the ball completely. Kowalski shook his head again.

"Nothin'?" Guittierez asked morosely.

Kowalski didn't answer right away, but watched two more pitches, a ball and the second strike. He thought about various possibilities, starting with—and discarding immediately—the notion that Mars was a hard, unemotional, programmed automaton possessed of no body language.

He ran down a few other possibilities. By now Zuke had joined up and was peering at him closely.

He watched Marshall swing and miss for a third strike.

"Holy cow," Kowalski said softly, sitting back against the dugout wall with his mouth agape.

"Holy cow, what?" Zuke asked. "How can this guy not have a giveaway?"

Kowalski closed his mouth, nodding slowly as realization sank in. "I don't think he knows."

"Don' know what?" Guittierez sputtered. "Go'damnit, kid, what in the hell are—"

"Guittierez, get your ass up to the circle!" Spinale barked.

"Move it, Freddy," Johansen affirmed, not entirely unsympathetic to the hangdog look on his hitter's face.

He sat down next to Kowalski. "Explains a lot, actually. Why he's so hard to hit."

"And to catch. Even his own guys don't know what he's going to throw. Jeez . . ."

"It's like Marshall playing cards," Johansen said, causing Kowalski to finally snap out of it and laugh. "Only guy that scares me in poker is the guy who doesn't know how to play. You can never figure what the heck he's got."

"Unless you watch him," Kowalski said as the others began drifting away. "Watch closely enough, it's like reading a neon sign. So how come they call you Zuke?"

"How come they call you Marvin?"

"How come—" Kowalski turned away from the field as Guittierez swung and missed for his second strike. "That's the name my parents gave me!"

Johansen stood up. "So what? Do I ask them why they picked 'Marvin'?"

As he walked away, Sal Spinale spat a particularly foul-looking plug of dripping chew out onto the field. "It's on accounta he's skinny," he said, waiting to see if Kowalski would pick up on the rest himself.

"Like a zucchini." Kowalski looked at Johansen's receding form. "Who came up with that?"

"Henry Schmidt. Who else?"

A loud *craaack!* distracted them, followed by a deep groan from the Yankee Stadium crowd. Johansen jumped up to watch Guittierez, one of the fastest runners in the American League, tearing from first to second even as the ball he'd hit was bouncing off the deepest part of the right field wall. Third base coach Bink Iverson was waving frantically for him to keep going, which he did, beating out the throw with a head first slide.

Johansen nodded approvingly. "The old-fashioned way."

Right fielder Vince Salvanella was up next, and waited patiently through a full count until Lee walked him on a curveball that got away. By that time Donny Marshall, who'd struck out a few minutes before but had just finished sulking, had joined the others in front of the dugout.

"Crandall's gonna pull him," Johansen said, even as Chi Chi los Parados put a bat up on his shoulders in the on-deck circle.

"Pull him?" Marshall said in surprise. "He only let two guys on!"

"He's losing his stuff," Kowalski said.

Spinale nodded. "You could see it in that last batch of pitches. Guy had five days of rest, thinks he's indestructible, threw too many fastballs . . . wears you out quick."

"Didn't look to me like he was losing his stuff," Marshall said, a comment the others didn't see any point in responding to.

Lee was replaced by Tim Macalvey, and Chi Chi los Parados sauntered over to the dugout as the relief pitcher took his allowed warm-up pitches—no more than eight, no longer than a minute, and then he had to be ready to throw for real. That was the rule, anyway, but it was rarely enforced. With all the television commercials lined up and waiting for a pitching change, Macalvey could've thrown twenty pitches and taken a shave by the time the ump got the word from the broadcast booth that the game could resume.

Los Parados grinned as he ducked his head down toward the dugout, bat still up on his shoulders. "This guy's an easy read, right, kid? I remember from before."

"Don't get carried away," Johansen warned sternly, "and don't forget the fundamentals."

"Don' worry about me," los Parados assured him, although there was nothing reassuring about the shit-eating grin that stayed plastered to his face. He lingered over the three bats he'd been swinging loosely, staring at them, rolling them around, hefting each one individually and looking at all sides of the last one . . .

Macalvey nodded his readiness and the ump looked over at los Parados crossly. "What'sa matter, Chi Chi . . . you lookin' for the instructions?"

Los Parados, who'd been described by *The Sporting News* as a self-made man who worshipped his creator, stepped to the plate, cockiness radiating from him like gamma rays. Over on third Guittierez was taking a moderate lead, making sure to do so in foul territory so if he got hit by a batted ball, it would be a foul and he wouldn't be out.

The first pitch was a breaking ball inside, and los Parados stepped away from it disdainfully, almost, or so it seemed, before it even left the pitcher's hand. A slider next, down and away, and once again los Parados signaled his contempt by standing upright before the ball reached the plate.

Macalvey hesitated, puzzlement on his features, then threw a fastball straight up the middle. Los Parados was ready and took a mighty swing but pulled it foul down the left field line. Another fastball, outside the corner, and this time los Parados stepped away from it completely, grinning and swinging his bat up over his head, for his third ball.

Macalvey launched a screaming fastball right at his head.

Los Parados, smile suddenly gone, ducked away so quickly dust rose up from his spinning feet, but the ball nicked him on the shoulder anyway.

"Whadda fock . . . !" Dirt still clouding around his head, los Parados looked at the mound, stunned. "Whadda hell'd joo—"

When asked once by a sportswriter what his favorite pitch was, Macalvey had responded, "The second knockdown. That way the guy knows the first one wasn't an accident." It was said of him that he'd bean his own mother if she fouled away on an 0-and-2 pitch, and he was equally deferential to los Parados now: "You're stealing the goddamned signs, you greaseball muthafu—"

Macalvey never got to finish, because by that time the benches in both dugouts were as barren as those in Central Park in winter, all the former occupants having departed in pursuit of the pitcher, the hitter and any exposed cranium or throat topping a uniform whose colors didn't match their own.

As a blizzard of fists, gloves and hats flew around the infield, Zuke stuffed a fresh piece of gum in his mouth and stood with his arms folded across his chest. About half a minute later, Yankee manager Augie Crandall stepped up beside him. (He'd been named for his idol, Yogi Berra, but with deference to that legend's greater stature, "Yogi" had been forgone in favor of "Augie," Augie Doggie being the younger sidekick of Yogi Bear.) They watched the melee in silence for a few seconds.

"Hell's a matter with your boy, Augie?" There were several levels of meaning in Johansen's question. The obvious one was why Macalvey would try to bean los Parados in the first place, but a more important one was why he'd purposely put the batter on first base when the count was 3-and-1. It was a sign of how badly something had rattled the pitcher.

Crandall scratched his crotch and looked around the stands before answering. "He don't like it, people steal signs on him."

Zuke tried to blow a bubble, but it snapped limply and he re-wadded the gum with his tongue, taking his time. He unfolded one arm and gestured outward. "You see any men on base sending signals?" He was, of course, implying the past tense and referring to the last time anybody at all was out in the field.

Crandall thought about it. "Nuh uh."

Zuke nodded. "And my base coaches . . . still as statues, right?"

Crandall pursed his lips but didn't answer right away. He regarded the umpires, who had stepped back several paces as the brouhaha intensified, and winced at what he thought might have been a tooth flying his way. "Gotta give you that."

Four men—two from each team—had joined forces to stop the pitcher from gouging out los Parados' eyes. The big man was dragging all four inexorably forward, so that their feet began forming ruts in the grass between the mound and home.

"So how do you figure my guys were stealing signs?"

Crandall remained quiet. They watched together for a little while longer. Three more men, including the batboy, had jumped on the pitcher and finally managed to stop his forward motion, but now they were trying to figure out how to negotiate for his release. Elsewhere, fearsome grunts attested to an escalation from a little steam-venting to some serious bloodletting.

"Don't gotta figure how, Zuke. But sure as shit they're gettin' stole."

The chief ump cast a sideways glance at them.

"Ready?" Zuke suggested.

"Yep," Crandall agreed.

Together, they sprinted from their positions toward the human maggot swarm as though they were shocked—*shocked!*—at the rumpus and had immediately swung into action as soon as they'd noticed it.

After it was all over, the umps tried to figure out whom to eject from the game; it seemed that there was no way to do it without kicking everybody out, including the batboy. Finally the crew chief said, "Fuck it; let the league figure it out from the video. You guys ready to play a little baseball yet?"

Back in the dugout Johansen took los Parados aside. "One more bonehead stunt like that," he said menacingly, "you'll be warming a bench 'til you're in a walker."

AFTER THE GAME Henry Schmidt was waiting in the players' parking lot as Johansen and Spinale walked out together. "Hell was that all about?"

"Macalvey tried to brain one of my guys," Johansen answered.

"I saw that. Got time for a drink?"

"Can't," Johansen said. He was in no mood for Schmidt today. Or any day, for that matter.

"Asshole pitcher," Spinale said. "Pro'ly someday they'll make a movie about him."

"Assholes only become colorful with the passage of time," Schmidt observed. "We may smile at the old stories of gamblers who sat in the stands and fired shots at players, but there wasn't a damned thing funny about bullets zinging toward an athlete's legs just because he didn't want to corrupt a game he loved."

He turned with Johansen and Spinale as they resumed walking. "It's all about time passing, see? The only people who look back at Ty Cobb with affection and a wink are those without firsthand knowledge of what a truly nasty prick he was. You think guys going weeks without a shower, players tanking games as favors to the mob, managers slipping mickeys to opposing pitchers . . . you think any of that sorry shit was *colorful*?" He shook his head ruefully. "It was a disgrace, and only by the grace of God and a fast infield was the game strong enough to survive it."

"Got a point there, uhright." Spinale shot a last wad of chew onto the pavement. "Known a few shitheads in my time, I have."

"Show me a pitcher throws a ball at a guy's head, I'll show you a Grade-A piece'a shit of a human being. And I'm talking about the manager, not the pitcher. 'Retaliation,' he says? For what . . . stealing signs? Razzing the catcher? For this you risk braining a guy?" They reached Schmidt's car and he tapped a finger on the hood. "Bullshit!"

"Fuhgeddaboudit," Spinale agreed.

"Come on, Sal," Johansen said. "Gotta work on tomorrow's lineup."

It wasn't lost on Schmidt that there was no need to work on tomorrow's lineup, since it was going to be the same as today's lineup except for the pitcher, unless somebody was injured, which nobody was.

Six

A LL YOU'RE SWINGING IS your upper body. Practically just your arms." Batting coach Lefty Peterson made a swiveling motion with his hips that turned his whole body. "Power comes from the legs."

"It does?" Kowalski said.

"Yep."

"I don't get it."

"What do you mean, you don't get it?"

"Your legs are planted on the ground. How do you get power from your legs?"

Peterson blinked several times. "*Everybody* knows power comes from your legs!"

"Didn't say I don't believe you, Lefty. I just don't understand it."

"I'll explain it later. Meanwhile, what you gotta do, you gotta get your hips into it, use 'em to bring your upper body around. Otherwise you're gonna spend a whole season makin' right turns at first base."

Kowalski had never really watched hitters before, having concentrated solely on pitchers, but he watched them now. He especially watched Juan-Tanamera Aires, trying to figure out how he hit so many practice pitches over the center field wall without seeming to half try. Bueno wasn't lunging or straining at the ball, just swinging smoothly and easily and belting long balls one after the other. "The toughest part of this game," Spinale once said, "is taking a round bat to a round ball and hitting it square."

Eventually the science of it began to dawn on Kowalski. Aires accelerated the bat through the entire swing, his arms fully extended to maximize his leverage. Because the bat kept speeding up, there was no need for him to jerk it forward at the beginning of the swing.

And Lefty Peterson had been at least partially right: Aires didn't actually transfer power from his legs, but used them to optimize the force generated by his upper body, in much the same way as a pitcher or a golfer did. By getting his hips out in front of his hands he created a slingshot effect, the stretched and leading lower half pulling on the upper to bring it around with a whiplike action.

"It's like if you hit a tree with a thin piece of bamboo," Kowalski said to Peterson. "You bring the bottom part of the bamboo forward and it gets out in front of the tip, which then tries to catch up and whacks the tree at a much higher velocity than your hand could ever move."

"I knew that," Peterson said. "Now how come you can't do that?"

"Didn't understand it."

"Well now you do, right?"

But it still didn't feel natural to Kowalski. Putting that much effort into swinging the bat made it difficult for him to keep it under enough control to meet the ball squarely. He spent some time with Aires, getting him to swing the bat slowly, watching him from various angles, asking him questions, until he figured out that batters must not be controlling the swing at all; they committed to it at the very outset and there was nothing they could do about it once they were underway. So if the ball did something unexpected once the point of no return had been passed, they couldn't make a midcourse correction.

And that was the source of Kowalski's problem. He was so used to taking his time to size up a pitched ball that there wasn't enough time to mount a really good swing at it. And if he guessed the pitch rather than really saw it, he'd be like every other hitter except without the power and coordination, and he'd have no business being on this team or in the game of baseball at all.

Unless a pitcher grooved him a forty-mile-per-hour cream puff, there was no way he was going to take a real swing. And big-league pitchers didn't groove forty-mile-per-hour cream puffs.

Still, as long as Aires and Peterson were willing to spend time trying to teach him, he was willing to spend time trying to learn. And since very few pitchers were willing to show Aires any real stuff, batting practice was the only chance he had to belt balls out of the park and have a little fun, so he was more than willing to throw a few tips at Kowalski.

He showed him how to hold the bat with the label facing up, because the bat is branded where the grain is widest, and therefore weakest, so if you could see the label you'd be hitting with the strongest part of the wood. He told him to check the ball's color as it came in, because if you see mostly white it's probably a fastball with the backspin blurring the red seams, but breaking balls and sliders had some topspin and would look reddish.

Lecturing Kowalski on seeing the ball to know what kind of pitch was coming was like tutoring van Gogh on the difference between red and green paint, but the rookie listened patiently and didn't object. He was more interested in things like the length of the batter's stride, and understood instantly that stride length was limited by the width of the stance. If you had your feet closer together, you could lift your front leg and drop your foot down farther out than where it was, which added power in much the same way a pitcher did. If your feet were too wide apart, you couldn't gain that advantage. So the short stance seemed preferable, and Aires explained that some hitters also favored it because it produced a more compact, easily controlled swing. A big stride encouraged overswinging, and that was why guys like los Parados, who was a power hitter, hit long balls but also struck out a lot.

Hold the bat back so you were precocked and wouldn't have to take it back once the ball was on its way to you, but not so much that you can't cock naturally a bit when you take your stride. Hold the bat loose, so you don't waste energy being tense. You want to hit the ball in front of the plate, not over it. After you connect you can take your top hand, the dominant one, off the bat and let it swing around on its own. Use a light bat so you can check the swing before the halfway point and avoid a strike if you see the ball going out of the zone. Don't lunge with your shoulders. You can see faster than you can swing, so don't wait too long to make a decision because you don't have enough strength to get it around. Don't open your shoulder too soon . . .

"An' here's anodder one, Marvin. You mus' to loosen up a little, hokay? These guys, you team guys, they not jus' guys like you work on dig a ditch, righ'? You don' gotta kiss 'em, but you gotta be friends. They gotta *trus'* you, and das more'n just play on the same field, hokay? Hokay. You be a nice, frien'ly guy."

May 15

"Tried everything, skip. You can't believe how embarrassing the whole process is."

On the team train going through Illinois, young relief pitcher Bryce Thomason, in an unguarded moment, was lamenting to Zuke Johansen about his and his wife's inability to conceive a child. "It's like you get sucked up into this flying saucer and aliens with no sense of humor dream up awful ways to poke and prod you."

Unfortunately for Thomason, Chi Chi los Parados was passing by at the worst possible moment.

Los Parados was a supremely arrogant Mexican whose particular brand of vaunting machismo involved not only building himself up but tearing down every ego that came within arm's length of him. The only drawback to ridiculing his bragging about an endless series of truly unbelievable and patently absurd sexual exploits on the road was that every one of them was true.

Overhearing Thomason at the crucial moment of confession—"Nothing we do is working"—he slapped the vulnerable young boy on the back in what might have been seen to be a comforting and reassuring manner, then said, "Sounds like we gotta put more men on it!"

Only Johansen's quick grab of Thomason's wrist in its windup prevented the young hurler from ending his career by breaking several crucial bones against Chi Chi's skull.

"Hundred and sixty two games," Kowalski said, shaking his head, as the still-smirking los Parados finally made it to the back end of the car. "Don't know how you guys can play that many games year in and year out." As a designated hitter who never took the field, Kowalski wouldn't experience near as much wear and tear as those who played both offense and defense and who were only too aware that baseball was a marathon, not a sprint.

"The game is easy," Bobby Madison said. "It's the season wears you out."

Early in his career Madison had taken to writing the name of the city he was in on a piece of paper and putting it next to the clock in his hotel room. It was easier to just look over at it than to try to remember where he was. After two years, though, it occurred to him that there was really no need to remember where he was until he got to the stadium.

"Whyda fock are we on a train, anyway?" Los Parados sat down and reached for a beer.

Sal Spinale tossed a pair of red chips onto the table. "Two better. On account'a Canfield the Cheapskie says it's safer than flying."

"Safer, yeah," Donny Marshall snickered as he matched the bet. "Must really love us, him flyin' around on a frickin' Concorde."

"Concorde doesn't fly to Chicago," Kowalski said.

"Says who?" Marshall snapped back at him.

"Says the laws of economics." Kowalski hadn't yet made his bet, but was staring at Fredo Guittierez, who'd made the first raise. "What's the point of flying a Mach 2 airplane five hundred miles, especially one that uses as much fuel as a 747? And you can't go supersonic over populated areas anyway."

"Hey, Einstein," Spinale prodded, "you gonna bet, or what?"

Kowalski continued studying Guittierez. "*Naahhh . . .*" he said at last, dragging out the single syllable as he tossed his cards into the middle facedown. "He's got 'em."

"Bullshit," Cavvy Papazian said as he took some chips off the stacks in front of him. "Hasn't got squat." He threw in three reds. "One better. Bueno, up to you."

"*No más,*" Aires conceded as he tossed his cards on top of Kowalski's. "The kid say Fredo got 'em, Fredo got 'em."

Guittierez matched the raise and bumped it again. "Last raise. Who's in?"

Marshall, Spinale and Papazian saw the final raise, then turned over their cards: a pair, three of a kind and two pair.

"Read 'em and weep," Guittierez announced happily as he threw down his hole cards, revealing a straight.

"Fuck," Papazian spat, annoyed not so much at having lost the pot as having failed to read Guittierez as Kowalski had.

"How's he do that?" Marshall said in wonder.

"Don' matter how he does it, man," los Parados said. "What matters, how'da fock come you never believe him when he tells you he's doin' it? Whyn't you fold, asshole?"

"Why don't you go, um, go fuck yourself?" said Marshall uneasily. The rookie shortstop, from whose mouth you could practically see a stalk of wheat still hanging out, hadn't quite gotten used to the easy profanity of the Bigs but was doing his best. Fiercely desirous of fitting in, he was a terrible poker player but craved the camaraderie, and somehow couldn't shake the notion that folding a hand was somehow an admission of defeat.

"One time, this guy Trump," Spinale said to him as los Parados gathered up the dead cards, "he was bidding against some other guy for this casino in Vegas, and—"

"Merv Griffin," Kowalski said.

"What?"

"He was bidding against Merv Griffin."

Spinale turned to him. "Who gives a shit, Kowalski? Point is, the—"

"And it wasn't Las Vegas, it was Atlantic City."

"You wanna sit on the bench the rest of the season? Let me tell the goddamned story!" Spinale turned back to Marshall. "Point is, these two guys, they kept bidding the price up and up, and finally Trump, see, he gives up and this other guy—"

"Griffin."

"I'm warning you, Kowalski! This guy Griffin finally buys the joint, and everybody starts yelling how Trump got beat, somebody else snatched the hotel out from under this big-deal big shot, what an asshole, right?" Spinale tapped two fingers on the table. "But Trump, he waits until the whole deal is done and then he says, he says, 'I got beat?' he says. 'Whadda you, kiddin' me? This other schmuck, this Griffin, he paid *fifty million* more than the joint was worth and got *I* beat? Hah!'"

Spinale grinned idiotically, but it began to fade as Marshall stared back at him dumbly. "I don't—did he lose it in a poker game? What's the, uh . . . there's a point here, right?"

As Spinale, incredulous, stared at Marshall, Kowalski began shuffling the second deck for the next hand. "Donny, the most important move in poker is folding. Quitting when you should is really the only thing you can do to come out a winner in the end."

"But what about betting?"

"That only determines how *much* you win or lose," los Parados pronounced.

"It's more than that," Kowalski said. "You use betting to fool guys into getting out when they're holding better cards than you, or staying in when they don't. But Donny—" He turned back to Marshall "—folding is the key to whether you win or lose. You can't ever get to the point where you can bluff if you stay in on every hand." He waved a hand around the table. "You're sitting there with one pair in your hand and three other guys are betting against you. Did you really think that *none* of those three was going to be able to beat you?"

"I wasn't sure . . ."

"You're never sure. You can only figure the odds. Keep your eyes open, watch what the other guys are doing. Pay enough attention, and they're practically *telling* you what they're holding."

Marshall smiled skeptically. "Gidadda here, Marvin!"

Kowalski shrugged and sat back. There was no need for him to call attention to the relative size of their stacks of chips.

"I need a break," Spinale said as he stood up and squeezed his way into the aisle. He passed by Johansen's seat just as a disconsolate Bryce Thomason was getting up to leave. " 'Sup, kid? You look like shit."

"Nothing, Sal. Just nervous." Thomason was scheduled to start the next day. It was a big break, because heretofore he'd been used strictly as a reliever, a specialist who could be relied upon to come in and close out a tight game.

Truth was, there was a marked difference in the mentality of starters and relievers. Starters were more calm and collected, endurance athletes given to careful planning. They pitched according to a schedule every four or five days and followed a highly regimented routine in between starts.

Relievers, on the other hand, were firemen, always on call and ready to respond to emergencies, sprinters who just wanted to get the damned ball and be let loose. Spinale had said of Bryce Thomason that he pitched like he was double-parked.

Somehow, though, the best could manage to get icy in the face of impending catastrophe, just like Thomason had during a crucial game in Oakland when he'd been called in with the bases loaded, the score tied and no one out. Taking the ball as he reached a mound conference full of men about to implode with anxiety, he'd inquired smoothly, "And what seems to be the problem here?"

"There's only two relievers in the entire Hall'a Fame," Spinale had remarked after Thomason had put the game away, "and one of 'em ain't Goose Gossage." He made it sound like the legendary closer's absence from the Hall was both a crime and a warning.

Converting closers to starters was a rarity, and Thomason was determined to demonstrate that he had great endurance as well as great stuff.

As Spinale made his way up the aisle, reliever Rafael Fuentes reached up from his seat and grabbed his arm. "Hey, how the hell come he never lets *me* start?"

"It's on account'a you always lose control at the same point in every game," Spinale answered.

"Oh yeah? When's that?"

"Right after the national anthem."

Spinale shook his arm loose and resumed walking, then sat down opposite Johansen. "Thomason gonna pull himself together?"

Johansen shook his head. "We need to scratch him."

"He know?"

"No."

"So what's—"

"Forget it."

Spinale forgot it. "Hey, I meant to ask you . . . how come you blew Schmidt off the other day in the parking lot? He just wanted to have a drink and you—"

"I was tired. Had stuff to do."

"Yeah, but—"

"Sal, you in a Chatty Cathy mood here, or what? I need to take a nap."

"Good idea. Me, too." Spinale, an accomplished catnapper, threw his head back and was asleep in less than five minutes.

Johansen's eyes were closed but he wasn't sleeping. He was thinking, as he so often did, about his rookie year in baseball.

Specifically, he was thinking about Henry Schmidt . . .

New York, years before

Schmidt's lower lip trembled visibly, even in the dim light of the wharfside bar. Johansen stared at him with a mixture of disgust, anger and not a little pity. "How much you in for?"

Schmidt wiped at his mouth. "Eighty large," he muttered resignedly, wincing in anticipation of Johansen's reaction.

Johansen exhaled noisily. "Holy Christ, Henry . . . !"

Henry Schmidt was the kind of inveterate gambler who'd seen no irony whatsoever when he once bet a friend a thousand dollars that he could go a week without gambling. He hadn't even seen the irony when he'd lost. While it was true that he was genuinely pained by loss, he didn't seem to receive much pleasure from winning either, because, like any astute and forward thinking businessman, he felt compelled to plow any short-term gains back into the business. But since the business was gambling, ending up in the black was a statistical impossibility. This logic was completely lost on Schmidt, who'd been telling himself for some forty-odd years that he'd for sure quit once he hit the big score, which was a bit like a high school junior promising a lifetime of celibacy if he could boink the prom queen just once.

"Walked away a winner from Vegas three times last year," Schmidt averred to Johansen proudly.

"I don't doubt it, Henry." And he didn't, figuring that three times a winner was about right, considering that Schmidt had made at least two dozen visits there altogether, as well as to Reno, Atlantic City and several seedy, Formica-bedecked Native American casinos in California.

The clatter of a wooden ball dropping into the roulette wheel, the soft *swish-swish* of cards flipping their way around a blackjack table, even the muted clicks of the solid-gold cigarette lighters favored by tuxedo-clad baccarat players . . . all of those familiar and comforting sounds were a harmonious symphony to Schmidt, but he'd bet on which of two sugar cubes a fly would alight on first if there was no more formal game immediately at hand.

Like most degenerate gamblers, Schmidt was perpetually in debt, chronically unhappy, constantly in fear and living in a state of denial so profoundly persuasive that, were he not such a truly warm and generous soul, he'd be clinically diagnosable as a sociopath.

"This mare at Belmont, Zuke," Schmidt pleaded as he grasped Johansen's arm, "there was no way she could lose. No way, I'm tellin' you, and this—"

"Except she did lose." Johansen snatched his arm away. "They always lose, Henry!"

"I had this tip—"

"Tip?" Johansen's eyes burned into Schmidt's. "Why in hell would anyone give you a sure thing, Henry! Why would somebody want you to bet a pile'a dough that would only cut into his own winnings, tell me! What are you, Al Capone, that you could ever return a favor like that?"

Schmidt turned his head away, ashamed at the truth of what he was hearing, that some wiseguy smarter than he had just upped his own take on the horse that was really the sure thing. Schmidt's wasted bet had only added to the pari-mutuel pool from which the winners drew their prizes. "Zuke, you gotta help me out here."

Johansen, embarrassed at a desperation so profound it could make Schmidt beg even before the harsh glare of his stupidity had begun to fade, shook his head. "I'm just a rookie, Henry, practically at league minimum. I couldn't begin to make a dent in eighty thousand. Maybe I could—"

"I need you to dump the Chicago game."

Johansen felt the world he thought he had known so well suddenly seem to shift slightly, as if crossing into another dimension parallel to his own but totally separate from it. He was acutely aware that Schmidt already knew everything that was going through his mind and there was no need to voice any of it out loud.

"I'm in some seriously deep shit here, Zuke. No more markers, no more promises, no more payoffs over time . . . the hard guys, they know I'll just piss it all away before they see any of it."

Johansen could guess the rest. The established bookies weren't so much concerned about the money as they were about their reputations. People were starting to figure out that the flamboyant, smart-mouthed Schmidt had been stringing his creditors along, pyramiding fresh losses on top of old ones in a kind of weird, self-cycling Ponzi scheme. Were they to allow it to continue, others might feel less pressured about making good on their own losses. So Schmidt either had to pay or he had to suffer, and suffer visibly, as an example.

"You owe me, Zuke," Schmidt said, which snapped Johansen out of his chilling reverie. "You were flinging cow shit at barn walls when I pulled you out and got you to the Bigs!"

"*I* got me to the Bigs, Henry. You got me signed."

It was unnecessary to point that out, because what Schmidt had said was essentially true. Without his uncanny eye for hidden talent, Johansen never would have been in baseball at all. It was also true that Schmidt had gambled away his entire bonus for finding Johansen within two days of the contract being signed.

Johansen wasn't a brain surgeon, but he knew right from wrong, and it didn't take him long to figure this one out. "Henry," he said softly, "if you needed a kidney, I'd rip one out of my side and hand it to you. But if I tank this game and get you square with the hard guys, a week later you'll be asking me to do it again."

"Zuke——!" Schmidt began to wail, sensing where this was going.

"Lemme finish." Johansen moved his eyes around the room, then leaned in closer. "I wouldn't help a junkie by giving him a fix, and I won't help you by paying off your debt."

"You owe me!" Schmidt hissed back at him.

"Yeah, I owe you. But how much? You're asking me to risk my career, maybe even prison, to fix something that won't stay fixed. You figure my debt's that large?"

"Zuke . . ."

"I've stood off to the side and watched you self-destruct for over a year, Henry. Now you're asking me to help you do it."

"Zuke, I'm begging you!"

"You got no right, Henry, you hear me?" Johansen kicked back the chair as he stood up. A few eyes turned their way, but just as quickly went back to their own business. "You got no right to ask me a thing like that!"

Johansen, watching as Schmidt put a shaking hand to his forehead, knew he couldn't stand another second of watching without doing something he might regret. He reached into his pocket for some bills, threw them onto the table and headed for the door.

He crossed the street quickly and put his hands on the rough surface of an old and crumbling concrete wall, drinking deeply of the raw, humid air as he leaned forward. A hundred yards away, luminescent foam churned behind a tugboat slowly pushing a garbage scow toward a landfill at the south end of the city.

Johansen knew that throwing a game would be as impossible for him as breathing underwater. But he also knew that the sight of the forlorn and terrified Schmidt sitting alone in a bar would haunt him forever if he just left him there. Maybe there was another way, some middle ground that would get Schmidt clear without requiring Johansen to shame himself so badly he'd never be able to walk into another ballpark.

He turned and began walking back to the bar, and saw Schmidt just as he emerged from the doorway. Johansen raised his hand and prepared to call out to him, but was stopped by the sight of three hulking shapes who appeared to materialize behind his friend.

Schmidt saw them, too, and hurried his steps, but it was like outrunning a disease, and before Johansen could fathom all that was happening, the shapes had enveloped Schmidt and then the entire ensemble disappeared.

Johansen ran across the street, frantically scanning the deep shadows . . .

"Jesus no!" a strangled, muffled voice cried out, and Johansen followed it without considering the consequences.

Shuffling, grunting noises punctuated by several thudding sounds drew him to an alley he hadn't noticed before. A dim, orange light flickered against one of its walls, and as Johansen's eyes adapted he saw that it was a cigarette lighter held high by small-time hood

Argenio Spazzarella, the sputtering flame illuminating a scene whose monstrous brutality was obscenely out of proportion to the transgression in question.

There was no way Johansen could have left it alone and lived with himself, and he threw himself hard against one of the shapes, knocking a surprised thug into a brick wall.

A cigarette fell out of Spazzarella's mouth. Still holding the lighter high, he hadn't yet quite figured out what was happening, and Johansen took that opportunity to ram his elbow into the face of the other animal who'd been working on Schmidt. The man emitted a startled squeal and dropped back, his hands flying to his broken nose.

As the first goon picked himself up and quickly assessed the situation, Johansen reached down and got his hands under Schmidt's arms and tried to pull him to his feet. The smell of urine and feces released amid bottomless fear surrounded him and threatened to leech into his heart, and that's when Spazzarella finally sorted himself out.

"It's the fuckin' pitcher!" he rasped out hoarsely as he dropped the lighter.

"Sonofa—" The first man pushed back from the brick wall. Johansen turned to the side and kicked out as hard as he could, knowing from the feel of contact that he'd broken something vital of the man's, and knowing with equal certainty that a barrier had been crossed and that he and Schmidt were dead if they didn't somehow get out of there within the next few seconds.

By now Schmidt had managed to rouse himself and start running, fueled by the possibility of escape that temporarily overcame his pain. Johansen, still off-balance from the roundhouse kick he'd delivered, got his footing and took a step toward the street.

"Here you go, pitcher . . ."

Before Johansen could process the words or discern what it was that had just flashed high above him, Spazzarella's hand shot down toward his shoulder at the speed of light.

He could feel each individual molecule of the stiletto blade as it pierced his jacket and then his skin, and knew as surely as if he were watching an X ray that it had gone on to sever his rotator cuff and a handful of other muscles with it.

The rookie pitcher barely noticed the physical pain in his arm, which was a distant tickle compared to the agony that descended like a shroud over his soul.

Seven

O UT ON THE MOUND AGAINST the Blue Jays, Majestyks starter Zacky Ghirardelli was getting killed. He got the first batter out, then it was single, double, walk, double, two more walks . . .

Ghirardelli was a junkball pitcher. No longer possessed of sufficient strength to fire the fastballs, curves and sliders that were the bread and butter of healthier arms, he resorted to pitches like the knuckleball, which could be thrown with hardly any effort but, if done correctly, could be counted on to bob, weave and meander so radically it was anybody's guess if the catcher could even handle it once the batter missed it completely. A good knuckler was a freakshow of a pitch, but also a risky one: Fail to release it just so, and it was a slow-motion invitation to be launched over the fence for a home run.

Orin Mathias came up to bat. Ghirardelli threw. Mathias smashed it over the left field wall, just foul.

"Watch out for him!" Sal Spinale yelled from the dugout steps. "He's a first pitch hitter!"

A dumbfounded Ghirardelli stared at Spinale: Of what possible use was that bit of information *now?* He shook it away and threw again, and this time Mathias caught it flush and put it on the other side of the foul pole for a home run. He might as well have hit a line drive at Ghirardelli's head.

It hadn't always been like that for the struggling pitcher, who in his younger days had some of the best speed and control in the league. He'd often compared pitching to golf, another sport he played with consummate skill: If you've thrown or swung enough in practice to nail your technique down, then you've got to trust your systems to do what they need to do. Your job was to completely forget technique and instead visualize the throw. See the ball leaving your hand, watch it curve and dive, see exactly how it's going to meet the catcher's glove when the batter swings and misses. Do nothing but that and your body will take over and do the rest. It already knows how—you've spent enough time training it—so what you need to do, you need only to give your body the mission by visualizing the desired result, then get the hell out of its way and let it go to work.

Except that it was no longer working for Ghirardelli, and he found himself becoming one of those pitchers who didn't think about winning, they thought about not embarrassing themselves out there. If they gave up only five hits but their team still lost 1-0, they were deliriously happy. If they won 12-10 and they pitched a lousy game, they felt awful. For them, a good game wasn't one they won; it was one they escaped from. If they did it with style, with a lot of strikeouts and very few hits, so much the better, but for those on the edge, pitching a baseball game had become like landing a plane: If they walked away unscathed, they did good. If the plane or their arms were still usable, they did great.

Almost without his realizing it, Ghirardelli's mantra had transformed itself from "Mow 'em down and take no prisoners" to "Please don't let me fuck up." This from a man once so fanatical about his craft that he wouldn't even help his wife with the dishes, for fear of softening the calluses he'd worked for years to build up to exactly the right proportions.

Now, like nearly all pitchers at one time or another who found themselves in a tight spot with their stuff abandoning them, he resorted to whatever he could get away with, annoying legalities be damned. He'd elevated the spitter and its variations to a fine art, altering the ball to skew its aerodynamics, doing it in ways that were either not immediately detectable or, if they were, not demonstrably intentional on his part. Despite the term "spitter," it wasn't necessarily about saliva, but could include such substances as slippery elm or Vaseline and even K-Y Jelly, secreted about various parts of the pitcher's anatomy and applied with stealth that would make a stage magician envious. He'd survived several friskings that had been administered by umpires whenever his pitches suddenly began falling off the table in late innings. He'd even been known to *fake* doctoring the ball, just to throw off batters by tricking them into thinking the spitter was coming when it wasn't.

At just about the time he lost count of how many men he'd put on base today, he saw Zuke Johansen come up out of the dugout with one hand in the air, signaling the ump for time. Ghirardelli hung his head and squeezed his eyes shut.

"Don't pull me, skipper," he said when Johansen was still ten feet away.

"Zacky . . ."

"Lemme pitch to this guy. I got him out last time."

"That was in *this* inning!" Johansen reminded him, trying to keep his voice free of sarcasm. "What's going on?"

Ghirardelli shook his head miserably and an old scene flashed into his mind, of the exact moment he knew his "younger days" were over. His manager at the time had walked out to the mound just as Johansen had today, and asked the same question: *What's going on?* "I'm throwing 'em twice as hard as I ever have," Ghirardelli had answered. "They're just not getting there as fast."

But now he didn't throw hard at all, and he had no answer for Johansen. He slammed the ball into his glove and then let his hand dangle at his side.

Some days the knuckler worked; some days it didn't. "Today's one of those days, Zacky," Johansen said, not unsympathetically. "You'll get it back."

It didn't make Ghirardelli feel any better. If he had some idea *why* it wasn't working, some flaw in technique he could spot, then he would know what to work on to correct it. But again like a golfer, one who swings the same swing that worked yesterday but today keeps sending them all to parts unknown, he could only clench his jaw in burning frustration and pray it would be better next time, because prayer was all that was left when you had no damned idea in the world what was wrong. He didn't want to become one of those desperate has-beens who hid sandpaper and nail files in their gloves, or who over-pomaded their hair so they could surreptitiously reach up and grab a glob, in order to do something—anything—to make the ball jink randomly on its way to the plate.

In the dugout Kowalski was fingering his lip thoughtfully. "I thought Zacky was the best knuckleballer in the league," he said to pitching coach Jimmy Hazeltine.

A piece of waxed paper with a blot of mustard on it blew past the dugout. One of the batboys ran to retrieve it, waddling awkwardly and bending down just as a fresh gust took it away again. "When it's working," Hazeltine said, "the only way to catch it is to wait for it to stop rolling past you and then pick it up. Problem is, every once in a while it goes completely to shit. And it usually goes to shit in this stadium, don't ask me why."

A couple of the other guys were laughing openly now as the batboy struggled to retrieve the errant piece of paper. Kowalski held his cap down to keep it from blowing off as he went up the steps and looked around the ballpark. Attendants were hosing down the infield sand to keep it from swirling up off the ground, and the flags festooning the scoreboard were flapping noisily as they stood straight out and pointed to home plate. "When'd it happen last time?"

"Cleveland, three weeks ago. Had to pull him after two innings.

Four days before that, in Anaheim? Guy was a magician." Behind them, Federico Guittierez winced as something flew into his eye. "Kinda like my golf game: Never know what the hell is going to show up."

"And before that?"

"Kansas. It was heartbreaking, and VandeMerve threw fastballs at us looked like they were fired out of cannons."

"Huh." Kowalski, still holding onto his cap, looked around once more and then went back into the dugout.

"Craziest goddamned thing," he heard Spinale mutter as he walked past him.

The bench coach stopped agitating for a moment as he watched Kowalski pull a laptop computer out of his carryall and then yank the phone cord out of the wall. "What the hell are you doing?"

"Checking something."

AS WAS HIS USUAL CUSTOM, Kowalski disappeared during the traditional postgame interviews, retreating into the sanctuary of the trainer's room, the confessional in which the trainer was the local priest and even writers didn't have access.

Coming into the locker room after he thought everybody else was gone, he saw Ghirardelli, slouched in dejection, staring at something Kowalski couldn't see around a bank of lockers. Coming alongside he eventually was able to see the object of Ghirardelli's apparent fascination: Billy Blyvelt sitting astride a bench, a needle in his arm.

Pulling back quickly so he wouldn't be spotted, Kowalski stifled a gasp and slapped his hands over his mouth, but he needn't have bothered. Ghirardelli was too engrossed, and Blyvelt too busy, to take notice of much else.

"I don't know . . ." Ghirardelli was saying, somewhat wistfully.

"Less than stellar today, Zacky."

"But that stuff isn't gonna help a knuckleball."

Blyvelt laughed. "Hell with the knuckler. Don't you want your fastball back?"

"Not *that* bad." But his voice lacked conviction.

Kowalski stole quietly out of the locker room and back up to the field, where Geoffrey Slagenbach was still gathering up equipment.

"Hiya, Marvin. Why you still dressed?"

Kowalski waved off the question and wandered to the dugout, where he sat for about half an hour staring at the field, and then made his way down to the visiting manager's cubicle.

"Why're you still dressed?" Johansen asked him.

Kowalski didn't answer, but took a seat in front of Johansen's battered wooden desk. "Zuke, I saw . . . one of the guys is, uh . . ."

Johansen sat down facing him. "One of the guys is what?" he asked, tensing up.

"He had a needle." Kowalski slumped back and put a hand to his forehead. "He, uh, he was . . ."

"Oh." Johansen relaxed. "That come as a surprise, did it?"

It had, but not as much as Johansen's cavalier attitude upon being told. "You knew?"

"Who was it?"

"I'm not going to—"

"Thomason? Bombeck? Blyvelt?"

Kowalski sat bolt upright. "What?"

Johansen waved him back down. "Not much of a secret, kid. If I told you how many guys in the league were on the juice, you wouldn't believe me."

"Juice?"

"Steroids. Stanazolol, Dianabol, Pronabol, Andriol, Anadrol, Deca-Durabolin, Maxibolin—"

Kowalski, his mind reeling, held up his hand. "How on earth do they get past the drug tests!"

"This is baseball, Marvin. There are no drug tests."

"No drug tests? How is that possible! Doesn't anybody care?"

Johansen wasn't sure whether to laugh at Kowalski's naiveté or sympathize with his shock. "They only care when it's convenient. What they want is to see guys knock 'em out of the ballpark three, four times a game. Why do you think they lowered the mound?"

"Then why am *I* playing? I'm a DH and I can't hit worth a hoot."

"Because even more than big hitting, the fans like a winner. If you win, you can take drugs, beat your wife, sodomize farm animals and join the communist party, they don't give a shit. They'll let you back in every time. But if you don't win? Spit on the subway and they'll hang you from the highest yardarm and scream about how your lack of good old American family values will be the death of the game."

"But steroids, I mean . . . don't they know what that stuff will do to them?"

"They don't want to know, kid."

"How many?"

"How many what?"

"You said, if you told me how many big leaguers use the stuff, I wouldn't believe it."

"Wild guess?" Johansen shrugged. "Maybe twenty-five percent."

Kowalski shook his head, whether in shock or disbelief Johansen couldn't tell. "Did you take the juice, when you were playing?"

Johansen hesitated, but just for a second. "Yeah. I spent two years in the minors watching guys not as good as me shoot up and get called up, like the needle was a magic wand. I couldn't get off the farm, so . . ."

"The minors? They're doing it in the minors? Jeez, Zuke . . . don't those guys . . . didn't you know you were gonna die young?"

"There isn't a twenty-year-old in sports who really believes he's ever gonna die, period. Dangle a big-league contract to a minor leaguer and he'll swallow arsenic if he has to."

Kowalski was having a hard time digesting what he was hearing. "Baseball players . . ." he muttered disconsolately.

"Not just baseball players, kid. The trick in any sport is to do as much as you think you can get away with. That's why every Olympics has a scandal, the Tour de France, bodybuilding . . . even the Paralympics."

"Baloney!" Kowalski exclaimed reflexively. "The Paralympics? Baloney!"

Johansen nodded. "Anything they can get away with. Wheelchair athletes? They tie strings around their dicks so they can't pee. Doesn't hurt, because they can't feel anything down there, but it elevates their blood pressure and makes 'em go faster. Once in a while one of 'em ruptures a bladder, but what the hell, they get a trophy."

"But—"

"Look, nobody *wants* to take the juice. If everybody else didn't, they wouldn't either. But what the hell can you do when everybody else is using and you're getting left behind?"

Johansen could see what was going on in Kowalski's mind. The kid was probably running down a mental list of his ball-playing idols and trying to figure out who'd been on the needle and who hadn't. It wasn't hard to spot some of them: journeymen ballplayers who'd puttered around the league for years and suddenly started hitting like Ruth; severe cases of acne out of nowhere; a few great years and then a mysterious hospitalization for failure of some major organ; skinny marinks reappearing after the off-season with twenty pounds of fresh muscle.

"Try not to worry about it, kid," Johansen said, rising. "It's about money—big money—so there's not a damned thing you or I can do about it."

San Francisco—May 23

Today was Kowalski's first interleague game, a recent innovation by which a team from the American League could play a team from the National League in other than the World Series. Very exciting for the fans, although it cut deeply into the heart of baseball purists, who were certain it was the death of baseball. Of course, purists had been predicting the death of baseball ever since fans were no longer allowed to sit in the outfield in the late nineteenth century.

It was Kowalski's first interleague game but he couldn't play in it, because they were at the National League Giants home field in San Francisco. The National League didn't use a designated hitter, and in interleague games the DH could be used only when the home team was in the American League.

This was also the day that Majestyks center fielder John "The Deacon" Amos returned from intensive rehab following a calf injury.

As soon as he got up to the field, Amos headed straight for Kowalski. "Welcome to the league, Marvin," he said, sticking out his hand. In the nearby dugout, several audible groans emerged. "I'm John Amos."

"Thanks, John," Kowalski replied amiably, taking the proffered hand.

"Tell me, have you discovered Christ yet? Have you accepted him as your Lord and savior?"

Upon hearing this, Cavvy Papazian headed out of the dugout to rescue the unsuspecting rookie.

"What was that?"

Amos repeated the question.

Kowalski looked around, not quite sure if this was a put-on or not. "That's an awfully personal question."

Now it was Amos' turn to be uncomfortable. That was a response he'd not gotten before, and he'd asked the question hundreds of times. "Well . . ."

"I mean, how do you even know I'm not Jewish? Or Muslim or a Buddhist?"

Hearing this, Papazian decided to back off and see if Amos gave it up. But one thing about proselytizers, they never took anything personally. So long as someone was willing to even have the discussion, they'd stick with it no matter what. "Do you believe in God?"

"What do you mean by God?"

"You know: a supreme being."

"That's just another name. Tell me what you *mean* when you say 'God.'"

Amos, suspecting he was being played, couldn't keep some small annoyance out of his voice. "Listen, you know very well what I mean when I say 'God!'" He was willing to engage in any kind of intellectual discourse this kid had to offer up, but not if he was being baited.

Kowalski shook his head. "In all truth, I really don't know what you mean. I don't know you well enough."

"All right," Amos sighed, digging in for the long haul. "Do you believe that there is something out there that is bigger than yourself?"

"Of course." By now a half-dozen players had bellied up to the wire mesh screen to listen in.

Amos, initially pleased with that response, now grew suspicious as Kowalski stared at him patiently without expanding on his simple answer. "Wait a minute . . ."

Kowalski smiled. "Can I ask you something, John?"

"Sure."

"Seems to me that whether God exists, or whether somebody believes or not, well, that's about the most important, complicated question a human being can ever ask. You agree?"

Amos sensed a trap but saw no way out. "I'd say that was about right."

"Okay. So how come every time we ask that question we want a yes or no answer?"

Amos started to relax slightly.

"I mean, it takes more words to tell you what I want on my hot dog than it does to tell you how I feel about God. Doesn't seem right to me."

Amos thought for a second, then began nodding slowly. "You got a point."

"Thought you'd see it my way."

"Well stated."

"Thank you."

"So, do you believe in God?"

"Depends what you—"

Zuke Johansen whistled and began shouting orders to everyone. When people started finally moving around, he clapped Amos on the back and said, "Nice to have you back, John. Glad to see you're feeling better."

"In the big inning," Wade Cogburn intoned somberly, "God created baseball . . ."

"Hey Kowalski, you're a'pposed to be practicing!" Spinale yelled.

"For what, Sal?"

It was a good point, but it annoyed Spinale anyway. "Everybody else is practicing," he mumbled, then decided to take it out on Ghirardelli instead, who *was* practicing. "Hey, Zacky, quit throwing already, goddamnit!" he called out to the sidelines where the pitcher was working out with Papazian. "You got a game today!"

Ghirardelli put his hands on his hips. "Told you a million times, Sal: I throw knuckleballs. There's no effort to throwing a knuckleball. But you gotta throw it a lot to keep the feel."

"Yeah, well," Spinale grumbled, "just don't wear your goddamned arm out."

Ghirardelli raised his eyebrows in disbelief. "I just told you . . . !"

Papazian walked up and handed him the ball. "Forget it, Zacky. He's so thick he don't even realize he makes no sense half the time."

At the sound of Ghirardelli's laughter, Spinale turned around and scowled, then yelled out, "Keep throwing, goddamnit!" which only made Ghirardelli laugh even harder.

He was still laughing as Kowalski walked up to him and said, "You shouldn't pitch today, Zacky."

The loopy grin left Ghirardelli's face so fast it was like watching a new slide go up on a screen during a lecture. "I shouldn't . . . hey, who the fuck're you, tellin' me I shouldn't pitch!"

Kowalski turned and let the stiff breeze blowing across the field tousle his hair. "You got a weird tailwind out there, Zacky. Must be blowing twenty, twenty-five knots."

"What's it to you?"

"To me? Nothing. But to you, a lot. Your knuckleball won't break. It'll be like hitting off a tee and these guys are going to clobber you."

"Yeah, well fuck you, Abner Doubleday." Ghirardelli took the ball he was holding and repositioned it so it was supported by his thumb at the bottom and his fingernails at the top. In actuality, the knuckles don't enter into a knuckleball. "I got a knuckler hops around like a bee buzzin' a flower."

"Not today, you won't." Kowalski held up the laptop he'd had tucked under his arm. "Last time out? When we were in Toronto? The reason you—"

"Yeah, well suppose you just mind your own damned business, okay? You get another ten years around here and then we'll let you be manager."

"Suit yourself." Kowalski, showing no obvious offense, did as he was told and let it go.

Spinale, quiet for once, was standing nearby. "Everything okay, kid?"

"Yeah. You know, Sal, I think ninety percent of this game is pitching."

"Damned right," the bench coach agreed. "And the other half is hitting."

GHIRARDELLI LASTED TWO-THIRDS of the first inning. He faced nearly the entire Giants lineup, getting two of them out only because of spectacular fielding by John Amos and Vince Salvanella, then gave up a triple on a play by Salvanella that was less than stellar but nowhere near bad enough to qualify as an error, and came back to the dugout looking like his dog had just died.

Johansen left Ghirardelli alone, but after the inning cornered Salvanella. "What the hell happened . . . you lose it in the sun?"

Salvanella looked crossly at Ghirardelli, who'd planted a cream-puff pitch as though the batter had ordered it off a menu. "Hell, skip . . . I lost it in a *cloud*!" This from the player sportswriters liked to call "Dr. Strangeglove," the man who never ran after a fly ball, but just seemed to be in the right place when it came down.

Ghirardelli's performance had been so abysmal the other players subconsciously shied away from him, as though whatever had caused such awful pitching might be catching. He buried his face in his hands and tried to fight off images of "Farewell Zacky Ghirardelli Day" at the Shit Hole in Des Moines.

Feeling a presence at his side he looked up to see Marvin Kowalski, and braced himself to deck the snot-nosed brat as soon as the I-told-you-so speech started.

"The reason your knuckler hops around," Kowalski said with normal inflection, "is because the ball isn't spinning. When the air hits the stitches it makes the ball move around randomly."

"I already know that," Ghirardelli said suspiciously.

Kowalski pointed out at the field. "But you've got a strong tailwind out there, blowing in from the bay. You only throw the knuckler a little over sixty miles an hour to begin with. Add a thirty-mile-an-hour wind from behind you and air is only hitting the ball at thirty or thirty-five." He paused to see if it was sinking in, then took a ball out of the equipment bag and dropped it into Ghirardelli's hand. "That's not enough to make it dance, Zacky."

Ghirardelli twisted the ball slowly, staring at the stitches as realization slowly dawned.

Pitching coach Jimmy Hazeltine had sidled up quietly to listen. "Always thought big tailwinds ruin a knuckler," he said, "but people say it's just old baseball bullshit."

"I checked the weather during your last few starts," Kowalski said. "Tailwinds killed you every time."

"So how come it don't move like a rabbit when he pitches into a headwind?" Spinale butted in smugly. "Tell me that, smart guy."

Johansen moved in as well. "Because a pitcher can't get a headwind unless you tear down the grandstand behind home plate," he said.

"How the hell come you din't tell me this before!" Ghirardelli demanded of Kowalski.

"I did."

"Well," Ghirardelli said, softening noticeably, "you shoulda told me louder."

Even by the time he finished the sentence, he found himself starting to feel better. Whether Kowalski's theory held any water or not, it offered hope. It explained what heretofore had seemed like purely random fluctuations in the efficacy of his knuckleball, why on some days batters would hit it like it had been set up on a tee, while on others it gyrated so madly Papazian had to use every square inch of an oversized glove to have any chance at all of catching it. "I liked it better when the mound was higher," he said in joking wistfulness.

"But look at it this way," Spinale chimed in over the ensuing laughter. "At least this way you're closer to the batter."

Kowalski rolled his eyes and did a quick mental calculation. "Yeah—" he plucked a hair from the back of his head and held it up "—by about this much."

Ghirardelli laid two fingers in a "Y" across the top of the ball he was holding, the classic throwing position, then slowly rubbed the bottom of the ball with his thumb. "Spend my whole life grippin' a baseball," he said, half to himself, "only to realize it's been the other way around all along."

"WHAT WAS THE POINT of jumping on the Deacon like that?"

Kowalski looked at Johansen in surprise. "You mean Amos?"

"I mean Amos. Think you were a little hard on him? He asked you a simple question."

"Asking me if I've found God isn't so simple."

"But what was the harm?"

"I don't like being preached to. Especially by strangers."

"You weren't strangers. You were teammates."

"But we'd just met!"

"Doesn't matter. You're on the same club, there's a whole culture goes with it. That's why John felt it was okay to start right in on you like that, something he wouldn't do with a stranger. Far as the Deacon's concerned, you wear a Majestyks uniform, you're family."

"Yeah, well I've had that stuff shoved down my throat all my life by family. They brag to everyone else about how smart I am, then they force-feed me all that—" He stopped before it became a rant. "Why do you think I'm going to MIT?"

MIT? Where the hell had that come from? "To get away, I suppose. I can understand that."

"Not so much away from something as *to* something else. A place where just asking questions isn't considered blasphemy."

And when the hell was it supposed to happen? Johansen shook the thought away, not wanting to get distracted. "Fine. But whaddaya say you don't saddle a well-meaning teammate with baggage that's yours, not his?"

Johansen saw that he'd made an impact, and didn't want Kowalski to feel overly bad about being chastised. "I'll grant you, John can get a little irritating wearing his religion on his sleeve, but I'll tell you something else: He's a good man."

"Never said he—"

"Not just a good ballplayer. A good man. He got Donny Marshall clean and sober, and he managed finances for some of these hotshot assholes who're seeing real money for the first time in their lives and don't know what the hell to do with all of it. He's the one who got Leffingwell's financial program going. He also got Papazian through a nasty divorce without him cracking up." Part of Amos' task during Papazian's painful split-up was to keep the catcher away from Chi Chi los Parados, whose advice to the nerve-wracked catcher had been "If your woman wanneda see more'a you, she shoulda become a pitcher."

They turned at the sound of a well-struck ball and watched as Vince Salvanella dropped his bat and took off for first. John Amos, who'd struck out in both his at-bats today, was the first off the bench and to the wire-mesh screen, clapping his hands and whooping loudly in support of Salvanella. "Move him around, Darryl!" he yelled encouragingly at Bombeck, who was getting ready to take his turn at bat.

"Zacky had a point, you know," Zuke Johansen said, changing the subject. He'd gotten his message across and saw no need to dwell on it, nor was he interested right now in psychoanalyzing Kowalski's apparent rebellion against his upbringing.

"About what?" Kowalski asked.

"About the mound. About how it used to be higher."

Kowalski nodded. "Pitchers were getting too dominant, so the league threw some advantages back to the batters."

"Well, it backfired," Johansen said with some bitterness. He wasn't just a manager but a true student of the game, the kind who could stand aside from the immediate issue and put things in context. Some of the players he dealt with barely knew who Ted Williams was, or could care less, and he was glad of the rookie's willing ear. "You got guys now who would barely have gotten noticed twenty years ago, they're knocking twenty, thirty homers a season into the stands."

"It's the drugs, right? The steroids?"

"It's not just that. Lower mound, the designated hitter . . ." Johansen shook his head. "There's no respect for tradition anymore. This isn't rhythmic gymnastics or indoor soccer, goddamnit, it's baseball! Guy should be able to go to sleep for a hundred years and wake up and go to a ballpark and know exactly what's going on. Baseball is like the paper clip—it doesn't change because it doesn't need to. You can't make it any better!"

He caught himself getting strident and tried to modulate his tone. "This is a game, what happens today isn't important, what happened *yesterday* is. What happens today won't be important for years. Everything that goes on is measured against what went on before. You can take a player today and compare him to a guy who was playing when Coolidge was president, or at least you could before they started fiddling with things that made the numbers fishy. *Designated hitters*, for cryin' out loud? It's like letting somebody else take Shaquille O'Neal's free throws for him." Johansen blinked and remembered where he was. "Meaning no offense, Marvin."

"None taken."

"Thing is, we don't own this game, we're just its custodians. You see museum guys touching up Rembrandts with a little more blue here and there? You can get sick, lose your job, we can have a war or riots or hurricanes, but the one thing you should be able to count on for a little stability in your life is baseball."

Kowalski waited for a few seconds, not wanting to jar Johansen out of the mood that had made him so voluble, then said, "One thing I don't get, though. With all that history, with all those statistics and the ability to compare players from one generation to the next, how is it that baseball is the only major team sport that plays on a non-standard field? How can you compare a guy who plays for the Cubs in Wrigley today to a guy who played in Ebbets Field in the fifties when the distances to the outfield fences aren't the same? Or what about how much easier it is to field on artificial turf where there aren't any crazy bounces?"

Johansen shook himself and looked around, remembering that a game was going on, however dull. With the Majestyks ahead by four and in obvious control, Johansen could afford to pull his attention away for a few minutes. "Damned if I know," he said.

Kowalski didn't want to lose him while he still had some question. "You were mentioning it's not just the drugs," he said quickly. "All that hitting, it's not just—"

"Pitching's gotten lousy, too, mostly because of expansion. Can't get enough good talent trained up to supply all the teams with decent arms. So we've got ordinary Joes racking up hits and thinking they're better'n DiMaggio, and it knocks all the historical stats out of whack."

"Fans sure do like home runs, though."

Johansen grunted contemptuously. "Home run's the most boring thing in the game. Everybody stands around with their thumbs up their asses because there's nothing to be done. You watch the ball sail away and everything that happens because of it is automatic. Every other kind of hit you have some drama, nine crazy fielders ganging up on one or two runners and doing everything they can to ruin their day." He pursed his lips and shook his head. "But whack one into the stands and there's none of that. All the men on base come home and there's not a damned thing anybody can do about it except hang their heads and let it happen. You call that exciting?"

Kowalski shrugged. "Some people think baseball's a boring game as it is."

Bryce Thomason had just checked his swing but gotten called on a third strike anyway and was staring daggers at the ump, as though about to start arguing the call. Johansen pushed back from the pole he'd been leaning against and headed for the dugout steps to stop his player from doing something stupid.

"It's only boring to boring people, son," he called back over his shoulder.

Eight

Des Moines—June 2

U M, MISTER, UH, MR. JOHANSEN?" said a familiarly absurd and timid voice.

Johansen felt a migraine coming on. "What is it,
Pudgy?"

"Well, uh, awful sorry to disturb you, I know you're busy, but,
uh . . ."

"I've got a plane to catch," Johansen squeezed out between
clenched teeth. "We've all got a plane to catch, so what's up?"

"Well, like I said, I sure didn't mean to—"

As Johansen began looking around for a small-bore weapon, Slagenbach finally revealed that Marvin Kowalski's parents were in the
general manager's office.

"WHAT WE'RE WORRIED ABOUT MOSTLY," Mrs. Kowalski admitted, "is he being in the city 'n' all."

Johansen tried not to be obvious as he looked at the clock behind them. The team's flight to New York was leaving in less than two hours, and the only worry *he* had about the city was how they were going to play the Yankees. Besides, the kid had already played in New York and nothing bad had happened. "Well, I really don't think you have much to—"

"I mean, Des Moines, well . . ." Mr. Kowalski's face screwed up with uncertainty and concern.

Des Moines?

"Used to was, only a couple dozen people even knew who our Marvin was. Now, well, seems the whole world knows who he is. Place like Des Moines, lotta bad stuff could happen."

Sure could, thought Johansen. *Could get a heart attack trying on gloves down to Younkers in the Southridge Mall.* "Don't know if you folks know it, but one of your son's best friends on the team is a lay minister in, um . . ." It occurred to Johansen that he didn't really know what the Kowalskis' religion was.

"You mean Mr. Amos?"

"Yes. He's a good man, straight as an arrow, and he spends a lot of time with Marvin." He saw the beginnings of a smile play around Mr. Kowalski's lips, and wondered if he was going to say anything about the fact that Amos was black. Or was it that he knew that his son and Amos were more like sparring partners than best friends, their debates having grown mythical in the range of topics they covered.

"We're not worried about bad influences, Mr. Johansen. Marvin's got a good head on him. It's people trying to take advantage of him, he bein' famous and all, but he dudn't have much experience outside of Osceola."

"Osceola?"

"County. Town'a Ocheyedan."

"Of course. Ocheyedan. Didn't realize that was in Osceola County."

"Uh huh," Mr. K said skeptically. "Anyways—"

"Baseball ends too late, Mr. Johansen," Mrs. Kowalski said anxiously.

"Ends? Oh, the season, yeah. Season ends in the fall." *For some earlier than others*, he thought but declined to voice, not wishing to get into the matter of playoff games.

"But college starts much earlier. You see, it's important Marvin go to college, on account of he isn't good for much around the farm. Does what he's told, but he doesn't seem much interested. Maybe he was cut out for better things . . ." She seemed to catch herself saying too much, straying outside the bounds of her Midwestern reserve, and pulled back.

"If he don't take over the farm," Mr. K affirmed, "he needs a way to make a living. Farm's probably not right for him anyway, tell you the truth. Too smart, see? Made his very own baseball machine, he did."

"He did?" Johansen bit his tongue, hoping he wasn't seen as ridiculing Mr. K's speech. "What'd it do?"

"Threw baseballs at him," Mrs. K answered. "Real fast, too. Used to scare the dickens out of us, how fast those hard balls were flyin' at him."

"Except it was a kinda flimsy contraption, see, and it didn't throw the balls so good. They come flyin' outta there ever which way, but Marvin could hit 'em, except I didn't know exactly where he was tryin' to hit 'em *to*, because he couldn't seem to hit 'em any better'n'at machine could throw 'em." Mr. K also seemed to catch himself growing voluble and came to a sudden halt. "Anyway, he needs a way to make a living."

"Baseball's not a bad way to earn a living," Johansen suggested.

"So what's he making . . . league minimum?"

"Uh, yes. Upstairs hasn't quite figured out what to do with him yet. Longer term, I mean."

"You're paying him league minimum because my boy doesn't much care about money and all he wants, he wants enough to pay for college. And you fellers don't really know what the *longer term* is, do you. One little change'a the rules and he's out of business, just another novelty act, another joke."

"Change the rules?"

"Sure, like whatsisname, that big guy, when he was playing basketball in New York. They outlawed the dunk just because of him, because he was too dom'nant, am I right? You don't think baseball could do the same thing?"

Johansen shook his head. "Baseball goes back before the Civil War, Mr. Kowalski. It moves like a glacier, not a jackrabbit."

"Except when it thinks it has to. I did a little research, see? Designated hitter, dropping the mound . . . I don't even know what I'm talking about, but it seems that whenever somebody gets a little too ahead they do something to get him a little more behind."

"Well, that's—"

"Look, I'm not knockin' your game, Mr. Johansen. It's just that our Marvin is a real good kid."

"Doesn't drink, doesn't get into trouble, doesn't do drugs," Mrs. K threw in.

"Course you don't know that for sure, do you." Johansen didn't know why he'd said that. Maybe it was because he felt he wasn't winning any points here and needed to gain the upper hand. But maybe he'd gone too far . . .

Mr. Kowalski looked at him for a few seconds, then said, "Well, you got a point there, sir." It came out like *Just because we're farmers doesn't mean we're stupid.* "We know you can't ever know that for sure."

"Okay, then."

"But what we *do* know is that he was a straight-A student, valedictorian of his class and had the highest SAT scores in the county. So even if he's shootin' heroin it dudn't seem to be affecting him much, does it?"

Johansen smiled in surrender, his efforts to shake these people up having backfired. "Okay, you got me there. But I run a clean club—"

"You don't have any control over—"

"You ever hear of a player named Harold Marbury?"

Mr. K stared at him, not knowing what to make of the interruption, then decided not to make anything of it since what had been interrupted was his own interruption. "Certainly, a troubled young man. Yankees, right?"

"That's right. But he played for Des Moines three years ago. For me. Got himself into a bit of a scrape over some substances he'd got caught with."

"I remember."

"I sat him down, told him if it ever happened again there'd be no more second chances. Well it happened again. So I put his a . . . I put him down on the bench and I left him there. Wouldn't let him play. Six million a year he was costing us and I wouldn't let him take the field."

"Rings a bell, that does," Mrs. K said.

Johansen nodded at her encouragingly. "Front office kicked and screamed and hollered at me, did everything but sue me and kidnap my family, but I wouldn't play him. Finally, they traded him to some people who worry less about stuff like that if the man's putting numbers up on the board."

Mr. K nodded enthusiastically. "You did the right thing with a man like that, Mr. Johansen. Why, I'da—"

"Don't misunderstand me, Mr. Kowalski. What a man does with his own life is his own business. It's when it affects the team that it becomes *my* business. I didn't ground him because he was a doper or got arrested but because he embarrassed his club. Let down his teammates. Even put on them some of his own stink and got people talking and it demoralized some of the others, couple of whom were making a fraction of what he was making and felt he oughta by God behave himself." He could see that he'd finally made an impact and stopped.

"So you won't let anything happen to him?" Mrs. K asked with hope in her voice.

"Not saying that at all, ma'am. Kid's over eighteen and I'm not his legal guardian. I'm just his manager. On top of that it's not my business to mother my players." He waited, for Mr. K to acknowledge with his posture the commonsense wisdom of what he was hearing, for Mrs. K to have a stab of anxiety that he could proceed to relieve.

"Only thing I can promise you is that I run the kind of club where bad things happening to him are less likely."

He waited for that to sink in, that his liability was well and truly limited, then softened his voice and his face and said, "But I like your son. A lot. And to the extent possible I'll watch out for him. Although, to tell you the truth, I agree with you, Mr. Kowalski: His head is screwed on real tight and he doesn't need much watching."

Now he had them, and it was time to close the deal. Into the thoughtful silence Johansen said, "By the way, you know how much money he *is* making?"

They both shrugged. "Now you mention," Mr. K said, "no."

Johansen told them.

They didn't blink, but just looked at each other. "Oughta just about cover it, Father," Mrs. K said.

"Cover what?" Johansen asked.

"Why, four years at MIT, Mr. Johansen."

"HEY SAL," JOHANSEN CALLED OUT during a light workout. "You ever hear of a town called Ocheyedan?"

"Yeah. Up near Trappers Bay."

"Small?"

Spinale grunted. "You wanna go huntin', you gotta walk *towards* town."

Johansen waved him over. "Tell me something, Sal, 'cuz I been wracking my brains: Can you think of any rules that got changed on account of somebody came along and took advantage?"

Spinale thought about it, started to shake his head, then his face lit up with a clearly delicious memory. "There was this guy once, Don Hoak?" He waited to see if Johansen would recall the name.

"Pittsburgh. About, jeez, forty years ago, right?"

"Right. This was in a game against, I don't remember who, but Hoak was on second and somebody hit a long line drive down the left field line. Hoak couldn't tell if it was gonna drop fair but he sees that the left fielder wasn't gonna be able to make the play anyway, so he runs like hell for third.

"Well, the ball drops foul, so it's dead, but instead'a heading back to second, Hoak hangs around about a foot away from third. The ump says to him, he says, 'Hey! Whaddaya think you're doing!' And Hoak says, 'I'm takin' my lead!' There was no rule said he hadda go back to second, see, and there was no rule said how long a lead he could take."

"Wait a minute . . ."

Spinale grinned. "Pitcher gets the ball and the ump says to play. Soon's the pitcher gets a toe on the rubber, Hoak takes one step and steals third!"

Johansen, incredulous, looked at Spinale for a long second then they both laughed.

"Anyway," the bench coach finally said, "they made a rule so's you can't pull shit like that anymore. Why'd ya ask?"

Johansen shook his head. "Just wondering."

New York—June 3

They arrived in New York the day before their game against the Yankees. They were feeling good, having just crossed the .500 mark, which meant that they'd now won more games than they'd lost this season.

With a free night to kill, some of the boys went to Mamma Leone's or the Stage, a big bunch ordered room service, but Marvin Kowalski, Chi Chi los Parados, Cavvy Papazian and Juan-Tanamera Aires went with Sal Spinale, who had a knack for sniffing out homier and more interesting establishments in whatever city he happened to be in. After many years he'd honed it down to a bunch of favorites, and never disappointed those who stuck with him. "The best way to avoid ballplayers is to go to a good restaurant," he'd announced before herding them toward the subway at Columbus Circle for the ride down to lower Manhattan on the A train.

"How come we ain' ridin' a limo?" los Parados said.

"Not enough time," Spinale said, leading them through a sea of gridlocked cars, some of which had their engines off. "Some of us'd like to eat *tonight*."

They'd had a blissful Chinese meal at Hong Fat's on Mott Street just south of Canal, then had walked north for less than three blocks and passed from the teeming bustle of Chinatown into the warmly inviting bosom of Little Italy, where they'd indulged themselves freely in cannoli and *baba au rhum* at Caffe Roma.

Fully sated and savoring the heady aftereffects of the sweet pastries, they'd put themselves willingly in Spinale's care when he'd suggested a walk and a beer and headed them up Mott to Broome Street, over to Sixth and then north again to Bleecker, everybody bragging unself-consciously about foods they'd eaten on other road trips—"One time in Houston," Papazian said, "had me some chili so hot it come with a childproof safety cap." Los Parados waved it away. "My mama makes salsa, you needed a *prescription*."—until they found themselves on the corner of Bedford and Barrow in Greenwich Village, which is when they'd felt the first pangs of uneasiness since they'd followed Spinale out of their hotel back up on Fifty-seventh Street.

"This where we all get jumped and robbed?" Papazian asked as he looked around and saw nothing but apartment buildings. Like most out-of-towners who knew the city only by reputation, it hadn't occurred to him that most muggers were basically cowards who preyed on the weakest of the herd and were not likely to take on a group of professional athletes when easier pickings were swarming everywhere you looked.

Then again, it was a pretty lonely corner they were standing on. "You say beer." Bueno Aires looked around and didn't spy anything that even remotely looked like there was a keg within. "What da hell?"

"Foller me," Spinale ordered, and led them into an alley that passed between two apartment buildings. They followed him across a dingy space and up to a door otherwise unmarked except for "86" in tarnished brass letters.

"Sal . . ." los Parados said skeptically.

Spinale pulled on the door and it opened easily, letting music, laughter and the smells of simple cooking spill out into the street.

"What da hell!" Aires said again, then followed obediently as Spinale led them inside and across a floor strewn with sawdust.

"Welcome to Chumley's, boys," Spinale said as he steered them to an ancient wooden booth and had them all slide in. "Used t'be this was a speakeasy. Case of a raid, everybody hustled out through that back alley we come through."

"You them ballplayers?" a brassy waitress asked as she came up to the table and looked them over.

"Yep," los Parados replied, puffing out his chest. "We're from—"

"Who gives a shit? What'll it be?"

Spinale said, "What's on the tap?"

"Beer, the hell'd you think?"

"Don't ask her what the soup du jour is," Spinale warned. "She'll tell you it's the soup of the day."

"You got a problem wi'dat? So what . . . fi' beers?"

After they'd ordered, Spinale explained that the term "86," meaning to toss a customer out on his keister, had come from Chumley's address of 86 Bedford Street. This bit of intelligence met with suspicious stares.

"I ain't kiddin' ya'. There's all kinds'a stories like that in New York. You know the Flatiron Building? Downtown?"

"First skyscraper in the city," the waitress said as she returned carrying five huge mugs of beer in one hand. "So whadda you, a tour guide?"

"Yeah. Twenny-five cents you can ride my—"

"Watch it, buster!"

When she'd gone, Spinale took a sip of beer and grunted gratefully, then set the mug down and folded his arms on the table. "When they built that, see, they didn't know anything about what big buildings would do with the wind. That it'd swirl around between 'em like crazy, like little hurricanes on account of, I don't know, something about eddies getting trapped and speeding up or whatever."

Kowalski nodded. "More like a horizontal tornado. When the wind hits a—"

"Kid, you tellin' this story or what? Anyways, what happened was, over on Twenty-third Street alongside the Flatiron, these little . . . sideways tornadoes would whip up from the street, see, and ladies' dresses would go *whooshing* up!" He shot his hands up into the air by way of demonstration. "And what with carrying pocketbooks and stuff, they'd dance around tryin' to hold 'em down, which they couldn't do without dropping something, so it was pro'ly one helluva show, lemme tell ya'."

He grinned and took another swig, a big one, closing his eyes as the beer, whatever brand it was, coursed deliciously down his throat. "And all these guys, whenever there was a wind, they'd hang around watching this for hours, until finally the cops got wise and they'd come around shooing them all away, telling 'em *skidoo*, see? And it being Twenty-third Street an' all, that's where *twenty-three skidoo* came from!" He sat back and spread his hands out, smiling again. "Get it? Twenty-three skidoo?"

The others blinked and exchanged glances. "Twonny-t'ree skidoo what?" Aires asked.

"Whaddaya mean, what? *Twenty-three skidoo*, goddamnit!"

Seeing no squiggles of recognition on the monitor, Spinale gave them all up for flatline brain-dead and hung his head. "You're in New York, you gotta know stuff like that, otherwise people gonna think you're just tourists."

"We *are* tourists," Papazian pointed out.

As Spinale muttered something unintelligible but unmistakably derisive, Papazian nudged Kowalski in the ribs. "Lookie here, kid," he said, indicating with his chin some spot across the room.

Kowalski looked but couldn't tell what Papazian was talking about. "What?"

Los Parados swung his head around and spotted it immediately. *"Ah, una chiquita, y muy buena, amigos!"*

Kowalski followed his gaze and saw a young woman who looked to be in her early twenties. She was alone and carrying a book, to which she quickly turned back after having been discovered staring at the table. Clearly embarrassed, she rubbed the side of her head and read furiously, as though she could negate the seconds she'd spent looking at the ballplayers if she read fast enough to cover the ground she'd lost.

"She was lookin' righ' at you, Marvin," los Parados reported with an undisguised leer.

"Baloney," replied Kowalski, reddening visibly.

"I t'ink she wass," Aires chimed in.

"Baloney!"

"Well, less jus' have a little look here," los Parados said, taking a sip of beer, smacking his lips and starting to get up.

"Holy cow, Chi Chi!" Kowalski hissed. "Siddown!"

"Nah. Can' let an opportunity li' this pass you by, *muchacho*."

Kowalski, unable to stop him, shook his head. "What a jerk."

Papazian laughed. "Jerk? Man's tryin'a do you a big favor, kid. You're, like, famous, and you spend a whole season'a off time sittin' on yer butt readin'. Kinda life izzat, a famous guy like you?"

"She wasn't looking at me."

They could see los Parados leaning toward the girl, talking, pointing back toward the table, then nodding and straightening up.

"Comin' back," Spinale said uselessly.

Kowalski could feel the others gearing up for some serious razzing at his expense, and steeled himself for the whole we're-gonna-get-you-laid horror show that was the bane of fresh and vulnerable young rookies everywhere who found themselves at the merciless mercy of the veterans of the pubic wars, of which there was always one imperial swordsman like Chi Chi los Parados to lead the way.

"Young *chiquita* over there's a big fan'a yours, *niño*," los Parados reported, purposely remaining standing in order to emphasize that there was nothing stopping Marvin from sliding out and getting moving, and the longer he stood there the more excruciating it would become as Kowalski did no such thing.

Kowalski picked up his mug and took a deep chug of beer, then plunked it back onto the table and wiped his mouth, after which he scooted across the worn wooden seat and stood up.

"'Bout damned time," he said, then spun on his heel and marched across the room, waving to the girl as he approached, and trying not to let his rubbery knees betray his bravado and send him crashing to the sawdust-covered floor.

Los Parados, still standing, blinked several times as he stared.

"Close you mout', Chi Chi," Aires ordered as he laughed.

"To Marvin!" Spinale said, holding up his mug as los Parados sat down.

"To Marvin!" the others responded, holding aloft their own beers.

An hour later, and with the girl's phone number in his pocket, Kowalski rejoined the others as they hailed cab after cab, rejecting each one until a Checker showed up. On the way uptown to their hotel, he completely ignored the obligatory wisecracks and, without a target rising to the bait, the snickering soon stopped.

The cab drew to a stop on Sixtieth Street. Spinale paid the fare, adding a generous tip, and the door was opened by a uniformed hotel doorman. Kowalski was last out and followed the others up the wide marble stairs leading to the hotel lobby. At the top of the stairs another doorman caught Spinale's eye and pointed to the street.

The coach turned and saw that the first doorman was still standing, somewhat expectantly, at the curb. "Hey, kid!" Spinale called to Kowalski. "Did you schmeer the guy?"

Kowalski stopped and looked up. "Did I what?"

"Did you schmeer the guy!"

"I don't . . . Criminy, Sal! How do I know when—"

"Ah, shit," Spinale growled as he started for the curb.

"What's going on?"

Kowalski looked up the stairs to see Johansen emerging from the revolving doors.

"Kid didn't schmeer da guy," Papazian explained, pointing toward the street.

Kowalski watched as Spinale slapped a bill into the doorman's hand and jerked his thumb toward the offender. The doorman shrugged knowingly—he'd seen rubes before.

"Jeez, kid." Johansen had his hands reprovingly on his hips. "You *gotta* schmeer the guy!"

Nine

June 4

S TARTING ON THE MOUND for New York was Romem-
allah "Rojo" Jones, an ebony-skinned first-generation
American of Ethiopian descent who'd won a modest
eleven games for Toronto last year. After becoming a free agent, he'd
been embargoed by his agent, who'd kept him out of the game during negotiations for a not-so-modest contract with the Yankees for
$300 million, making Rojo the highest-paid athlete in any sport in
the history of the human race. Today was his New York debut.

Rojo had a clause in his contract that required him to make a minimum of $1 million a season more than the next-highest-paid player
on the team. Interestingly, the Yankees were also looking at Manolo
Garcia, a shortstop from Texas, whose agent was demanding the same
clause. Were they to sign Garcia, both players would have to be paid
an infinite amount of money in order for the club to be in compli-
ance with both their contracts. Since that was a practical impossibility, the Yankees had informed Garcia that they would be unable to
hire him, at which point the shortstop's attorneys threatened to sue

to invalidate Rojo's contract, claiming that it constituted "tortious interference" with Garcia's right to obtain employment for which he was qualified. When the Yankees attorneys informed them that, were such a claim upheld, Garcia's own contract, which contained the same clause, would then itself be invalid, Garcia's attorneys said "Not necessarily," that it would only be a problem if somebody decided to make a legal issue of it. When it was pointed out to them that Rojo was damned well likely to make an issue of it, Garcia's attorneys replied that they were confident they could prevail in court. The matter was still pending.

Many had shaken their heads in disgust over the seemingly exorbitant amount of money New York was paying for Jones considering his less-than-stellar won-lost record for the Blue Jays, but wiser observers understood the real substance of the deal. The truth was that Rojo was a tremendously good pitcher; the problem had been that last season the Blue Jays had been awful on offense, and not too swift on defense, either. The star pitcher had done his bit, racking up an incredible ERA of 1.80, but even while he was holding opponents to one or two earned runs per game, his teammates were failing at the bat, often scoring only one or even no runs per game, while making an endless string of crucial errors in the field. There was nothing a pitcher could do about any of that, which only pointed up the utter absurdity of the "won-lost" statistic for a pitcher.

So here was Romem-allah Jones, a pitcher who could easily light up a World Series, with no way to get there unless he got acquired by a team with the ability to exploit his skills. The Yankees, meanwhile, had a gaping hole in the starting rotation. They also had a fanatically loyal fan base from which plenty of money was pouring in, but those fans were showing signs of moodiness, no doubt a result of constant humiliation at the hands of Mets fans. The New York baseball rivalry was not unlike the Civil War, in which families could be split apart by divided loyalties, and the close proximity of the enemy—your brother, your secretary, your boyfriend or, in the worst case, your *customers*—only hardened everyone's hearts and increased the overall intensity of the polarization.

The Yankees front office was smart enough to ignore the nobody's-worth-$300-million type of empty punditry of which media talking heads were so fond. The simple truth was that the only determinant of somebody's worth was what the market was willing to pay. As the suits added up the dollar value of declining ticket sales, dwindling ancillary merchandising and eroding advertising rates due to a drop in television viewership, and then factored in the additional effect of an escalating inability to attract free agents, who would be unwilling to sign with a losing club, $300 million a year for a savior began to look less and less ridiculous. Of course, whether a single pitcher who would be pitching only once every five days at the most could single-handedly lead a team to the Series was debatable, but such was the mentality of baseball, the only field of endeavor in which a man can succeed three times out of ten and everybody thinks he's doing a super job.

Rojo's biggest problem at this point in his career was the cold shoulder he was getting from a number of his New York teammates who bitterly resented how much money he was making relative to their own salaries. He'd tried to explain that they were taking it out on the wrong guy. "What do you want from me?" he'd asked right fielder Bobbie Ray Wurtz. "They were willing to pay it and I took it. What the hell was I supposed to do . . . say no? Would *you*? You don't like it, take it to the front office, but what'd *I* do to piss you off?"

In the style which so many professional athletes adopted as their model for vigorous and intellectual debate, Wurtz had riposted cleverly, "Fuck you, Jones," thereby pretty much ending that episode of witty repartee.

No matter how you looked at it, Rojo had something to prove. In truth, he really didn't need to pitch any better than he had in Toronto. With New York's powerful offense behind him, as well as a bullpen full of excellent relievers, all he had to do was settle into his groove and do what he did best. And what Romem-allah Jones did best was read batters and throw fastballs.

As far as batters were concerned, he was still in the American League, so most of the hitters he'd be coming up against would be the same players he'd pitched to before, a huge advantage which the Yankees had taken into account.

And when it came to fastballs, few threw them better. Rojo wasn't just a brainless hurler but a true artist, the kind of athlete the less-informed called "natural" but who spent countless hours honing his craft, taking nothing for granted, relentlessly self-critical and hell-bent on becoming better. His was a symphony of creative variations on the basic pitches, executed with all the precision of a first-chair violinist and with almost as many shadings of tone.

Best of all, he relished a challenge. "It's no fun throwing fastballs to guys who can't hit 'em," he'd told the *New York Daily News*. "The real deal is throwing them to guys who *can* hit 'em, and getting those guys out."

Rojo's repertoire of weapons was formidable, and all he needed to do was deploy them as he'd always done and not push the envelope unnecessarily. But he had something to prove today, his debut with his new team.

IT'S AN OLD TRADITION in baseball, that if a pitcher has a no-hitter going, nobody says a word, sometimes not even the local television announcer, lest they bring down some kind of jinx. And if there is a perfect game underway, nobody even dares *think* about it. You just keep playing and then analyze what happened afterward.

So after four innings the Majestyks dugout wasn't thinking about the fact that they'd put twelve batters up and not one had reached first base; they were just thinking about trailing 4-0 and their total inability to get past the mauling that Romem-allah Jones was dishing out.

"Fuckin' ump," Donny Marshall spat angrily, scowling as he

stomped back into the dugout after his third called strike. "Sumbitch's callin' a strike zone the size of a fuckin' pool table."

Because Zuke Johansen wasn't at all thinking about the perfect game underway, he was totally unprepared for the volume and intensity of the fearsome booing that would rain down from the capacity crowd when he decided to pull DH Grover DuBois right off the on-deck circle and put in Marvin Kowalski instead. All he was thinking about was how to put a dent in the wall Jones was putting up pitch by pitch.

What the crowd was thinking about was how Kowalski, who'd yet to be put out by any pitcher he'd faced, was going to get to first base and wreck what was shaping up to be the most spectacular debut in history. That Rojo could still pitch a no-hitter, itself a rarity comparable to a perfect ten in Olympic gymnastics, was of small consolation to New York baseball freaks, the toughest fans in sports if you didn't count British soccer. Yankees fans didn't go to sleep counting sheep; they went to sleep striking out the entire Boston lineup.

The more astute in the stands felt their already intense excitement grow to even dizzier heights: They were about to witness an irresistible force meeting an immovable object.

The normally implacable Kowalski was taken aback by the ferocity of the derision with him at its focus, and hesitated on the top step of the dugout. Remarkably, it was Sal Spinale who provided the measure of comfort to keep him moving. "Look at it this way, kid," he said, hand clasped tightly on the nervous rookie's shoulder. "Nobodies don't get booed."

If Kowalski had been hoping to see some small sign of weakness from Jones, some tiny indication of a failure of confidence, he was disappointed. The statuesque pitcher looked at him as though he wasn't a ballplayer, just . . . lunch. Maddeningly unperturbed, not even fiddling with the ball but just standing there, Jones waited calmly for the rookie to take a few practice swings and assume his stance at the plate.

Kowalski had been intently watching Rojo throughout the first four innings and watched him now as he positioned the ball in his glove. By the minute crook of his arm Kowalski guessed he was jamming his fingers outside the seams, and when he saw the throw come over the top, he knew it was a splitter that would come in like a missile but drop down just before crossing the plate. It did just that, and Kowalski let it go by as it traversed the plate several inches under the strike zone.

Umpire Howie Burke growled out something incomprehensible and made a motion with his right arm. Kowalski snapped his head to the side to catch the last of it, then looked back at the scoreboard to confirm the impossible: Burke had called it a strike.

Horrified, Kowalski turned once again to the umpire, who stared right back at him: *You got something you'd like to say?*

"Cream puff," the catcher, Willard Fenoke, razzed.

Wisely, Kowalski looked away. If an ump made a lousy call at first or failed to see a base runner miss the bag at second or misjudged how wide the turn had been at third or didn't spot the catcher's glove touch the runner sliding into home, you could scream and yell and give him a mountain of righteously indignant guff, but you never—*never*—argued with his call of balls and strikes.

"Like it was on a fuckin' tee," Fenoke taunted again. "You shoulda hit it outta the park."

Kowalski willed it away and got ready for the next pitch. Rojo took the sign with an approving nod, then looked down at his glove as he positioned his fingers on the ball. Kowalski couldn't read him at all, and didn't know that he was laying his middle finger down along a seam and nestling his index finger next to it, but he saw the cutter once it was released and knew it would break violently sideways without the down-and-away predictability of a slider. Since it was heading for the right edge of the strike zone and would break still further right, Kowalski again let it go and pulled back slightly to avoid getting hit. It missed him by less than two inches.

"*Sdraagggghhh!*" the umpire bellowed again, shooting his right hand out to the side.

This time Kowalski spun his whole body around and regarded

Burke with undisguised hostility, some small part of his brain noticing that Fenoke had refrained from razzing him again, probably out of embarrassment at the absurdity of the call.

"Play!" the ump yelled, pointing to the mound, and again Kowalski turned away without saying anything.

Anything much. "You're missing a really good game here, ump," he muttered.

"Whuwuzzat?" Burke snarled.

"Just clearing my throat."

Kowalski took up his stance once more but suddenly realized he was in some very deep trouble. A thrill of heat ran up his spine and instantly weakened his arms, and he took a step back and prepared to call time when Fenoke stood up and beat him to it. As the catcher trotted out to the mound to confer with Jones, Kowalski stepped back and looked toward the dugout, hoping Johansen would come out to talk to him.

"What's going on?" Johansen asked when they met near the on-deck circle.

Voice trembling, Kowalski tried to explain. "He's going for the edges. Figures if he can get them real close and I let them go by, maybe the ump'll call them strikes."

"Looks like that's what happened."

"Bullshit, skip! This umpire's either got cataracts or he's a Yankees fan! The way he's calling them, Jones could throw one into the goddamned *stands* and he'd still call it a strike!"

Alerted by this uncharacteristic use of profanity to his player's state of agitation, Johansen purposely kept himself calm, hoping to transmit some of it to Kowalski. "So swing at everything that's even in your zip code. He's throwing everything hard and I don't care who he is, he can't keep that up forever. Let him grind himself down and let's get him the hell out of our hair."

Fenoke turned away from the mound and began trotting back to the plate. "I'm not used to hitting that far out of the zone," Kowalski said, on the edge of a whine. "I don't . . . what if . . ."

Johansen smiled and poked him in the chest. "Chrissakes, kid: So you strike out or whatever. Not the end of the world, and—" he pointed to the dugout "—you'd sure as hell be in good company today!"

Johansen's smile disappeared in an instant at the sight of Kowalski's face reacting to his little pep talk. Jaw hanging open, the kid looked as if he'd been socked in the stomach. "Strike out?" he barely breathed. "Jesus, Zuke . . . don't you get it?"

"Play!" the umpire yelled.

Kowalski continued to stare at Johansen for another second. "I *can't* strike out!" he said, then turned and headed back to the plate as Johansen, shaken for reasons he couldn't explain, returned to the dugout.

With two strikes on him, Kowalski couldn't bunt any balls foul or they'd be counted as a third strike and he'd be out. He had to take a full swing at everything even remotely reachable and hope he could hit it foul. Anything hit fair against the Yankees fielders and he was dead at first if they didn't catch it in the air beforehand.

Rojo's fast-sinking two-seamer was a near-guaranteed groundball out for any hitter sucked into swinging at it, unless that hitter knew exactly what was coming, and Kowalski did. He was sure it was too low to be a strike but, taking a full but gentle swing to be sure to connect, grounded it foul anyway. A near-flawless four-seamer was next, the "standard" fastball gripped across the stitches for maximum speed and rotation. It spun with only the white of the ball showing to the batter, normally making it difficult for him to lock in on, but again Kowalski got hold of it and sent it foul. He was mildly gratified that at least that one was legitimately in the strike zone.

Because he was hitting everything that came his way, the umpire was essentially out of the picture and Kowalski started to relax, content to be doing his job, gobbling up Rojo's pitch quota, tiring the man out and thereby opening the way for his teammates to finally get some hits off whoever came in to relieve.

Then Fenoke stood straight up and pointed off to his right. Rojo hesitated for only a second, then nodded his agreement with the decision that would ruin his day. He lobbed the ball well away from the mound for an intentional ball. Then he did it again, and again, and one last time.

The noise from the stands was confused, some in the crowd machine-gunning contempt at Kowalski, some hysterically cheering Rojo's selfless sacrifice, many trying to do both at the same time. As Kowalski tossed the bat away prior to taking first base on four balls, he paused for a fraction of a second to look at the pitcher, who he was sure dipped his head barely perceptibly as if to indicate some modicum of respect at Kowalski's having kept his cool and done his job despite the clearly rotten umpiring.

Kowalski came back with a half-nod of his own, letting Rojo know that it wasn't just the quality of his pitching that was admirable, but the depth of his smarts and consideration for his team that led him to agree to throw away a possible perfect game rather than risk compromising a likely win.

Three hits by Majestyks batters in later innings spoiled the "no-no" anyway, although the Yankees still won it, 5-0, but that one move in the fourth inning made Jones an instant hero in New York. The next day he was on the cover of every newspaper in town and had dinner with the mayor and several members of the city council. It would have been the entire council, except that the ones who'd publicly ridiculed the Yankees for making the deal for Rojo in the first place judiciously elected not to attend.

While all that was going on, Kowalski for his own safety was driven out of town in an unmarked police vehicle, although he would have felt a good deal more secure had the NYPD not chosen— no doubt unknowingly—to assign two rabid, and heavily armed, Yankees fans as his escorts.

They'd kept him and Johansen down below the stands for two hours after the game, in the only truly private space at Yankee Stadium, the umpires' locker room. After some awkward moments, Johansen had broken the ice by asking the umpire-in-chief, "How the hell do you guys call balls and strikes, anyway?"

The umpire-in-chief hadn't called them that day, that was just happenstance; all four umps rotated positions game to game so all eventually took a turn at home plate.

The crew chief looked up from his Diet Pepsi. "I calls 'em the way I sees 'em."

The second base ump pushed aside his Perrier. "I call 'em the way they are."

Howie Burke took a deep swig from his Budweiser and set it down empty, then stared directly at Kowalski. "They ain't nothin'," he growled, "til I call 'em."

Ten

WHAT I WANT TO KNOW," barked Holden (né Homer) Canfield, "is how come we're nearly halfway through the season and he hasn't signed a contract for next year yet!" Maybe *Canfield* would have called it a bark, but it was more of a yelp, a kind of bravado attempt to hide a whine behind a demand.

"Damned if I know." Johansen was immediately sorry for how that came out. There was no sense antagonizing the man who paid his salary. "That's not the kind of discussion I normally have with—"

"I'll tell you why: The little sonofabitch is gonna hold out on us, that's why. Gonna keep taking his minimum from us and then let himself be sweet-talked by the Yankees or Boston or some other'a those sonsabitchin' clubs got more money'n we do."

"So you've spoken to him?"

"He won't talk to us, Zuke! Somebody's got this kid's ear, I'm tellin' you!"

"I doubt it, Holden."

Johansen tried not to laugh as Canfield stormed around the room in some ill-conceived imitation of Patton or Bill Gates or George Steinbrenner. The owner was all of five-foot-five, balding, paunchy and pasty-skinned. He'd probably been beaten up regularly in grade school and, without realizing it, had spent the rest of his life plotting some misbegotten psychic revenge. He'd considered going into law, an arena in which the least physically prepossessing could wage war without regard to classical definitions of strength, but at a crucial moment in his life something better had come along: the Internet.

Canfield, a fair but not brilliant computer nerd, had conceived of a compression scheme that would make a slow data-transmission line look much faster than it actually was. He'd rounded up some venture capital, stolen a few bright minds from the supervolatile job market in Silicon Valley, and hired one of the best public relations firms in Los Angeles. The only thing DeMinimus Data had ever produced was a press release, but ten months after its founding Canfield had IPO'd it, and six months and one day after that he'd sold the whole thing to a giant competitor who wasn't quite sure what it was going to do with it, but was terrified of someone else getting it. Overnight Canfield had been transformed from a socially inept and self-conscious geek into a supremely rich, socially inept and self-conscious geek, a truly dangerous creature riddled with delusions and with entirely too much leisure time in which to indulge them. Like many who strove to assert themselves in the eyes of people they've never met, Canfield had never won the war for self-respect but only escalated its intensity, using the weapons salvaged from each interim victory to wade into the next futile battle.

Now, the *schlemiel* who'd never gotten picked for kickball games in the fourth grade owned his own professional sports team, which in itself wasn't so bad, except that he wasn't content to let people who knew what they were doing run it, but instead insisted on headline-grabbers such as blowing the entire player budget on an Argentinean superstar without having consulted with people who would have told him how easily a lone superstar could get neutralized in baseball.

"You gotta talk to this kid, Zuke. You gotta talk to him before he figures out how much he's worth."

Johansen frowned. "Not very sporting, Holden."

"Sporting? This is business, goddamnit! Besides, I'm not trying to hose the kid—" Who, Johansen thought to himself, doesn't even have an agent to represent his interests "—I mean, hell, he'll be looking at more money than he ever thought of in his life! What's he, from a farm, for God's sake? In two months he goes from kicking shit in a barn to playing major-league baseball and making major-league money. What, we're bad guys for looking to pay him something reasonable without losing our shorts? Without us he'd be hosing down pigs and probably *losing* money!"

Canfield saw that he hadn't completely convinced his manager. "Look," he said, calming himself and taking a seat just opposite Johansen so their knees were almost touching.

Johansen braced himself, knowing he was in for a dose of the owner's laughably ham-fisted style of enlightened personal management, the kind where he thought he was looking deep within your soul with the kind of penetrating insight magically conferred on successful businessmen.

"You and I both know the kid is better off with the Majestyks," Canfield said, his voice dripping with sincerity and concern. "Playing for you, the kid'll keep his head screwed on right, he won't get dazzled by all that heavy jewelry, big cars and fur coats bullshit. You care about shit like that, and a lotta guys don't. So he'll make decent bucks, he'll be in a good environment . . . we'll do right by the kid, Zuke. You and me, buddy."

"Doesn't make sense for me to negotiate, Holden. We've been through this before. I gotta manage these guys, and the last—"

Canfield jumped up and began pacing again. "Who's asking you to negotiate? All I want is for you to get the kid to talk to us!"

There wasn't much arguing with that line of logic. Johansen saw that, and Canfield saw that he saw it. "Where is he, anyway? Didn't see him down at pregame."

"Stayed over in New York," Johansen explained. "He—"

"I knew it!" Canfield stopped his frantic pacing and pounded a fist into his palm. "I *knew* it! Somebody's talking to him already. Goddamnit, Zuke, I—"

Johansen held up his hand. "Relax, Holden. He isn't talking to anybody. It's just some family business and he needed . . ."

Johansen spun a plausible story, the truth being that Kowalski was so hopelessly enamored of the woman he'd met at Chumley's that he might have melted into a puddle on the spot if his manager hadn't promised him leeway to spend an extra night in New York. Johansen had started to give him a fatherly lecture faintly reminiscent of a high school health class taught to horny teenagers by absurdly inept and secretly jealous teachers, but quickly realized how out of touch he was and how tuned-in Kowalski, like most of his peers, probably was.

He sat back on his chair and rubbed at his lip. "You know, Holden, from Marvin's perspective there's really no need for him to negotiate a contract now. What's the rush? I mean, who knows, we win the pennant, due in no small part to him, and suddenly his worth is—"

"Or he gets beaned next Tuesday and goes cross-eyed, and then he's back to slopping hogs."

"True . . ."

"And I gotta tell you something: That may be *his* perspective, but you're paid to worry about *my* perspective. And mine says we sign this kid up before we can't afford him. Nothing wrong with that, Zuke, that's the way the system works."

"What system?"

"Capitalism, that's what. Wasn't for capitalism there wouldn't be any baseball."

"They got baseball in Cuba."

"Oh, you mean where there's no capitalism?" Canfield shook his head, the enlightened lecturing the naïve. "Or maybe you think a guy hitting .325 in Havana lives in the same apartment building as a cab driver. Is that it? Maybe you think an Olympic hockey player in Moscow waits in line to buy toilet paper just like the guy who cleans the locker room."

Canfield had a point, and Johansen wasn't about to argue it. "Just because it's business doesn't mean you can't do the right thing." Johansen was sorry he said it before the sentence was finished because he was sure he was going to get another knee-to-knee lecture about why the Majestyks were about to be so good to Marvin Kowalski, but Canfield surprised him.

"Let me tell you something, Zuke," the owner said as he crossed his arms. "Capitalism is a wild beast without a thought in its head. It doesn't cogitate about who it's hurting any more than a shark does about what it's eating. It does it because that's what it does, and your only mission is to figure out where on the food chain you are. Once you either make that decision or fall into it by accident—two things an awful lot of people tend to confuse—your course is set, and second-guessing it leads only to depression, guilt or, if worse comes to worst, a career in politics. Now—"

Canfield sat down behind his desk and slapped a hand on the arm of his chair. "You gonna talk to Kowalski?"

"I told you, Holden, it doesn't—"

Canfield snapped his fingers. "Hey, wait a minute! Why the hell am I even—" He hit a button on his intercom. "Angie, get me Henry Schmidt!"

Johansen lunged forward on his chair. "Henry Schmidt? What're you calling *him* for!"

Canfield smacked the side of his head. "I must be going senile. Why'm I talking to you when I should be talking to his agent? I completely forgot how we—"

"Schmidt's not his agent, Holden!"

"Course he is. Isn't he the guy who brought him here in the first place?"

"Well, yeah, but—"

"So there you go."

"I'm telling you, Schmidt's not his agent! There's no contract be-tween 'em, not even an understanding. Schmidt doesn't get a cut of Kowalski's salary, and—"

"I don't really give a shit, Zuke. I wave ten percent in front of him he'll *become* his goddamned agent." He stabbed at the intercom again. "How you comin' on that call, Angie?"

Expecting to hear Canfield's secretary break in any second to an-nounce that Schmidt was on the line, Johansen sat back, trying to think, unaware that, as he did so, Canfield was staring at him pa-tiently, the beginnings of a shit-eating grin playing about his lips.

A few seconds later Johansen stood up, his mouth set in a grim line. "I'll talk to him, Holden."

"Excellent," Canfield replied, but made no move to tell his secre-tary to cancel the call.

On his way through the outer office as he left, Johansen noticed that the secretary's phone was still in its cradle on her desk. Angie herself wasn't even at the desk, but across the room dropping fold-ers one by one into a file cabinet. She smiled prettily at Johansen, then went back to her filing.

"MARVIN, HOW YA' DOIN'?"

"I'm good, skipper." More like positively glowing.

"Happy being on the team?"

"You bet. Having a ball." He looked delirious, happy just to be alive.

"'At's the spirit, kid."

Later that day Johansen called Canfield. "Sorry, Holden. Kowalski won't budge. Couldn't get a thing out of him."

"Christ, Zuke . . . what're we gonna do!"

"Nothing's broke, Holden, so don't let's fix it."

By mid-June the Majestyks had climbed out of the cellar and into third place in the Central Division, six games out of first behind the Chicago White Sox. Since the Sox had recently lost two of their star pitchers for the season because of rotator cuff and knee injuries, it was a pretty good bet they'd soon be getting out of the way, which gladdened the hearts of the Des Moines Majestyks.

There was great controversy about whether it was Marvin Kowalski who was pulling the team up from obscurity and into the limelight. His on-base percentage of 1.000 had certainly played a role, but other players still had to hit behind or ahead of him to exploit all those free trips to first. It had taken a good deal of experimentation by Zuke Johansen to figure out the best place to put him in the lineup, but it had definitely begun to pay off.

Others thought Kowalski's real impact on the team may have been more subtle, and had to do with his role as a point around which the other players could rally themselves to higher levels of performance. Hitting statistics had improved dramatically, but whether that was due to Kowalski's tutorials on reading pitchers or was simply a result of greater motivation because of all the public scrutiny or that some real pennant hope glimmered on the horizon, no one could say. As with most human endeavors, nothing succeeded like success. The more the Majestyks accomplished, the more they were driven to accomplish. Each victory was like a food pellet to a lab rat, positive reinforcement that built on itself, and even defeats only made them stronger and more fiercely competitive.

Predictably, the sports media were not given to subtlety. They were not given to *anything* that took more than ten words to describe in a headline. Studied analyses of the complex emotions driving elite athletes were left to post-career retrospectives, and what was needed on Sunday mornings were sound bites.

"Kowalski's lifting that team up single-handedly," one would open.

"He's a one-man freak show," the next would shoot back. "How long do you figure—"

"Why doesn't he give interviews?"

"Freak show? The kid's a *phe*-nom. Three at-bats and he uses up half a guy's pitches!"

"You call that a skill?"

"You try it. Got eyes like an eagle."

"Eyes but no hands. What good's that kinda vision if he's got no—"

"Thinka those reflexes, for Pete's sake. We're talking about a guy who *never misses!*"

"Where'd he come from, this *mook*? How come he won't talk to the press?"

"Let's get down to the real business of today's game . . ."

The real business of today's game, as it was for every Majestyks game, was whether the opposing pitcher was going to try to take Marvin Kowalski on or just let him get to first and save his arm for the next batter.

It wasn't always an easy decision, because an additional happy outcome for fans everywhere as a result of Marvin Kowalski was the return of Juan-Tanamera "Bueno" Aires.

Baltimore—June 27

"What the hell do I do now?" Tony Wilson asked.

Good question, thought Orioles catcher Pete Brannigan as he conferred at the mound with his pitcher. That Kowalski pain in the ass had put himself on first, as usual, and had also moved John Amos, who'd earlier grounded one past the shortstop for a single, to second base. The Majestyks had two outs, but now Juan-Tanamera Aires was up at bat and the decision facing Baltimore was fairly straightforward: Should Wilson load the bases by intentionally walking Aires and then try to get Federico Guittierez out to end the inning, or pitch to Aires and try to get him out right away instead?

"How ya' feelin'?" Brannigan responded to Wilson as their manager walked up from the home dugout.

"How'm I throwin'?"

"Don' get much better."

The manager agreed. "Control, location . . . stuff's good tonight, Tony. Real good."

Wilson had given up no runs and only two hits in six innings, while Majestyks pitcher Bryce Thomason, who'd only recently been moved from relief to the starting rotation, had given up eleven hits

and a run. He'd seemed distracted all night, and his and his wife's inability to conceive were starting to become a team problem.

"Sure hate to walk him with two guys already on," the manager
said.

Wilson nodded, knowing the decision had just been made.
"Ump's callin' 'em pretty wide. I go for the corners—"

"He'll go down swingin'," Brannigan agreed. "They're down by
one, there's two outs on 'em . . . they'll take chances."

"Yup," the manager concurred, hiding his misgivings well. He'd
caddied at a country club as a teenager and had carried one lesson
from those days into baseball: Once a decision had been made, you
never gave your player cause to second-guess it. You slapped the
club or ball into his hand with a reassuring smile or nod and let him
know he'd made the right choice.

"Bueno" Aires, watching the little confab carefully, could tell
what had happened and felt his heart leap. Had a decision been made
to intentionally walk him, the trio would have looked sheepish and
depressed, the pitcher's shoulders would have slumped and he'd be
pressing his lips together and looking at the ground in resignation.

But this bunch was standing straight up, determination in their
faces, jaws jutting forward defiantly. Brannigan and the manager
both trotted rather than walked away from the mound, the catcher
back to the plate with obvious anticipation, the manager slapping
his hands together and snapping his fingers and nodding toward the
dugout, delivering a body-language pep talk.

On the mound, Wilson was throwing the ball forcefully into his
glove, as if he could hardly wait for everybody to get back into position so they could get going and put this Argentinean bastard away.
Meanwhile, the Argentinean bastard was standing off to the side
taking a series of full swoops of the bat to loosen up his shoulders
and groove the perfect swing into his muscle memory.

All that on-field testosterone sprayed its way into the stands, too,
the fans sensing a serious confrontation brewing and reacting via the
only means available to them, which was making noise. Had the decision been made to walk Aires, tidal waves of freely expressed deri-

sion would have crashed down on the home team from the surprisingly large number of Majestyks fans who'd traveled to Baltimore to see the game.

But now that some *gen-yoo-wine,* good ol' fashioned country hardball was in the offing, two prize steers banging heads for all they were worth, the crowd turned its attention to its own team and sent down a raucous cacophony of wild clapping, bone-jarring foot stomping, shrill whistles and hoarse screaming, as if each fan had the ability to personally make a contribution to the megawatts of strength and confidence being zapped directly into the bloodstream of "Our Bueno." They were aware that Zuke Johansen usually put Bueno up before Kowalski, so he'd have a chance of stealing a base while the pitcher drove himself nuts dealing with the kid. But this time Johansen had changed his mind. If Aires could knock one out of the park with Kowalski on base, it would be worth two runs rather than just one. And there was an unanticipated bonus, because John Amos had gotten himself on base as well, and was now on second, crossing himself repeatedly and muttering feverish entreaties for divine intervention.

As much of a motivation as all that grandstand noise from the Des Moines contingent in the crowd might have been to Aires, it was equally so to Wilson. He was anticipating that most delicious of sounds, a loud, crashing, deafening and instantaneous silence, an almost palpable hush, the same sweet music that occurred when a basketball player sank a crucial free throw in the opponent's arena just as the home crowd had succeeded in raising the decibel level dangerously high in their efforts to harass him into missing.

It was the sorrowful melody of disappointment, and Tony Wilson was getting ready to order it up on the jukebox especially for this moronic mob of small-town boobs so enamored of the novelty act called Marvin Kowalski.

WILSON HOWITZERED ONE DOWN the middle. Aires, who'd been trying to anticipate everything it could possibly do, was taken by complete surprise when it did absolutely nothing. He started to swing, guessing he could alter the path of the bat in midcourse depending on what the ball did, then abruptly checked up altogether, but the ump thought he'd passed the halfway point and called a strike anyway.

"Whoa!" Brannigan yelled as the ball hit his glove. "You believe this guy's control?" He stood up to return the ball and Aires could sense his shit-eating grin right through the mask. Brannigan was not a razzer by nature—it would always come back to haunt you—but he could talk trash when the situation called for it. Besides, he wasn't actually dissing Aires, just praising his own man.

Wilson's backdoor slider started out aimed at Bueno's hands but swung back to the outside edge of the strike zone. Bueno went after it but caught it late and with the tip of the bat, sending it foul into the right field stands.

"Damn, sometimes I don't believe this myself!" Brannigan made no attempt to hide the glee in his voice, staying down this time as the ump handed him a new ball and he threw it out to the mound.

Bueno let the 0-and-2 pitch go by for a ball, then almost got suckered into going after a sinker but checked up successfully. Now 2-and-2, he watched carefully as Wilson, pitching from the stretch to keep Amos from taking too big a lead off the base, grunted with the effort of an apparent fastball, but Bueno saw it for what it was, a change-up that only looked like a fastball.

He swung with everything he had and the ball leaped for the heavens. The crowd began to roar, but Bueno stayed put, realizing that the ball had come in so slowly he'd caught it a bit early. Sure enough, it drifted further and further toward the stands left of the foul pole, although it wasn't lost on anybody that it made it all the way to the third deck before it finally disappeared.

With the count still at 2-and-2, Bueno was pretty sure Wilson would go for a corner next, and he did, but it wasn't quite as wide as Bueno had expected and he went for it. This time his timing was perfect and he caught it eight inches from the tip of the bat, but it was a splitter and therefore diving as it crossed the plate. The ball hit the bat slightly below center and took off at an angle somewhat less than the ideal trajectory for maximum distance, but the connection was otherwise solid.

It was a line drive through the hole between second and short and then the alley between the left and center fielders. With nothing to lose, Kowalski and Amos took off, Amos with strength and speed for third, Kowalski with . . . whatever, for second, both of them watching third-base coach Bink Iverson rather than what was happening in the outfield.

Iverson was waving wildly, keeping one eye on the outfield and the other on Amos, making sure his runner knew that the play was to run like hell for home, because Bueno's shot had bounced off the center field wall and away from the fielder who'd gone after it. Iverson wasn't too worried about Amos, but he did hope that Kowalski saw his frantic waving and understood what was going on so he'd keep going past second base to take third.

As the fielder scrambled to make a play, Iverson suddenly caught a flash out of the corner of his eye but couldn't quite make it out, then saw that it was Bueno Aires igniting the air into near-incandescence as he shot for first and made an impossibly abrupt left turn when he got there. As Bueno passed the halfway point on his way to second and appeared to accelerate rather than put his flaps down in preparation for landing, Iverson's brain did a quick calculation and then froze in horror: Aires was going for the triple, but there was no way the vastly slower Kowalski was going to be able to vacate third base and make it to home. Then he caught another movement, and it was the fielder, who'd finally managed to snag the ball, rearing back to throw it in.

Iverson threw his arms as high in the air as he could and started screaming "Stop! *Stop!*" at the top of his lungs, jumping up and down to increase his visibility. Even as he began his wild dance, though, he saw the error of his ways. Kowalski, who hadn't yet reached third, began to slow down and wonder if he was being told to go back to second. Now Iverson was faced with the conundrum of how to let Kowalski know he was supposed to keep going to third and that it was *Aires* who was supposed to hold up at second.

Fortunately, Kowalski's brain was a lot faster than Iverson's. Since he was already three-quarters of the way to third, there was no circumstance under which it would make any sense to go back. Furthermore, since Amos had already taken two bases, it was a sure bet Aires would, too, and that meant that there'd be no room on second even if he did try to get back there.

He also realized something else, and that was that the play from the outfield wasn't going to be at second base, because Bueno was so fast he'd be on the bag and have time for a beer before the ball arrived, and it wasn't going to be at home, because that was too far to throw the ball in time, and that left only . . .

Third base! Which would explain Iverson's apparent attack of apoplexy, his eyes nearly popping out of his head as he made the sign for Kowalski to for God's sake *slide!*

Only problem was, Kowalski had never slid. But he did his best, dropping down onto his left side and sticking out his foot, except he caught a little too much ground when he did so, which slowed him down, and he thought sure he wouldn't touch the bag in time, because he could see the third baseman's eyes watching the incoming ball, and he saw those eyes fall and fall which meant the ball was practically in his glove, and then Kowalski couldn't see anything because his foot was kicking up so much dust and powdery sand that it obscured the third baseman's face.

Obscured it so much that the third baseman couldn't see, either. Hand flying to his eyes, he ducked out of the way of the ball, which bounced crazily in front of him and shot off to the right toward the dugout.

"*Run!*" Iverson screamed like a wounded boar, bending toward the swirling dust cloud. Kowalski looked up in alarm just as Iverson, his face contorted with anxiety and his arm pointing toward home, screamed again. "*Run, goddamnit!*"

By now Kowalski's foot was on the bag and he scrambled to his feet and took off for home. Something ran across his path and he realized it was the pitcher, Tony Wilson, going after the errant ball because the third baseman was temporarily incapacitated and Brannigan had to keep his post at home plate. That left Wilson to try to make the play and it was obvious he couldn't do it in time, so Kowalski put his head down and went for it, crossing home plate standing up.

The Majestyks dugout was in a state of total frenzy, and Kowalski started to smile, but then he saw that they weren't looking at him but at third base, where the human mortar shell known as Juan-Tanamera Aires was sending up a rooster tail of sand as he brushed a foot across third base and reoriented his weapons radar on home plate. Kowalski turned to see the ball bounce off a railing in front of the Baltimore dugout and Wilson stagger-step to a halt in front of it. As the pitcher reached down to pick it up, the third baseman got back to his feet and into position.

Aires saw it all, too, and stumbled slightly with the effort of reversing his forward momentum. He threw himself down just as Wilson released the ball, and barely got his hand on the bag before the third baseman caught it, swept his hand down and tagged him.

The third base umpire leaned down and crossed his arms, then flung them out to the sides. *Safe!*

The score was 2-1, Majestyks.

Wilson retired the side by striking Federico Guittierez out on five pitches, which didn't make him feel any better about the earlier decision to pitch to Aires. Johansen pulled Thomason and called in reliever Rafael ("Three more saves and he ties John the Baptist") Fuentes, who held the Orioles to two hits and no runs. Wilson stayed in, and for the remainder of the game gave up nothing.

The White Sox had lost in Oakland an hour ago. The Majestyks were a few minutes away from being just five games out of first and one game out of second in the division.

"When we lose, I can't sleep at night," Johansen said as Fuentes was throwing to his last opponent. "When we win I can't sleep either, but I sure feel a damned sight better in the morning."

"Hey, kid," Spinale said when it was finally over, "you know we're only two blocks from where The Babe was born?"

"Really?"

"Yep. And his old man ran a joint on Conway Street. Ruth's Cafe, it was called." He pointed toward the field. "Right there."

Kowalski followed the line of Spinale's arm but couldn't see a way to look out of the stadium and onto a street. "Where?"

"Right there. Center field."

John Amos stepped away from the water cooler and held up his hands for silence. "How about we kneel down and give thanks to Jesus for this glorious victory?"

A dozen pairs of eyes looked past him to the end of the dugout where Cavvy Papazian was peeling off his protective gear. The veteran catcher had played a truly magnificent game, calling pitches perfectly, protecting the bases against steals by intimidating potentially aggressive base runners with his split-second reflexes and astonishing accuracy, and generally controlling defensive play with the uncanny feel for the total picture that his teammates had come to take for granted and the rest of the league admired and feared.

Papazian winced slightly as he grabbed at a zipper, and Kowalski took note of his hands. The ends of several fingers were bent at unnatural angles from having taken thousands of stinging jolts from balls tipped foul by batters. His face had areas permanently mottled from the times his mask had been driven forcefully into his skin. He shuffled slightly from foot to foot to try to relieve some of the pain in his tortured knees, and his entire body was a papyrus on which was written the history of every ball, bat and base runner that had slammed into it with little regard for the accumulating toll.

Battered, bruised and weary, he looked up when Amos had finished his summons to give thanks elsewhere, and the air in the dugout grew tense with expectation.

Papazian looked back down and let his hands drop away from the strap on his chest protector. Turning toward Amos he nodded, said "Okay," and winced again as he bent his knees and sank to the ground for the hundred-and-fiftieth time that day.

• • •

"WHAT I JUST CAN'T UNDERSTAND," Kowalski said later, when he'd returned to the locker room after his usual avoidance of postgame interviews, "is how it is that Thomason, who pitched six of the sloppiest innings you ever saw, gets credit for the win, while Wilson puts on a brilliant performance, gives up two hits and he gets the loss."

The only people left were Zuke Johansen, Sal Spinale, and reliever Rafael Fuentes, who was getting ultrasound and diathermy treatments for his arm from the team trainer unaffectionately called the "physical terrorist."

"Them's the rules," Spinale explained. "Thomason was ahead after five and we won."

"I know the rules, Sal. Just doesn't make any sense. If Rafael had given up two runs, Thomason would've gotten a loss, and there wasn't anything he could've done about it. Same performance, two different outcomes. What kind of sense does that make?"

"There're other statistics you look at for a pitcher, though," Johansen said. "ERA, for example."

Kowalski shook his head. "I look in the papers, I see 'Fifteen game winner Mars Lee,' or 'Jones is eight and three this season.' But if I want the ERA, I've gotta go look down in the fine print." The ERA, or earned run average, was a measure of how many runs a pitcher allowed per nine innings pitched. Only *earned* runs were counted. Runs scored because of an error on the part of a fielder were not included.

"Maybe that's what *you* do," Johansen said, "but the front office looking to buy a guy, or me trying to figure out how to use him? I look at all of it. And the won-lost *is* important. It's an indication of how a guy does under pressure, his sense of perspective. If you're ahead by a single run and hold 'em off for six innings, that's damned good pitching. If you're ahead by six runs and you give up a few, that's still good pitching. Maybe a guy's thinking, why mangle my arm when we can afford to go a little easy?"

"So it's like RBIs," Kowalski mused out loud.

"Exactly. A double is a double, but if a batter can get one with the pressure of one or two guys on base waiting to come home, it says something about his mental toughness. That's why RBIs are important." Johansen got up and went over to check on how his star reliever was doing.

"Except in your case, kid," Spinale said with a wink.

Kowalski smiled and took no offense. He'd walked seven times with the bases loaded and therefore had seven runs batted in to his credit, despite not ever having gotten a single hit. As it happened, he didn't even have a batting average, because all he ever did was walk and walks didn't count as a turn at bat. "Awful lot of numbers in this game," he said.

"Yeah, but me, I like the stats," Spinale replied, hoisting himself onto a training table and letting his legs dangle over the side. "Everything in baseball is about numbers, and you can't fake the numbers. You don't have to wait for no damned reviews to know exactly how you did. You can hire the best PR flack in the world, you can build kiddie hospitals and you can be good to your mother, but you got a 6.0 ERA or you're battin' .190, you suck and you're going down. But if you're twenty and five this season or you're hittin' .350, you can snort coke in Times Square and beat your wife and they're gonna figure out a way to let you keep playin'."

THEY HAD A DAY OFF and Kowalski flew to New York to see his girlfriend. Somehow, she never flew out to see him, or to see a game.

"She works," he'd explained to Donny Marshall.

"Weekends too?"

"Uh, sometimes. I guess."

Chi Chi los Parados had grunted upon hearing that. "Wunner what kin'a job she got," he said, without exactly asking.

Eleven

BLEARY-EYED AND DAZED, the Majestyks dozed fitfully in some kind of bus taking them . . . somewhere. They'd played a tough doubleheader against Texas, the games going into extra innings before the Majestyks won both of them, and hadn't finished up until well past midnight. Then their flight had been diverted owing to some weird wind conditions and they'd had to set down . . . somewhere else and get bused to . . . the first somewhere.

Game's easy; it's the season that kills you.

Marvin Kowalski, jarred awake by the wheels hitting a rough spot, blinked and tried to clear his head. Straightening up from his uncomfortable slouch, he looked out the window and winced as an angry sun, low in the early morning sky, lanced fire into his unprepared eyeballs. He shaded them with a hand and took in the landscape as it sped by.

Burger King. Wendy's. McDonald's. Del Taco. Taco Bell. Circle K. Kmart. Howard Johnson. IHOP. TraveLodge. Holiday Inn. Baskin-

Robbins. Home Depot. Home Base. Shakey's. Wal-Mart. Target. Costco. Sam's. Pep Boys. Payless. Jiffy Lube. El Pollo Loco. Radio Shack. Best Western. Big 5.

He looked away and rubbed at his eyes, only dimly aware of the various snores, snuffles, groans, scratchings and shiftings going on around him, then looked out the window again.

Pizza Hut. Jack in the Box. Sizzler. Days Inn. Winchell's. Krispy Kreme. Dunkin' Donuts. Rite Aid. Dairy Queen. Embassy Suites. Comfort Inn. Marriott. Residence Inn by Marriott. Courtyard by Marriott. Office Depot. Office Max. Staples. Blockbuster. Walgreens. Kinko's.

Across the aisle Sal Spinale stirred and stretched with a prodigious yawn, then turned to look around and see who else was up.

"Sal," Kowalski said softly, jerking a thumb toward the window, "where are we?"

Spinale scratched his head a few times, then stood up creakily and leaned over Kowalski to have a look for himself.

Sears. Kentucky Fried Chicken. Carrow's. Starbucks. Denny's. 7-Eleven. Carl's Jr. Super 8. Motel 6. Gap. The Outback. Banana Republic. Coco's. A&W. TJ Maxx. TGIF's. Barnes & Noble. Waldenbooks.

Spinale fell back across the aisle and into his seat, closing his eyes. "We're in America," he announced, and went back to sleep.

Anaheim—July 22

Turned out it had actually been southern California. The Majestyks were scheduled against the Angels, had landed in Palm Springs and then been bused through Banning, Beaumont, Moreno Valley, Box Springs ("Box Springs?" Grover DuBois had exclaimed in disbelief. "Bullshit! Ain' no such place as Box freakin' Springs! *Cain't* be no such place!"), Corona, Yorba Linda, Placentia ("Placentia?" DuBois had started up again) and finally Edison Field in Anaheim, less than three miles as the crow flies from Disneyland.

"Edison Field," third base coach Bink Iverson snorted contemptuously. "Dissin' the game, they are, selling the name to a corporation."

"Doesn't Disney own these guys?" Papazian asked. "Who the hell is Edison?"

"Utility company. Payin' a meg-and-a-half for naming rights. I hate this shit: Coors Field, Staples Center, Safeco, Pepsi—"

"Mahoney Fertilizer," Papazian said, reminding him of how the Des Moines ballpark got named.

"What do you think's a good name for a stadium?" Kowalski asked.

Iverson folded his arms across his chest and stuck his chin out. "Wrigley!" he declared, and Kowalski laughed but didn't have the heart to tell him that the venerable old park in Chicago had been named for the owner of a chewing gum company who'd bought both the club and the field in 1918.

But nothing could top the scoreboard in the minor-league Campbell Stadium flashing "Mmmm, mmm, good!" whenever a Camden player hit a home run.

It was an uneventful game, the Majestyks amped to the gills trying to make the playoffs, the Angels no longer in real contention. By the eighth inning it was 5-1 Majestyks, Johansen had already put in reliever Bobby Madison, and there were more fans in the parking lot trying to get out than were left in the stands.

After Darryl Bombeck singled to right, Kowalski was up at bat. Angels manager Cooty Cummings signaled for time to put in a new pitcher.

"Who the hell's this?" Spinale asked as the reliever walked to the mound.

Johansen frowned and looked up at the scoreboard. "Tim Moriches?"

"Never heard of him." Spinale pulled a thick book from his gym bag and riffled through some pages. "Nothin' from scouting. Must's just got called up."

They stood side by side as Kowalski took his place in the batter's box following the new pitcher's allowed minute of on-field warm-up. The first live pitch was a standard fastball down the middle, thrown somewhat tentatively, and Kowalski knocked it foul.

Next came a mildly breaking curve, also thrown with less than full confidence. Then a slider, another slider, a sinker, fastball, two more breaking balls . . .

Twenty pitches later the count was 2-and-2. Moriches was throwing every pitch in the book, most of them well within the strike zone.

"Hell, Zuke," Spinale said. "Dudn't even look like he's *tryin'* to get him out."

"Yeah." Johansen had turned his attention to the home-team side of the field, where Cooty Cummings was standing, peering intently at the mound.

"Hell's goin' on here?" Spinale asked.

Johansen watched a few more pitches, then said, "I think I know."

He stepped out of the dugout, stretched, then sauntered as casually as he could over to Cummings. "Hey, Cooty," he said easily.

"Hey, Zuke. 'Sup?"

Johansen folded his arms across his chest and watched another pitch, which Kowalski again blooped down the third base line. "Cooty, you using my boy here as a tackling dummy?"

Another pitch, down and away for a third ball. "Ain't a bad way'a puttin' it."

"Who's your guy, this Moriches?"

"Good kid. Great arm. Pitchin' in San Bernardino, thinkin'a bringin' him up."

Johansen thought about it and watched a few more pitches. Kowalski looked over at him and rolled his eyes: *What the hell . . . ?* "Lemme guess. Kid a little gun-shy of crowds?"

"Somethin' like that." Another fastball, this time a rocket. "Figured we'd bring him up to the Bigs and let him get a little wet with your *phee-nom*. Figured he could throw a couple-three dozen pitches that don't matter shit anyhow, see how he does." Cummings thrust his chin toward the mound. "Looks good, don' he? Gettin' a little more confidence with every pitch."

"Hardly sporting, Cooty."

"*Sporting?*" For the first time, Cummings turned to look at Johansen. "You're the last damned sumbitch oughta be talkin' about *sporting!*"

"My guy's playing legit ball."

"And what's my guy doin' . . . diddling altar boys?"

"But—"

"Listen here, Zuke: You insist on playin' that freak, tryin'a wear guys down pitchin' to him, you oughd'na be surprised to get a little'a yer bullshit right back at ya'."

Out on the mound Moriches hitched up a shoulder and craned his neck a few times. Cummings saw it and held up four fingers toward the catcher, who nodded, stood up and pointed to his right. Moriches threw the ball wide, purposely walking Kowalski.

Cummings signaled to the home plate ump for time, said "See ya' in the funny papers" to Johansen, and jogged out to relieve Moriches, who now had a taste of the majors and acquitted himself well.

ON THE SHUTTLE BACK to the hotel, Kowalski pulled Johansen to the rear seats and said, "What was *that* all about?"

"New guy, just up," Johansen answered. "Cooty figured you'd be a good test, see how tight a grip he had on himself. How'd he do?"

"He threw some good stuff. Really nice control. Kept it mostly in the middle but, my guess, he'll be pushing toward the corners before you know it."

The bus pulled to a halt in front of the entrance to the hotel. "Yeah." Johansen started to get up, but Kowalski grabbed his arm and held him back.

"Say, uh, skip . . . ?"

Johansen knew what was coming. They had another extra day off and Kowalski would want to go to New York. That was his right, but what he would be asking was if he could skip the team plane back to Iowa first and head off on his own. "Bright and early Thursday, Marvin," he said as he stood and led the way to the front door of the bus.

"Absolutely, Zuke!" Kowalski answered excitedly. He jumped off the last step and onto the sidewalk, began walking hurriedly and then slapped his head. "Darn!"

"What'sa matter?"

Kowalski was already on his way back to the bus and turned without stopping. "Forgot to schmeer the guy!" he called out as he reached for his wallet.

Twelve

W HERE'S KOWALSKI?" Johansen said, looking around
   the dugout.
      Billy Blyvelt pointed toward the hallway. "Phone."
Johansen bit down on his tongue and strode across the dugout as
players got out of his way. Stepping into the corridor that connected
the dugout to the locker rooms, he saw Kowalski, cell phone up to his
ear, leaning against a wall and giggling, murmuring into the phone
with his hand at his mouth, then giggling again.

"Hey, Kowalski . . . you busy?"

The startled player whirled, saw Johansen, then mumbled something into the phone and flipped it shut. "Sorry, skipper," he said,
then started forward quickly and headed for the dugout.

"Boy's distracted," Sal Spinale said as Johansen, head shaking,
reappeared.

"Pussy on'a brain," Chi Chi los Parados opined. "Man's useless,
he got pussy on'a brain."

"Not if she's watchin' him on television," Spinale countered. He pointed as Kowalski, first up for the Majestyks, grabbed several bats and walked—strutted—to the on-deck circle.

Normally a perfunctory stretcher, today Kowalski swung three bats in wide, swooping circles, then dropped two and took a couple of hard practice swings that looked more appropriate for a long-ball slugger. He moved his neck around as though working out some kinks, then strode purposefully and confidently for the batter's box, where he kicked a little dirt as he planted his feet, just like the sluggers did, ostensibly to give their cleats a good grip on the ground but really to put dirt onto the rearmost white chalk line of the box. That would supposedly obscure the ump's view so the batter could sneak an extra inch or two back and thereby get maybe one more nanosecond to look at the incoming pitch. Home plate umps typically warned rookies but let veterans get away with it, and this ump was savvy enough to know that, in Kowalski's case, it didn't make any difference.

It didn't make any difference to Johansen, either, that his designated hitter was showing a bit of style, a little hotdogging, as he twisted and turned, letting the bat go with his right hand so it whipped behind his head as he hit his typical series of foul balls before getting walked. Nor was it worth mentioning that he stood a little more upright as he loped to first, or tore off his gloves with some uncharacteristic panache, or that he had a few friendly words for the first baseman when he arrived, and bent way down as he took his lead, crabbing back and forth as the pitcher wound up, as though he were seriously considering stealing second, even though that was about as likely as a parakeet stealing the Hope diamond.

Despite the harmless preening, Kowalski kept his mind on business. In the middle of the fourth inning he came into the dugout after Federico Guittierez stranded him on first by striking out, and walked up to pitcher Bobby Madison. "Ump's a little lopsided, Bobby."

"Whaddaya mean?" Madison punched his glove a few times, getting ready to head for the mound.

"Not sure." Kowalski waved pitching coach Jimmy Hazeltine over.

"Almost like he's seeing the whole zone moved over a few inches. Called two strikes on me when the pitches were clearly outside, but called three balls when they were well within the inside edge."

"Huh." Madison looked out toward the field. "Explains why I walked Jhabouti. Thought the calls were bullshit."

"It's also why you struck out Carnega," Hazeltine added. "I didn't think you were inside on two'a those."

The pitcher turned back to Kowalski and punched him on the shoulder with his glove. "Well let's just have us a little look-see," he said, then headed out. He paused on his way to the mound to have a short conversation with catcher Cavvy Papazian.

Kowalski, who normally didn't bother watching the Majestyks pitchers, watched now. On his first throw, Madison sent a curve down the middle that broke sharply outside as it crossed the plate. Tampa Bay second baseman Roger Valentine let it go and straightened up as Papazian reached over to catch the ball. He wasn't paying much attention as the home-plate umpire turned and pointed, but caught it out of the corner of his eye.

Valentine's eyebrows rose in surprise. *Strike?*

The ump looked down at his hand and nudged a dial on his mechanical counter. Valentine frowned and took a practice swing before getting back into position.

Madison threw another one outside, and again Valentine let it go. The umpire stuck his arm out and pointed: another strike.

Valentine spit out a huge wad of chew. "You missed that one," he muttered.

"Wouldn'ta missed it if I'da had a bat," the ump shot back, raising a chortle out of the catcher.

Valentine tried to shake it off, then took his stance again, a few inches closer to the plate than he had before.

Papazian put his wrist on his left knee so his dangling glove would shield his sign from Tampa Bay's third base coach and tapped an index finger against the inside of his left thigh. Madison nodded, wound up and threw a fastball that headed for the batter's hands. Valentine raised his arms and let the ball pass under them. The ump looked down at his counter but otherwise did nothing, indicating a ball.

Valentine expected a sucker pitch, Madison trying to get him to swing at some piece of junk he could afford to throw because he was ahead in the count, 1-2. It came in the form of a slider that headed to a point beyond the outside corner of the strike zone, but not that far outside, and in the third of a second he had to analyze the pitch Valentine considered that this ump had already called two of those as strikes and so he had little choice but to swing, which he did, reaching for it much more than he was comfortable with and catching it above center so that it dropped down, bouncing its way toward shortstop Donny Marshall, who scooped it up easily and made the play at first.

As Valentine slowed and crossed first base uselessly, kicking at the dirt in anger and not a small amount of confusion, Madison widened his eyes and looked toward the dugout, where Kowalski shrugged and smiled back, lifting his hands: *Told you!*

Batting in the sixth with the count 2-and-2, Kowalski watched a sinker as it dove for the ground, and started to lift his foot to get it out of the way. But it wasn't a hard-thrown pitch and also looked like it might catch just his toe, so he stayed put. As soon as he was struck, he threw the bat away and headed for first.

"Hey!" the catcher yelled out after him. Kowalski ignored it, but then heard the ump call him back.

"Hit my foot," Kowalski protested as he walked back toward the plate.

"Bullshit," the catcher said. "Hit the dirt and never touched you." The umpire nodded his agreement and indicated that Kowalski should resume his position at the plate. "Count's three and two. Yer still up."

Kowalski refused to pick up the bat, and Johansen came out of the dugout. "What's the problem here?"

"Got me in the foot," Kowalski said, "and—"

"Tell your man to pick up his bat or I'll—"

"Let me see the ball," Kowalski said, cutting off the ump.

"What? What the hell's the—"

"Fuck the ball!" the catcher spat. "He told you to pick up your bat, so—"

"Let me see the ball!" Kowalski repeated.

Johansen, not knowing what his player had in mind, held out his hand. The ump shrugged and gave him the ball, which he in turn gave to Kowalski, who turned it over, then picked up his foot and held the ball next to it.

"What the hell's your point?" the catcher demanded.

"Look!" Kowalski said to the ump who, along with the catcher and Johansen, bent over to see what he was talking about.

On the ball along a seam was a brown smudge. Kowalski was holding it against the toe of his shoe, which had a rubbed spot on the outside edge. "Shoe polish," he said. "Off my shoe and onto the ball. How do you suppose it might've gotten there?"

"Sonofagun," the ump said as he lifted his mask to look and realization dawned. By that time the Tampa Bay manager had come out to the plate as well.

"Ah, bullshit!" the catcher exclaimed, turning away and flipping a dismissive hand at Kowalski.

"Ya damn right, bullshit!" his manager yelled in support, then, "What's going on, anyway?"

"Take yer base!" the umpire shouted, pulling the mask back down over his face.

Without waiting for further debate, Kowalski spun and ran back to first, clapping his hands and smiling as the local fans, who had no idea what was going on, booed anyway since the Majestyks had obviously won whatever they'd been arguing about.

BY THE EIGHTH INNING, Kowalski thought he was the second coming of Babe Ruth, invulnerable and invaluable. He was also insufferable, doing his best to make himself noticeable whenever a television camera with a red light glowing was pointed in his direction. He chatted up everybody in sight, always with a bat held loosely in his hands, taking casual swings and watching the path of the wood with what he hoped was being seen as a practiced and coolly professional eye. Somewhere in New York a girl was watching, and in the oldest dance of multicelled creatures, Kowalski was displaying his plumage, demonstrating his strength, offering his virility up for public scrutiny and generally certifying his genetic suitability for the further propagation of the race.

Part of that ancient ritual involved proving his superiority over competing contenders, and Kowalski was all smirk, strut and world-weary insouciance as he sauntered to the batter's box. But it was tough to convey power and potency when all you were doing was blooping balls foul, so he stepped up the display a notch, swinging harder than usual to put a little something on the ball and give the impression that he could damned well put a manly swat on 'em if he wanted to.

He took a hard swipe at a fastball and it rose high into the air before dropping foul into the left field seats. He hit the next one harder, and the next one even harder, putting it into the second level, and then he went after a slider and really put his hips into it and caught it a fraction of a second later than he'd intended.

In less time than it took to think about what he'd done, the earth beneath his feet seemed to open up and he was standing above an impenetrably black abyss. The crowd went quiet instantly, but as the ball he'd just struck climbed ever higher, the silence was replaced by a mounting cry of surprise and shock that was quickly metamorphosing into delight.

Kowalski still had his right arm across his chest, the bat wrapped around his back, as he assessed the trajectory of the ball and saw that it was barely going to clear the front row of the field-level seats just beyond the third base line. He knew without turning his head that the blur in the rightmost corner of his vision was Tampa Bay third baseman Pedro Aguilar, a rookie who'd only been in the Bigs for three weeks, racing like the wind to get to those seats and in a few short seconds make his bones and make history. Since Kowalski had joined the Des Moines Majestyks, nobody had ever gotten him out. He'd never struck out, he'd never been put out at first and nobody had ever caught a ball he'd hit into the air.

But Pedro Aguilar was moving as though a lion was chasing him, snapping his head back and forth between the ball and the seats, sizing up the angles, the distances, the rates of closure. As Kowalski watched in escalating horror, Aguilar didn't slow down as he approached the low fence separating the seats from the field, and the fans in those seats, who would normally be standing and jostling for position in order to grab the foul ball when it came down, in a remarkable display of collective loyalty were instead scrambling to get out of the area as quickly as possible.

Seeing the empty seats in front of him, Aguilar slowed slightly and took an extra half step and then launched himself into the air, clearing the fence and landing with his feet on two adjacent chairs. He took a fraction of a second to stabilize himself, then looked up and held out his glove.

Poised over the yawning chasm of his about-to-be-shattered myth, Kowalski felt dread overtake his bowels as he anticipated the inevitable, and could only hope and pray that the agile and athletic rookie third baseman had misjudged the ball and would not be able to shift his precarious position in time, but Aguilar was standing stock still and didn't move his glove hand even a millimeter as the ball neatly, smoothly and horribly dropped into it and stayed there.

The sound that arose from the delirious fans seemed powerful enough to lift Tropicana Field off its foundations, and Kowalski welcomed the diversion as his heart curled in on itself and shrank into an icy ball. He could feel the disappointment in his manager, his teammates, his fans and his girlfriend as though it had been pumped into him intravenously.

There wasn't even enough spirit left to cause worry when he saw Zuke Johansen and Sal Spinale, murder in their eyes, come storming out of the dugout to beat him to death with their bare hands. He just stood there, head hanging, shoulders slumped, and waited for the fatal pummeling.

But Johansen and Spinale veered off at the last second and made for the home-plate ump instead, yelling and gesticulating wildly, pointing to the field-level seats, pointing at Kowalski, stamping their feet and growing red in the face.

Puzzled, Kowalski stepped in closer to try to figure out what the rhubarb was all about. The ump stood there patiently, absorbing the diatribe and not saying a word. Kowalski had enough mental capacity left to notice that nobody from the Tampa Bay dugout had come out to join in the fray, and the catcher was standing patiently off to the side.

When Johansen and Spinale at last showed some sign of running out of steam, the ump bent forward and said over the din from the stands, "If you two assholes'd calm down for a second and let me make the call, maybe you could avoid a pair'a heart attacks."

He then turned to Kowalski. "Count's 3-and-2. You're still up."

Kowalski, not sure he'd heard the ump correctly, stood still and made no move to comply. The catcher stepped back behind the plate without protest and pulled his mask down, then punched his glove several times. As the racket from around the stadium began to degrade into confusion over why Kowalski was still standing at home plate, Aguilar came running in from the field, holding the ball high above his head for all to see. "I caught it!" he screamed. "I caught it!" Johansen and Spinale were already walking back to the dugout, nodding their heads in satisfaction.

"I don't get it," Kowalski finally managed to croak hoarsely.

"Pedro was off the field," the catcher said. "And standing still."

"But guys go into the stands all the time to catch fly balls!"

"If his momentum carries him in," the umpire explained, "he can catch it. But if he has time to establish himself in a stationary position, the catch is disallowed." He pointed to the pitcher to let him know it was time to resume play.

The crowd noise changed in volume and tone as the savvier fans explained things to their neighbors and word spread. Kowalski let the next pitch, a breaking ball down and away, go past him unmolested.

The wind completely gone from his sails but with his legend thankfully still intact, Kowalski went from The Babe back to Marvin in less time than it took him to make the jog to first.

Thirteen

Arlington, Texas—August 13

AWFULLY SORRY to bother you, Mr. Johansen."
Johansen could sense hesitancy and embarrassment at the other end of the line. "No trouble at all, Mr. Kowalski. What's on your mind?"

"Well, uh, sounds kinda silly . . . but is everything alright with Marvin?"

Is everything alright? No, Mr. Kowalski, everything is not alright with your son. Everything's dead damned wrong because the kid is hopelessly, absurdly in love. He's gaga moony and has to force himself to keep his mind on business. We went into extra innings in Seattle and I thought he was going to have a stroke because he wanted to catch the last red-eye to New York. "Why do you ask?"

"Tell you the truth, he hasn't called in a while. Which is no big deal, believe me. I mean the boy's got a right to a little privacy, right? But he's also stopped sending money home."

Johansen nodded his head and closed his eyes. *Always comes down to money, doesn't it?* "Things a little strapped on the farm, are they?"

"The farm? Oh. *Oh!*" Marvin's father laughed, then said, "No, no, Mr. Johansen. No, things are fine. It's just that Marvin's always sent most of his money home for us to put in his college fund, is all, and last couple of weeks he hasn't sent any, so we were, you know, kind of wondering . . ."

Johansen marveled at the strange mix of naïveté and sophistication that seemed to be at play within Kowalski's parents; didn't they realize that their son was now worth more than all of Osceola County and was more likely to *endow* a new building at MIT than take classes in one? "Tell you the truth, Mr. Kowalski, things have been a bit hectic around here. Don't know if you've been following, but the team's doing real well and that kind of tends to put more pressure on everybody . . ."

He did as good a job of assuaging the anxious parent's fears as he could without either overtly lying or violating the implied confidentiality he felt toward his players, until Mr. Kowalski said, "Is he still reading in his spare time? Is he studying?"

"As hard as ever," Johansen managed to say while biting his tongue. Since the close call in Tampa Bay, Kowalski had put aside his physics texts and bought a stack of books about the rules of baseball. Not just the 208-page official league publication, but books about interpretation complete with real-world case studies, history books that described the evolution of the game and put the rules in context, trivia books and quiz books and books about bizarre situations and odd calls and unusual plays and bitter disputes and how they got resolved. Even with that, he never stopped asking questions of the coaching staff and veteran players every chance he got.

"That's good," Mr. Kowalski said. Then, "Might be good for the boy to read something else besides science once in a while."

Oh boy. "Think so?"

"I do. He dudn't believe in anything he can't see."

"Not such a bad philosophy."

"Well, I think sometimes you just have to have a little faith, Mr. Johansen. I tell that to Marvin, he says, Well how do you know what to have a little faith *in*?"

Johansen was getting itchy, shifting from foot to foot. "It's a good question."

"He's always askin' good questions." There was a chuckle over the line. "Once, when he was a kid? I mean, a little kid? I read him 'Casey at the Bat.'"

"One'a my favorites." *I gotta get off this call!*

"Yeah. Well, you know what he says to me, this skinny little runt? He says, 'Pop, why didn't they walk Casey?'"

Johansen stopped stepping back and forth, and frowned as he tried to remember the details of the classic poem. *Then from that gladdened multitude went up a joyous yell, for Casey, mighty Casey, was advancing to the bat* . . . "The other team had a two-run lead, first base was open—"

"Dudn't matter, 'cuz I don't know enough about the game. All I'm saying, this is how the boy thinks."

August 19

"Hey Sal, did you know Marvin was spending all his money on that girl in New York?"

"Not any more he ain't." Spinale pointed to the back of the locker room, where a half-naked Marvin Kowalski lay on his back along a bench, arm thrown over his face and hiding his eyes.

"They broke up?" Johansen asked.

"Not sure. But he hasn't been on his cell phone in nearly an hour. Some kinda record."

Johansen watched the inert form for a few seconds, then called out, "Kowalski! Get a move on!"

Kowalski jerked his arm away and sat up, trying to blink away the harsh overhead light. He dutifully continued getting dressed, but his movements were desultory and laconic, and stayed that way as he moped onto the field.

Kowalski took a deep breath and inhaled the steamy aroma rising from the infield of the ballpark eight miles east of Fort Worth. Although only in the league for less than a season, he was already beginning to draw comfort from fields that felt like a second home. Kicking the fine sand between home and third, surveying the keen edge that divided the emerald grass from the base paths, drinking in the fresh chalk lines and the endless rows of seats and the smell of popcorn, hot dogs and even stale beer . . . all of it was powerful enough to revivify the most jaded and battle-weary cynic if he'd ever gotten them into his blood in the first place. The more he played ball, the more Marvin Kowalski grew to understand and appreciate one of Sal Spinale's more subversively penetrating homilies: "Home is where you go when you go home."

The familiarity that intoxicated him, the oceanic blueness of the dome of sky above, the unimprovable perfection of the day, only served to deepen his sense of loss and self-doubt. But as long as he insisted on wallowing in a pit of misery, who better to try to pull him out of it than that perennial nominee for the Mr. Sensitivity Award, Manuel "Chi Chi" los Parados?

"You don' become a man just 'cuz you get you nose wet a firs' time."

Sitting in the dugout, Kowalski turned to regard his teammate. "What?"

Thus encouraged, los Parados expanded on his thesis. "You don't know yet s'only nooky, so you don' know shit, man. You think iss *love*, all flowers and son'shine 'n' shit." He shrugged with the studied indifference of the world-weary. "You lose a'first one, 'slike the whole world is ending. Til you get a *good* one, and then you realize whudda piece'a shit da' odder one was, and *thass*—" He poked Kowalski in the chest "—*thass* when you become a man."

Kowalski rose up off the bench. "She wasn't a piece'a shit! You didn't know her!"

Los Parados smirked and cocked his head. "Oh yeah?"

At the other end of the dugout, Sal Spinale nudged Zuke Johansen and pointed toward the bench with his chin. "Uh oh . . ."

"Her name's what . . . Dee Dee?" los Parados said. "Or was it Trixie this week. Don' matter. She's got a place on Fi'ty-third, pictures of her foggin' dogs on the wall and a mole right here." He pointed to a spot near his sternum. To Kowalski's drop-jawed look of astonishment he added, "Wodda hell'd you think, kid . . . nice *muchachas* hang around in bars pickin' up ballplayers they don' even foggin' know and cook their *huevos* for 'em?"

Kowalski, unable to speak, could only stand there and stare, complying autonomically when los Parados patted the bench for him to sit back down.

"Okay, so now you got you nose wet, da' part's over. Now, you find you'self a nice girl, smar' like you. Trus' me, amigo: this one gonna fade like las' night's *cerveza*."

Kowalski let out a long breath. "Doesn't make this one feel any better right now."

"I know tha', li'l brother. Belie' me, I know. Ah not tryin'a make you feel better, I'm jus' tryin'a give you son' *hope*, is all."

Kowalski, smart enough to sense the wisdom beneath the crass delivery, nodded and looked down at his shoes.

"What happened, anyway?" John Amos asked after a decent interval.

Kowalski waved it away. "Doesn't matter."

Detroit—August 20

Kowalski shot from the first stage of death—denial—right to anger without passing Go. He convinced Johansen to let him bat first against the Tigers, and summoned up all the sneering contempt he could squeeze onto his face as he purposely crowded the plate as closely as he thought he could get away with.

"You nuts or what?" the catcher asked him.

Sure enough, "Steely" Dan Andresen threw the very first pitch of the game right at him, to the great amusement of the Detroit players in the dugout. Expecting it and already poised to duck away, Kowalski timed his spin perfectly, so that the ball brushed by his arm, unambiguously snagging the fabric but not doing him any real damage.

Without waiting for the ump's call, he flipped the bat away and took a fast trot to first, never taking his eyes off the mound as he went.

"Pussy!" he mouthed at Andresen as he turned sideways and adjusted his cup. To the pitcher it looked like a New York–style crotch-grab mocking, which is just what Kowalski had intended.

When he got to the bag he said to the first baseman, "First pitch of the game and we're on base already. Big guy really showed me something out there." He knew the remark would get back to Andresen in the dugout.

As Aires came up to bat, Kowalski took a long lead, scuttled back to the base and took another lead. Andresen knew he was being taunted, but he also knew that he didn't want to be the first pitcher in baseball to have a base stolen from him by Marvin Kowalski, so he threw several balls to first before pitching one to Aires. Rattled, he let Aires get 'hold of one, a grounder to right field that got him on base and advanced Kowalski to second.

Now Andresen had faced two and let them both on base. The catcher, knowing like all catchers exactly what was going through his pitcher's mind, called for time and went out to settle him down. Andresen let out a long breath and nodded, then the catcher patted him on the fanny and went back to the plate.

Andresen took hold of himself and struck out Billy Blyvelt, got Darryl Bombeck on a pop fly to center and Cavvy Papazian on a fly to left. Relieved to have gotten out of the inning alive, he wasn't prepared when Kowalski ran by him on the way to the dugout and said, "Want me to just start out on first next time and save you four bullshit pitches?"

To Kowalski's surprise, Andresen didn't take out after him, but he could practically feel the smoldering rage radiating off the pitcher.

"What the hell are you doing, Kowalski?" Johansen asked in the dugout.

"Neutralizing him," Kowalski answered as he dropped onto the bench. "Isn't that what I'm supposed to do, throw these guys off and make 'em harmless?"

"No need to get him all riled up like that."

"Why not?"

"Because it's not your style, that's why."

"And what exactly is my style . . . stand up there like a human dartboard and let the pitcher control what happens?"

"Worked pretty good so far."

"Well it's not enough."

"Listen—"

"Zuke, if I screw it up you can fire me, okay? Trust me; I'll get this shithead out of here before the sixth inning."

Johansen regarded him curiously. "When did a fellow ballplayer get to be a shithead?"

"When he tried to take my head off."

"You were crowding the plate! And he didn't go for your head, he just brushed you back."

But Kowalski wasn't listening anymore.

HE CAME UP AGAIN in the fourth inning. To everyone's surprise, he'd left his batting gloves and helmet in the dugout.

"You plannin' to bat like that?" the ump asked.

"You call this batting? You think this ape is going to pitch to me?" He shook his head contemptuously.

"He *is* gonna pitch to you," the catcher said.

"Yeah, right," Kowalski responded. "Come on, let's get this over with."

"Shaddap, the both'a yuz," the ump warned. "Kowalski, get your helmet on your head or your ass in the showers."

"But—"

"I don't give a rat's ass if yer grandmother's on the mound . . . we got rules in this game."

The batboy, knowing the rules better than Kowalski did, was already waiting with the helmet and handed it over. "Who're you guys kidding?" Kowalski muttered at the catcher as he put it on.

The catcher shrugged. "Whatever you say," he responded in amiable singsong as he squatted down and flashed a sign toward the mound.

The fastball came screaming in right for the middle of the strike zone. Kowalski was fully prepared—he'd goaded Andresen into taking him on—and batted it high into the left field stands for strike one.

Andresen threw the same pitch again. This time Kowalski sent it dribbling down the third base line.

A change-up. Kowalski shifted his stance and hit the slow pitch down the *first* base line.

In the dugout Johansen, Spinale and batting coach Lefty Peterson jumped immediately to their feet. "What the hell was that!" Johansen exclaimed. Kowalski, a righty, never hit balls in that direction.

"Tryin'a get Steely's goat," Spinale said. "Show him he can do any damned thing he wants to those pitches."

Really angry now, Andresen threw a monster fastball toward the inside corner. Kowalski lifted his hands and arched his back, letting it go by for a ball. The next one was down and away for a second ball, and Kowalski flashed a smile at the mound: *Giving up already?*

Andresen pressed his lips together and ground his teeth. He shook off the catcher's first sign, then the second, then rejected a third with an irritated toss of his head. Kowalski knew exactly what was going on: The catcher wanted him to give up a walk and get on with the game, but Andresen wanted to teach this snot-nosed punk a lesson.

Finally relenting, the catcher let out an audible sigh and got ready. The pitch broke away so sharply he had to lunge after it, and it was another ball, for a full 3-and-2 count.

The next three were all in the zone, each one thrown harder than the last, and Kowalski was almost flippant in how easily he swatted them away. Andresen was fuming openly now, his growing exasperation in full view. He was shaking off an alarming number of signs until finally the Detroit manager came out of the dugout and called for time.

Kowalski watched the mound conference, the manager arguing something and Andresen spitefully dismissing it with small, rapid shakes of his head. Finally, the pitcher smacked the ball into the manager's outstretched hand and stormed off the mound.

When Kowalski got back to the dugout after the reliever put him on first and got Aires to ground out, Johansen said, "I think you made an enemy there."

Kowalski got a drink from the cooler, crushed the paper cup and threw it to the floor. "Fuck him. Not my job to be friends with pitchers."

On the way out of the park after the game, he passed through the horde of kids waiting for autographs as though they weren't there.

"I know this great barbecue place over in Bricktown," Spinale said. "What say we—"

"No thanks," Kowalski said curtly, cutting him off. "I got plans."

"Alright, well . . . we got an eight o'clock plane in the morning, so don't—"

Kowalski turned away from his locker. "Hey Sal, you gonna ask me if I did my homework next?"

"Just reminding you that—"

"I don't need reminding." He slammed the locker shut with a bang that turned heads all across the room. "Jesus Christ . . . !"

Dark clouds behind his eyes, Kowalski left just before the media were allowed in.

Fourteen

BEEN TWO WEEKS SINCE THE KID got dumped by that broad," Spinale said. "How long you figure'a let him go on like this?"

Johansen looked around at the players on the field. Two coaches were hitting fungoes to fielders standing in pairs and talking and occasionally fielding a ball if it didn't require too much effort, while the pitching staff jogged around the outfield at speeds slower than a brisk walk. It was an easy warm-up and Johansen didn't mind; his team was having a terrific season and, during games when it counted, everybody was playing like it was bottom of the ninth in the last game of the Series. He'd never seen such enthusiastic and joyful hustle, so if the boys wanted to loaf during a workout they didn't really need, there was no sense being hard-nosed about it. "Where is he?"

"Don't know."

Usually the first on the field, Kowalski hadn't even shown up for the last three pregame warm-ups and didn't seem to care about the fines. He'd barely shown up for the games, either, trudging in bleary-eyed and unfocused.

Los Parados had reported that the rookie phenom had discovered the world of groupies and seemed hell-bent on starting at one end of the line and working his way down to the other with no pauses in between. He'd also discovered bourbon, and was apparently behaving as if he could make up for all the valuable drinking time he'd lost in the eighteen years of life before he'd begun boozing. "Smar' as he is," los Parados had said, "he don' seem to unnerstan' the shit hits the fan *later*."

"You hear he bought hisself a Porsche?" Spinale pronounced it *por-shee*.

Johansen finally took his eyes off the field and turned to his bench coach. "You're shitting me."

"I shit you not. 'Pussy catcher,' he called it."

Johansen inhaled deeply and let it out slowly, his lips set in a grim line. "Don't even pay him enough to keep fining him. Bet he didn't show up for his hitting lesson, either."

"Thing is," Spinale said, "he's basically a good kid. All of this . . . whatever . . . it's not like him."

It's not like anybody, Johansen thought to himself, *until it is*. He couldn't begin to count the number of "good kids" in professional sports who'd gotten smacked with fame and adoration so suddenly they'd had no time to prepare, who got treated with the kind of deference more appropriate for someone who cured cancer, and who were showered with so much money that they immediately began spending it as fast as they could for fear it would be taken away as precipitously as it had appeared. They snorted coke, drove too fast, abused women—sometimes all three at the same time—always pushing the outside of the envelope to see how far it would stretch. They were *all* good kids once. No one was immune. And nobody tried too hard to stop them as long as they kept winning.

But it had never happened on Johansen's watch. It was an understanding he had with the owner, and also with the owner of the stadium, and no one understood better than Robert Leffingwell, who gave no more thought to pressuring Holden Canfield to get rid of a self-destructive prima donna than he would to ridding his house of termites.

Leffingwell wasn't a prude or a Puritan. He didn't care if the players chased tail or caroused til all hours. He didn't care about anything they did so long as it was legal, was gone by morning and didn't hurt the team. He'd even formed a subsidiary of Mahoney Fertilizer playfully called "Income Fertilizer" that provided financial management for the less astute players, which was nearly all of them. John Amos had the original idea when he played for the Marlins, but had been so impressed with Leffingwell's attitude toward his players that he'd joined the Majestyks when he became a free agent and gotten the financial management program going full bore in Des Moines. It was so well handled and so successful that players from other teams had asked to become clients as well.

Johansen didn't fully understand the relationship between Leffingwell, who'd built the stadium, and Canfield, who owned the team, but he knew enough to understand that Leffingwell swung considerable clout on all matters concerning the Majestyks.

Leffingwell hadn't yet said a word about Kowalski, but Johansen knew it was just a matter of time.

KOWALSKI HAD FINALLY SHOWN UP, excusing his lateness with some mumbling about a "stomach virus," which was so lame Johansen didn't even bother to call him on it. Kowalski was like a hand grenade with a loose pin lately, and everybody was afraid that if they jiggled it too much it would come loose and explode in unexpected but probably unpleasant ways.

He hadn't even said anything when Johansen pulled him out of the starting lineup. He sat, sullen and unapproachable, yet still watching the pitchers.

But today the team needed him. They were down by one to the Oakland A's in the bottom of the ninth, with Aires on first and one out. Kowalski dutifully got himself walked as usual. Darryl Bombeck was up next and executed a perfect bunt down the first base line. The Oakland catcher ran after it, but wisely declined to make the play to first because Bombeck was a real runner and it would be close, so he threw to second instead and got the much slower Kowalski out. Aires was now in scoring position on third, with two outs, and John Amos was up.

Kowalski took his time heading for the dugout, and heard a pitched ball hit something, then saw the ball dribble foul across the first base line and roll his way. He bent over and picked it up, flinging it toward the catcher without looking, and resumed walking toward the dugout.

That's when the noise started. It came from up in the stands and sounded something like he imagined a mama grizzly must sound like when a wolf got too close to her cubs. It was not a friendly noise.

Kowalski turned in time to see the catcher, to whom he had just thrown the ball, tag Bueno Aires out and end the game.

"YOU'RE TELLING ME this has happened before?" Skeeter Phalango asked the ESPN reporter who was commenting on the monitor.

"Believe it or not. Guy named Max West, playing for the Red Sox."

The ESPN reporter's face faded away and was replaced by a replay of the afternoon's festivities. It showed the routine pitch, low and away, which John Amos let go by for a ball. But it was so far out of the zone the Oakland catcher couldn't hang on to it. It bounced off his glove and rolled away.

Seeing the wild pitch, Aires immediately took off for home. He had so much time he wouldn't even need to slide to get the tying run.

"Only thing I can think of—"

"Kowalski never does interviews," the ESPN reporter reminded him.

"Right. So what I'm thinking, Kowalski must have assumed that

Amos had swung on it and fouled it away. He figured it was dead, so he just picked it up and did the catcher a favor by tossing it back."

"Mr. Johansen?"

Sal Spinale turned his head away from the television. Geoffrey Slagenbach had picked the worst possible moment to intrude on the Majestyks manager.

"He did him a favor, alright." Now the monitor showed Johansen, Spinale and Cavvy Papazian coming out of the dugout to see what they could do about preventing Aires from decapitating Kowalski with his bare hands. Even the Oakland catcher and the ump were trying to restrain the furious Argentinean from killing his own team-mate.

"What do you suppose was on this kid's mind Skeeter?"

"Not baseball, that's for sure. You're talking about a player who's normally as attentive as a border guard."

"And smart, too."

"What is it, Pudgy?" Johansen snarled.

"Well . . ."

"You said it," Phalango responded. "But let's face it, Marvin Kowalski has looked like a visitor from another planet these past couple of weeks."

"Are we gonna hear about him entering rehab before the season's over?"

"We have no hard evidence of that, but, well . . . you never know, right? We'll be right back with more after this . . ."

Johansen hit the remote and the screen went dead. He turned to look at Slagenbach, and some exotic form of nuclear energy beaming out of his eyes set off warning alarms in the equipment manager's brain, causing him to bypass his normal routine of hemming-and-hawing and stepping from foot to foot and excusing himself endlessly, and made him get right to the point.

"Kowalski's parents are on the line."

Fifteen

I T WAS EXACTLY WHAT Marvin Kowalski needed. Loud, garish, bustling and crowded, with three separate bars scattered around the room. Music—pounding, mindless, heavy on the bass and generally relentless—came from a DJ perched on a tiny balcony sticking straight out of the wall above the crowd. People dressed like extras in some low-budget, futuristic punk-rock music video gyrated on the wooden dance floor, whatever athleticism they might normally have displayed now rubberized and uncoordinated owing to a combination of alcohol and an impressively wide variety of recreational pharmaceuticals.

Chi Chi los Parados poked Kowalski in the ribs. "Whud I tell you, man!" he yelled over the noise.

Kowalski nodded. "Let's get a drink!" he shouted back, and led the way to the closest of three bars.

Los Parados grabbed him by the arm and pointed across the room. "Thass a better one."

Kowalski shrugged and let himself be maneuvered across the

169

floor. He was surprised to find himself unaccosted, and assumed everyone was too drunk or stoned to recognize him. It also occurred to him that this place probably wasn't a hotbed of baseball fans. He might actually have to do some work to hook up.

He pointed to a bottle of Jack Daniels rather than try to be heard over the din, and as the bartender turned to grab it, Kowalski saw los Parados in the mirror, talking to a woman dressed in relatively terrestrial clothes and still able to hold her head upright. She lifted her eyebrows slightly at something los Parados had said, and Kowalski did a quick assessment: nice-looking, not too much makeup, and another quality he couldn't quite put his finger on. She looked more self-confident than most of the women he'd been with recently. Cool, in other words. Unhurried, and measuring things with a critical eye. Just then her eyes found him, but rather than look away, he met her unabashed gaze and straightened up, sensing as she blinked that she recognized him. Then it was gone, and she returned her attention to los Parados. Too bad; Kowalski would like to have moved on her himself, and the pickings among the rest of the crazies looked mighty slim.

He went back to his drink, then casually looked over, but los Parados and the woman were no longer there. He figured he might as well drink up and go elsewhere, as he was not likely to see los Parados again this night.

"Hi there," said a female voice at his elbow.

He turned and, sensing a riot of sequins, bright red lipstick and enough perfume for a chemical warfare attack, smiled automatically, a practiced, PR grin with no warmth behind it, then looked forward again. He waited until the bartender was turned his way, then began reaching into his back pocket. Slowly . . . slowly . . . slower still . . .

"Your money's no good here," the bartender finally said, holding out his hand.

"Thanks." Kowalski abandoned the pretense of reaching for his wallet and shook hands perfunctorily, then turned and walked away without another glance at the girl next to him.

As he walked toward the door he spied los Parados, still with that woman, but now another girl had joined them. Los Parados was looking back and forth between them, a pained look on his face, which was when he spotted Kowalski and gestured animatedly.

"Yo, Marvin, my man!" he called out loudly, then began steering both women over. The new one was different; brassier, more showy . . . *larger*. Kowalski wanted no part of her, and eyed the door, gauging the distance relative to the trio headed his way, but it was too late.

Kowalski stared hard at los Parados, trying to flash him the *No go!* sign, then gritted his teeth as the message got lost amid the sensory clutter filling the room. Los Parados smiled brightly, stepped to the side and held both his hands out toward . . . the *first* woman.

"This here Jannine," los Parados said. "Jannine, this here is *mi amigo*, Marvin Kowalski he very own self."

Her eyes locked onto Kowalski's, but no words were exchanged.

"Joo gonna say hello or wha'?" los Parados shouted.

"How you doin'?" Kowalski said. Did Chi Chi really intend for him to take this one?

She shrugged. "You?"

"Good."

"Ahngonna take this little one for a drink," los Parados said, moving the second, distinctly *un*-little woman away. And then they were gone.

"Thirsty?" Kowalski asked Jannine.

"Sure."

They went to the bar, they ordered drinks, they chatted aimlessly while waiting, clinked glasses when they arrived, and chatted aimlessly some more.

A few more minutes passed and then Jannine put her mouth next to his ear. "You want to stand around doing the bullshit bolero or you just want to get out of here now?"

HE WOKE UP RELATIVELY ALERT, having gone out of the club so fast he'd barely had time for one full drink there, and only one in his hotel before Jannine had begun orchestrating the various melodies of an astonishingly varied sexual fugue.

A rustling had woken him, and now he became aware of New York City street noise that no amount of sound proofing could block out completely. Across the room he saw Jannine pulling on a shoe. "Where you going?" he yawned sleepily.

She didn't answer right away, but got the other shoe on, then stood up and grabbed her purse from the dresser. Fully assembled and ready to part, she turned to face him. "To report a rape."

"What?" Kowalski's eyes snapped fully open, but he was momentarily unable to speak, and she turned for the door. "You're . . . wait!" he finally managed to croak.

She turned, impatient and annoyed at the delay.

"What rape?"

"What you did to me last night."

"What I . . ." He sat up straight and tried to clear his head, holding out his hand to beg for time. "What the hell are you talking about!"

"Nothing but another big-shot athlete who thought he could abuse women just because he can hit a baseball."

"Jannine . . . !"

"See you, Marvin."

"Hold it a second!" He threw aside the bedcovers and stumbled to the floor, intending to stop her, then looked up to see a gun pointed at him. He froze in horror, falling back onto the bed. "Jesus . . . what . . . why would you do something like that!"

"For a hundred thousand dollars, that's why."

Kowalski, who'd grown up in the rural Midwest and understood guns, noticed how steady her hand was. "A hundred . . . what? What hundred thousand dollars?"

"The hundred thousand you're going to pay me to keep it quiet."

He concentrated, trying to make his brain work despite the battering ram of thoughts threatening his grip on reality. "I didn't do anything!"

She eyed him suspiciously: Could even this yokel be that stupid? "Doesn't matter. I just want a hundred grand."

"Are you crazy? I don't have that kind of money!"

She laughed humorlessly. "Right. And Alex Rodriguez clips coupons for the supermarket. Good-bye, Marvin."

"Wait! Jesus!" He rubbed the side of his head. "I'll get it. I can get it. They're offering me . . . they want me to, uh—"

"Good. That'll make things easier." She put her hand on the door-knob.

"Where are you going?"

"I already told you. To report a rape."

He stopped rubbing. "But . . . I just told you I'll get the money!"

"And I said good."

"Then why—"

"Because, *Marvin*, if I don't report it now, then you split and I'm left with nothing."

"No! I mean, I won't do that! I—"

"Right now, see, the evidence is, um . . ." She rocked her head back and forth. "The evidence is fresh, know what I mean? I report it, then we deal. Less chance for mistakes."

Kowalski wasn't too addled to recognize a negotiation in the middle of a shakedown, a possible way out of the mess. He'd seen plenty of movies. Sure! She shakes him up but good, scares the hell out of him, then they dicker. All he had to do was glom onto the game and play it out with her, see what she'd settle for, figure out what the bottom line was that would make this go away. And if he was very smart, he could throw in some delaying elements that might make it possible to really whittle it down. Maybe even turn it all around and scare the hell out of *her* and avoid paying anything. Yeah! Show her what kind of street savvy this fresh-from-the-farm rube had going for him.

He got hold of himself and prepared to get it on with her, to start a little dancing and identify the real issues. "Okay, here's—"

"Good-bye, Marvin," she said as she opened the door, and then she was gone.

•   •   •

THE PHONE RANG FOUR TIMES before he picked it up. "Hello?" he said in a small voice.

"Marvin?"

Kowalski leaned against the wall and closed his eyes. "Zuke. Yeah."

"What—you okay?"

"Yeah, fine. Why . . . uh . . . what's up?"

"Bus for the airport's leaving early. Bad weather or something. Downstairs in thirty minutes. Marvin?"

"Skipper, I . . ."

"You sure you're okay?"

Thirty minutes and he'd be on his way to LaGuardia and back to Des Moines. The thought perked him up. "Of course I'm okay! See you downstairs."

He hung up hurriedly and took a quick shower, trying to wash away the awful events of the morning with some vigorous scrubbing. It was probably all just a trick, he thought as he dried off. Scare the bejesus out of me then come back and extort some money.

He put on a fresh shirt and reached for his pants. No way was she going to the police or to a hospital. Put herself through that, all that publicity, and then risk not getting anything if she made any mistakes at all?

He pulled on his shoes. Next time he was in New York she'd try to see him, but he'd call on the same team resources the other superstars used, the ones that kept eager fans and groupies away. No clubs, no restaurants, just stay in his room and lay low, and if she decided to go to the police then, what of it? Who'd believe her? Nobody'd even seen them together except los Parados, who wouldn't tell, and as for the "evidence," well, that would be long gone. She'd be just another gold-digging, piece-of-shit groupie.

He was really starting to feel better when the door burst open and two uniformed policemen stormed in, pointing shotguns at him. As he stood there, paralyzed, a third uniform walked in, obviously of higher rank, and said, "Marvin Kowalski?"

He could only nod dumbly as his eyes frantically caromed back and forth between the two high-powered weapons aimed at him.

The third uniform spun him around and grabbed his arms, pulling them behind his back. "I'm Deputy Inspector Edwin Knowles, and you're under arrest on suspicion of rape." He began putting on hand-cuffs. "Complaint was sworn out by a Florence Rassmussen."

"Florence?" Kowalski whispered hoarsely. "She said her name was Jannine!"

"Oh, yeah? Who did?"

"The girl!"

"Ah. You mean the one you raped?"

"I didn't rape her!"

"But she was here."

"Wh-what?"

The cuffs snapped closed. "You just said the girl who reported being raped was here. With you. Just like she said she was. You just said that, right?"

"Wait a minute!"

Knowles spun him around. "You admitted she was here."

"But I didn't rape her!"

"You had sex with her . . ."

"Yes, but . . . listen, this isn't right! She's the one who . . . I didn't . . ."

"Eddie . . ." one of the other cops said.

"Huh? Oh, yeah, almost forgot. You have the right to remain silent . . ."

They hustled Kowalski roughly down the hall and into a service elevator. "She's just trying to extort money from me!" he cried out in a strangled voice. "You've got to believe me! She pointed a gun at me and said—"

"A gun!" one of the cops chortled. "Pointed a gun and made you do it, did she?"

"Made me . . . no, she didn't make me do anything! She said—"

"Woman was upset," the higher-rank growled. "What you did . . ." he shook his head and looked away.

"I'm telling you, I didn't—*aaagggh!*"

The cop who'd poked the rifle barrel into his belly put his face up close. "Scumbag athletes," he hissed menacingly. "Make all that dough and think you own the fucking world."

Kowalski, bent over, looked up and tried to answer. "Look, I—"

"Shut up!" the cop screamed in his ear, and raised the butt of the rifle.

"Not here!" the higher-rank said, holding out his hand to stop him. "Wait'll we get him to the house."

Kowalski groaned and collapsed.

SEATED BY HIMSELF in the back seat of the squad car, Kowalski started the ride in mortal terror and on the edge of vomiting, and it only got worse during the half-hour it took to go the six blocks to the Midtown North precinct on West Fifty-fourth Street. Passing Tiffany's on Fifty-seventh, he noticed a clock in the window and realized that he should have been on the team bus to the airport ten minutes ago. By now somebody would have called his room, gotten no answer and grown angry at the latest fuck-up by the king of all fuck-ups, who'd really gone and done it this time, even though he'd actually done nothing at all.

Somebody was staring into the car as it crept along in traffic and Kowalski dropped his head down quickly to avoid being recognized. The cop in the passenger seat turned at the movement and grunted, but otherwise said nothing. Neither of them had uttered a word the entire trip, not even on the radio.

At the precinct house, the squad car pulled into a space close to the front entrance. One of the cops opened the back door, put a hand on Kowalski's head and pulled him out, then led him through the green doors, across the lobby and into a back room.

"Listen," Kowalski said, "you've got to believe me! I didn't—"

The cop spun him around, grabbed him by the collar with one hand and cocked the other one into a fist. "You open your mouth again, I'll shut it permanently."

Kowalski looked at the poised fist and felt his bowels begin to let go. Trembling and sweating, he stayed still, not knowing for sure if he was supposed to nod or say okay or just stand there and do nothing.

The cop, fury boiling in his eyes, waited, then opened his hand and shoved him forward. Unable to stop himself because of the handcuffs, he stumbled and fell.

The door closed and he was alone, too afraid to move. Voices came through the door, quickly growing louder and angrier. He couldn't make out complete sentences, only words and the occasional phrase. "You crazy? . . . reporters . . . screamin' 'bout brutality . . . resisting . . . him alone . . ."

The voices grew even louder, then the door burst open and the rifle-toting cop, now carrying only a baton, walked in with Deputy Inspector Knowles hard on his heels. The door shut behind them and the voices became quiet. Kowalski could see silhouetted shapes congregating on the frosted glass that formed part of one wall.

The cop with the baton stepped forward and straddled Kowalski, then turned to look at Knowles, who waited a moment, nodded, then left the room.

The cop waited for the door to click shut, then turned back, steadied himself and raised the baton.

Kowalski screamed, a gurgling and piteous wail of the purest terror, and tried to shrink himself into the floorboards.

With his eyes squeezed shut and his head pulled tightly into his shoulders, he barely heard a voice shout, "Hold it!"

No blow came, and another second later he risked opening his eyes slightly. Knowles was back, staring at him, then looked at the other cop and waved him off.

The cop hesitated, as if deciding whether to obey, then reluctantly stepped away.

"Can you take his cuffs off?" a familiar voice said. "Please."

Zuke? Kowalski opened his eyes fully and saw a grim-faced Johansen in the doorway. Knowles made a hand motion at the cop, who pushed the prisoner onto his side and fiddled with the cuffs until they came loose.

Kowalski rolled onto his back and slowly brought his arms forward, surprised at how much they ached, and rubbed first one wrist then the other, not looking at Johansen. He sat up, suddenly conscious that he was on the floor while everyone else was standing, and got to his feet. Not trusting his shaking legs, he sat down slowly on a cheap folding chair next to an aluminum card table.

"We'll be right back, Marvin," Johansen said, and then he was alone.

Kowalski felt hot tears streaming down his cheeks. Terrified, ashamed, confused . . . and he hadn't done anything!

Except be a complete and total asshole, letting a low-life, celebrity-hounding groupie bimbo break his stupid heart and send him whirling down a black tunnel to the point where he'd behaved like some secondary character in a cheap novel. His parents had clucked and shaken their heads reading stories about those dim-witted, animalistic jocks who'd gotten too much too fast and reacted not with grace and strength but weakness, falling heir to every temptation that wafted past their supersensitized and overcompensated nostrils.

And now he, Marvin Kowalski, valedictorian of Ocheyedan High in Osceola County, Iowa, had become one of them, letting down not only his parents and Mr. Schmidt but his teammates, his coaches and his manager. They'd welcomed him into their close-knit fraternity, their band of disparate brothers bound by their love of a game, and now here he was, sitting alone in a New York City police station, his life in ruins, bringing down shame and disgrace on everybody who'd had the misfortune to have known him.

•   •   •

HE SAT THERE for what felt like an hour. Voices again, more subdued. Shapes on the frosted glass, then the door opened. It was Johansen, standing alone, his face foreboding.

Kowalski, anxiety-ridden and thoroughly wrung out, stood up. He wanted to say something but couldn't think of anything, and his mouth was so dry he probably couldn't have gotten the words out anyway.

"Let's go," Johansen said.

Kowalski couldn't comprehend the meaning right away, and knit his brows together in confusion, then shook his head back and forth questioningly.

"Come on," Johansen said, flapping a hand toward the lobby. "We're leaving."

Kowalski gulped, and decided it wasn't important if he understood or not. They were leaving!

He stepped gingerly forward and let Johansen, an arm across his back, lead him through the lobby and out the front door where a cab was waiting. The door opened from the inside and he saw Sal Spinale sitting there, beckoning him inside.

"Gotta take care of a few more things," Johansen said. "Get in and I'll be back in a minute."

Kowalski did as he was told, noticing his overnight bag and carry-on sitting on the floor of the cab. He sat down next to Spinale, who handed him a bottle of water and patted his knee.

"Don't worry about it kid," the bench coach said. "We're gettin' it taken care of."

Kowalski looked into Spinale's eyes to see if it could possibly be true, then almost fainted at the waves of relief that washed over him like icy rain.

"JESUS, ZUKE," Deputy Inspector Edwin Knowles said as Johansen returned to the lobby. "Thought the poor sumbitch was gonna puke right on the spot."

The cop with the baton grinned. "I gave him one'a these," he said, losing the smile and glowering, making Knowles laugh.

"Hated to do it to the poor kid," a female voice said from off to the left behind the desk officer's podium.

Johansen snickered as he took an envelope from an inside jacket pocket, and Knowles and the cop guffawed openly, the cop making an obscene and derisive pumping motion with his fist.

Jannine rolled her eyes and told them to fuck off, then took the envelope with a faux-demure, singsong "Thank you."

Johansen reached into a different pocket and pulled out a sheaf of tickets. "Here you go, boys," he said, stepping forward and holding them out. "Field-level, first base line."

Knowles reached for them eagerly. "And you better remember—"

"You guys get to the Series—" the other cop added.

"Or the playoffs . . ."

Johansen handed over the tickets and held up his arms in mock surrender. "I know, I know. Of course, that assumes that *you* guys get to the Series or the playoffs . . ."

The police officers *harumphed* knowingly. "Gimme a freakin' break, Johansen," Knowles sneered. "With Rojo pitchin', Malinowski, Perpado . . ."

"Yeah, I know. A sure thing. Well, I got a plane to catch." He turned to Jannine. "Might be best, you stayed away from my boys for a while."

The high-priced hooker waggled the envelope at him. "Might just go to Tahiti."

"Not a bad idea."

"Well . . . you give that Chi Chi a big wet kiss for me."

"Not even if you give me back that envelope."

BACK WITH THE TEAM three days later, Kowalski braced himself for a storm of retribution from the teammates he'd disappointed, but none came. Spinale had been right after all: You could shoot heroin, commit murder, hurl racial epithets on national television and rape women, but so long as you were a winner on the field, all would be forgiven.

Kowalski promised himself to take that as a one-time blessing rather than a continuing license.

Sixteen

Des Moines—September 28

IMPOSSIBLY, MIRACULOUSLY, the Majestyks were tied for first place in the Central Division of the American League with Kansas City.

Whom they just happened to be playing against today, right here in the Shit Hole, the final day of a three-day stand.

It had become a happy team, and a happy place to be. Habits that to some had seemed irritating at one time were subtly transformed into colorful eccentricities, team oddballs now being referred to in picaresque and roguish terms absent the kind of derision that tended to surface in circumstances less congenial.

Kowalski had even made peace with John "The Deacon" Amos, coming to enjoy the sparring Amos was perfectly willing to engage in without seeming to take any offense.

"Let's all take a moment to give thanks to Jesus," Amos had said after the Majestyks had thoroughly trounced Toronto in a lopsided 9-1 win.

"I'd a thunk we oughta give thanks to Bueno," los Parados shot back, referring to the Argentinean's 3-for-5, 5 RBI hitting.

"With Jesus at our side we can do all things. We prayed for a victory and we got it."

"Hey, John," Kowalski piped up, several of the other players in the clubhouse turning their attention his way in anticipation of another set-to. "What do you figure, the other guys didn't pray?"

"I'm sure they did, Marvin," Amos replied.

"So, what then . . . they didn't pray hard enough, is that it?"

"I'm sure they entreated the Lord fervently."

"So why do you figure He liked us better'n them?"

"Well, I wouldn't look at it that way."

"Then how come He made us win and them lose?"

"Well—"

"What do you figure the Blue Jays are doing while we're thanking God, John . . . you figure they're giving Him a hard time?"

"Your arrogance will be your undoing, kid. You have to humble yourself before the Lord and give thanks for this splendid victory."

"I don't know. Sure would feel funny thanking God for making Toronto lose."

Amos smiled indulgently. "He didn't make them lose, Marvin. He made *us* win."

"Ah. Well, that explains it. But if God gave you a triple last time up, how come He struck you out the time before that?"

"Never underestimate the power of prayer, son."

"If it was that simple," Kowalski shot back, "the Pope'd be hitting .350."

"You must walk with the Lord, Marvin."

"I'd rather he walked with the bases loaded," Johansen said. "Don't you guys have some work to do?"

Kowalski turned to Sal Spinale. "You hearing this, Sal? How can a guy get away with that kind of mindless nattering?"

" 'Cuz he's hitting .323 and he's made only two errors in ninety games. *You* hit .323 and you can become a twirling dervish, for all I care."

And so it went, but there had been no rancor in it. Kowalski enjoyed the intellectual give-and-take, and Amos figured that as long as the kid was willing to at least discuss things, there was yet hope of saving his soul. So long as you were winning, no offense was taken and everything was forgiven.

Almost everything.

WITH THE TWO TEAMS TIED and the regular season almost concluded, today was for a lot of marbles. Des Moines and Kansas City had only two more games each after this one and a win here was crucial for a realistic chance of advancing to the playoffs.

In the playoffs, four teams would compete and two would survive to contest the American League pennant, so-called because the team that won got an actual pennant to fly from its home field flagpole. Teams advancing to the playoffs would be the winners of the West, Central and East divisions, with one additional "wild card" team to round out the field to four. The wild card would be determined by the team with the best record that didn't win a division.

On the mound for the Royals was Fanagalo VandeMerve, a former South African cricket player with an arm like an aircraft carrier catapult but who'd had a tough time learning to pitch while standing still; in cricket he'd been able to run and release the ball like a javelin thrower. Pitching a baseball for him was like Carl Lewis doing the long jump from a standing start.

For the Majestyks it was Zacky Ghirardelli, in a stadium so calm the flags were hanging straight down. Except one, a giant American flag standing straight out in what looked like a Force 5 gale. But it was only one of stadium owner Robert Leffingwell's little patriotic tricks, compressed air piped up through the staff and blown out of little vents to make the stars'n'bars flutter regardless of wind conditions.

The game began as a classic pitchers' duel: very few hits, a walk here and there, but no runs. By the fifth inning no batter had even gotten as far as second base, and then Ghirardelli, hand cramping but unwilling to flag it to Johansen because of how well he was doing, started to fade. The knuckler that had been bouncing around like a heat-crazed wasp suddenly found a flight path straight as a light ray and the Royals started hitting it.

With men on first and second, no outs, one run already scored and no fingernails left in the Majestyks dugout, Johansen pulled Ghirardelli and put in Bryce Thomason. Although Thomason had been made a starter earlier in the season, there was nothing that precluded his being drafted to close out a game in the event of an emergency. He hadn't pitched in three days so his arm was well rested, and there was nothing it needed to be saved for: If the Majestyks didn't win this game, the next time he'd be on the mound would be April of the following year.

His first pitch was hit by a disrespectful batter who blasted it just to the right of Chi Chi los Parados so fast the second baseman barely managed to stick out his glove before it went rocketing past him. He turned to see John Amos, cap falling off his head, thundering in from center field, catching the ball just before it hit his toe.

One out.

Los Parados reacted quickly and was already stepping back to second base to await the flip from Amos which would put out the runner, who had to return because the ball had been caught. The runner hadn't believed it *could* be caught, and had taken off for third for what he assumed would be an easy base. Now he'd be forced out as soon as los Parados had the ball in his hand and his foot on the bag, after which los Parados might be able to get off a shot to first before that runner got back for the same reason.

But Amos didn't toss the ball to second. He was moving so fast that he doubted he could make a controlled throw without slowing down first, and at his present rate of speed he'd reach second not much later than a thrown ball would, so he just kept on going.

Los Parados saw it and got off the bag, moving toward the pitcher's mound rather than third so he wouldn't get called for interfering with the runner, whom he could see Amos was easily going to beat anyway.

Amos saw it too, but he also saw the runner from first, who had obeyed his third base coach, who'd also failed to believe the ball could be caught and had waved him on, but was now screaming for him to get back to first. He was just in the process of trying to stop his forward momentum when Amos veered off into a slight detour and tagged him with the ball.

Two outs.

Now Amos executed another midcourse correction that would take him back to second. He sized up the situation and saw that the base would fall in between his next two strides if he didn't either stretch way out on the next one or knock half off the second one, and he also saw the base runner fling himself out parallel to the ground in a desperate attempt to get a hand on the bag. There was no time for the extra step and he wasn't sure he could make the reach, so he dropped onto his left side and slid into the base jamming his toe against the bag and lying still so it would stay there.

All was deathly stillness for a brief moment and then the second base ump shot a finger toward Jupiter and rasped, "Yer out!"

Amos had gotten all three outs by himself. It was only the eleventh unassisted triple play in major-league history and the first ever by an outfielder. Majestyks benchwarmers poured out of the dugout and joined the players on the field who were mobbing Amos as they came in following the end of the inning. Many in the park that day would later tell their friends that the noise exploding up out of the stands made the 1945 V-E Day celebration in Times Square look like a poetry reading in a village library.

Back in the dugout Amos credited it all to Jesus.

"No problem," Sal Spinale said. "Where you want us to send his check?"

Out on the mound at the start of the new inning, Fanagalo Van-deMerve was feeling feisty, and as soon as he got Kowalski out of the way by walking him, got the sign to go ahead and pitch to Juan-

Tanamera Aires, who let two perfect fastballs go by for strikes, then a down and away two-seamer for an expected ball.

As soon as VandeMerve let the next one go, another fastball, he knew he'd made a terrible mistake. It was supposed to kiss the inside corner high but missed, heading for the exact spot Bueno liked more than any other.

Barely before he'd even finished his swing, Aires casually dropped the bat and sauntered to first without bothering to look at the ball, which he probably could have seen easily because of the supersonic shock waves trailing behind it as it headed into orbit somewhere in the upper deck.

BUENO'S SHOT DEEP INTO THE STANDS had made it 2-1. A Royals solo round-tripper in the next inning tied it up at 2-2.

In the bottom of the ninth, Kowalski had walked—so what else was new?—then Bueno hit a grounder to the shortstop, who'd easily gotten Kowalski out at second but couldn't make the double play and left Aires safe at first. He was the last hope to score a run for the Majestyks, and when he stole second without getting a permission signal from the dugout, Johansen wasn't sure if he was going to give him a medal or a fine after the game.

With one out and Aires on second, VandeMerve was starting to get angry, and when VandeMerve got angry he got calm, any pain or fatigue that might have been nagging at his arm evaporating in the wash of a special kind of adrenaline known only to golfers, Zen masters and pitchers. With Donny Marshall up at bat he went for the corners but didn't push the envelope, banking on the read of the umpire that he'd been cultivating all game.

Sensing VandeMerve's confidence cranked up to high, Johansen sent a sign out to the third base coach, who nodded his understanding, then looked at Marshall and tweaked his right ear, swiped a hand across his chest, patted his hip, clapped twice, touched a forefinger to his cap, rubbed his right forearm, rubbed his left forearm, banged two fists together twice, touched his nose, hunched his shoulders up, then did the whole thing again—twice—and finally folded his arms across his chest.

The only thing in the entire performance that counted was touching his nose the second time. Marshall looked over at second to make sure Aires had seen the sign, then took a perfunctory practice swing and got ready.

VandeMerve, trying to hold Aires to as short a lead as possible, took a last look at him before starting his pitch, but as soon as his forward leg left the ground, Aires took off for third and Marshall squared his bat around into position for a bunt.

The infielders saw it and reflexively started forward, but as soon as VandeMerve committed to his pitch Marshall brought the bat back over his shoulder and adjusted his stance for maximum swing power, lifting a leg and beginning what was sure to be a massive all-out swing.

Then he just stood there as the ball shot by him.

The charade only flustered the catcher for a split-second but it was enough, and Aires beat out the throw to third.

VandeMerve, now enraged, fired a slider at an outside corner and Marshall went down looking. Two outs.

Chi Chi los Parados stepped out of the on-deck circle, preening as arrogantly as ever. Normally this was standard operating procedure in order for a batter to intimidate the opposing pitcher, but in los Parados' case it was just plain conceit.

Smirking openly, he took VandeMerve's very first pitch and hit a so-so shot to shallow left. Royal left fielder Joey Badalucca scooped it up and, correctly ignoring a potential play at first, pegged the ball home to make sure Aires wouldn't score. The catcher, having already torn off his mask as soon as the ball was struck, stood up in preparation for running Aires down, but the canny base runner had already assessed the entire situation and begun returning to third, where he now stood with his foot on the bag.

Over on first los Parados peeled off his batting gloves and stuck them in his back pocket, then took a lead and stutter-stepped back to first, then did it again, and again, all the while staring at Vande-Merve, daring him to throw. Unlike a left-handed pitcher, who faced first base in the stretch and had an easier time keeping an eye on the runner, the right-handed VandeMerve had to face away from the base. The best he could do was look over his shoulder occasionally, and then he had to sacrifice some of his mechanics in order to get the pitch off quickly and keep the runner honest.

VandeMerve, growing grimmer and darker and more menacing by the moment, looked like he was about two seconds away from putting a fastball down los Parados' throat, but soon got himself back to the task at hand, which had just come up to bat in the form of John Amos.

VandeMerve's first throw was to first, but los Parados had anticipated it and easily beat it to the bag, where he widened his disdainful grin. Thoroughly rattled by now, VandeMerve then threw a hard-breaking curve which Amos let go for a ball well outside.

Los Parados and Aires were both stepping on and off their respective bases, trying to shake VandeMerve up as much as possible, then took serious leads as the pitcher sent a fastball right down the middle, slightly high and slightly outside.

Just the way the Deacon liked it. Amos swung and connected solidly, sending the ball into shallow right. By the time the outfielder let it bounce once and then got a glove on it, Aires was already home, and los Parados halted his run to second, leaped high into the air and flung his arms skyward, then sprinted toward his teammates who were already spilling out onto the field and flinging their gloves into the air. The outfielder threw the ball down in disgust and dropped onto the field, his head buried in the crook of his arm.

Johansen could literally feel the ground shake as thirty thousand Majestyks fans stomped their feet in chaotic joy: Impossibly—unbelievably—Des Moines was one Kansas loss away from making the playoffs.

The players didn't know whether to laugh or cry, so many of them started to do both, pounding each other on the back, piling body upon body in the infield just beyond home plate, high-fiving and shouting . . .

All of them except Marvin Kowalski.

"Hey, kid!" Sal Spinale yelled. "The hell's a'matter with you! Get the hell on out here, goddamnit! You had as much as anybody to do with—"

Kowalski, remaining placid amid the storm, just pointed out toward center field.

Zuke Johansen, grinning and happy but wondering about Kowalski's odd behavior as well, looked where he was pointing.

Royals second baseman Jefferson Rickover was standing on the base with both feet, gesticulating wildly at second base umpire Nelson Barry. As Barry shook his head in non-understanding, Rickover stomped up and down on the bag and held out the ball for the ump to see. This seemed to give Barry pause; he put one hand on his hip and scratched his head.

Meanwhile some fans had broken through the security cordon and were storming onto the field with the kind of gleeful frenzy that the players knew spelled trouble. Even as they tried to get off the field and down into the locker room, their way was blocked by a small army of reporters and cameramen jockeying for the best angles and the juiciest interviews.

"What's going on?" Johansen asked Kowalski after half a dozen security guards had walled them off.

"Not sure." Kowalski narrowed his eyes and kept watching, as though if he looked harder he might understand better. "I think it's something about Chi Chi not having touched second."

"Who gives a hoot?" Spinale asked. "Bueno already scored."

Now all of them were watching the strange goings on at second, and then Johansen said "Uh oh" as Barry held out his hand for the ball, got it, stared at it for a few seconds and then nodded at Rickover, who made a fist and pumped it forcefully.

"This is not good," Spinale agreed.

"I know what happened," Kowalski announced.

All eyes turned toward him. "I'm afraid to ask," Johansen said. "What?"

The umpire, lips grimly set in a straight line across his face, started making his way through the unruly celebration. "The play wasn't really over until the out was made," Kowalski explained. "I think Rickover picked up the ball and stepped on second."

"So what?" Spinale said. "Aires was already home!"

"But it was a *forced* out at second, Sal. There was no run scored."

The ump finally landed in front of the Majestyks dugout. "Got a little problem here, Zuke."

"And what might that be, Nelson?"

The umpire turned and pointed. "Los Parados never touched second."

"Congratulations," Spinale said. "Now you can get rid of that seeing-eye dog."

The controversy, which displaced a 6.8 earthquake in Guatemala, the death of a Supreme Court justice and the failure of a Middle East peace agreement on the news that night, eventually went all the way up to the commissioner of baseball, who declared the game a tie and ordered it replayed, but only in the event that the Majestyks and Kansas City were tied at the end of the regular season and had to resolve who'd won the division.

The end of the regular season, of course, was two days away.

THAT MAKE-UP GAME WAS NEVER PLAYED. The Royals dropped both games of their final two-day stand against Texas, and the Majestyks won both of theirs against Tampa Bay. With Des Moines now ahead by two full games, there was no way a make-up game against Kansas could change the fact that the Majestyks were officially in the playoffs.

They then took on the Boston Red Sox and won that series 3-1, an outcome that lost a stupendous amount of money for people who'd bet against Des Moines at fifteen-to-one at the Vegas books, and now they were to meet the New York Yankees in the best-of-seven contest for the American League pennant and the right to move on to the World Series.

"Criminy," Sal Spinale had remarked to no one in particular as he'd rubbed his stomach in the bottom of the ninth of the final game against Boston. "These goddamned cliff-dwellers give me a freakin' ulcer."

Seventeen

PAPAZIAN, AMOS, MARSHALL AND KOWALSKI walked into the Oyster Bar at the ground floor level of their hotel, the Plaza. Marshall hadn't gotten two steps inside the door when he cocked his head slightly and said, "Ah jes' loves New Yawk!"

Kowalski followed his gaze and saw five stunning, if overly made-up and garishly dressed, women lounging at the far end of the brass rail. "Who are they?"

"Well, lessee," Papazian said. "There's Tiffany, Ashley, Brittainy, Asia and Morgana."

"Which one's which?" Kowalski asked.

"Doesn't matter," Marshall answered.

"That way lies iniquity, my son," Amos warned.

"Leave the kid alone, Deacon," Marshall whispered. "Hell you doin' in a bar, anyway?"

"Even our Savior drank wine, Donald."

"Wine? But you drink bourbon!"

"The translation from the original Greek biblical sources was hazy," Amos explained, "and all that is known for sure was that alcohol was involved."

"So what are you saying, John," Kowalski asked. "Jesus might've changed water into Jack Daniel's?"

"Another mistranslation. It was actually 'water on the side.' Shall we?"

As they headed for the bar, the young ladies straightened up and began fiddling with their hair. "Well, well," said one of them, "heard you mud rats made the playoffs but I thought maybe my radio was acting funny."

"Har de har har," Papazian said, stepping up without hesitation and giving her a firm squeeze of the rump, to which she responded with a giggle. "Then how come you fillies're hanging around the Oyster Bar?"

"Hoping some'a them fine Yankees might show up, is why," said another, a statuesque Nubian who looked graceful even standing still, "before they gotta rest up for the Series."

Donny Marshall had gravitated naturally to her, the only black woman in the bunch. "You get that kinda disrespectful mouth at Bradcliffe?"

"That's Radcliff, bwana," she said, losing the faux-'hood accent and appraising Marshall with a practiced eye. "And it was Vassar."

"She's not bullshittin'," Papazian said in an aside to Kowalski. "Now she's a lawyer with a weakness for athletes. Don't stare, f'Pete's sake!"

Kowalski jerked his head away so quickly he'd have been less noticeable had he just kept staring.

"And what have we here?" another woman said in a high-pitched voice as she came around to stand next to Kowalski. "Don't tell me this is the *phe*-nom that's turning baseball on its ear, hmmm?" She put out a hand and ran it along his collar.

"Actually," Papazian said, "he's just the batboy."

She pulled her hand back as if from a bee sting before realizing it was just a joke.

"She don't even talk to nobody ain't hittin' at least three-ten," Marshall said as the others laughed.

The woman smiled and reached out to touch Kowalski's shirt again. "My name's Tiffany," she breathed provocatively.

"Pleased to meet you," he answered easily. Two months ago he might have been flustered into semicoherence, but he'd come a long way since.

"Pleased to—Oh, I do love a man with manners!" Tiffany-for-the-moment hooked her arm through his and rubbed a shoulder against him.

Amos, sensing Kowalski's discomfort, rubbed his hands together briskly and turned away. "Well, must be off."

"Me too," Kowalski said, disentangling himself from the aggressive groupie and stepping toward Amos.

Marshall came scurrying over and leaned in toward Kowalski. "No reason'a be a monk, kid, just on account'a one little bad experience. Take y'self a bite!"

"I don't think so, Donny."

"Well why the hell not!"

Kowalski edged closer to Amos, but bent back toward Marshall. "I'm allergic to penicillin."

Once outside the door and back on Central Park South, Amos said, "What really happened with that girl, the first one? The one you met at Chumley's?"

Kowalski looked over toward the statue of José Marti. "I told her I was going to college in the fall."

Amos stopped dead, right in front of Rumplemeyer's Ice Cream Parlor. "College?"

"Yeah. Why?"

"You're going to college?"

Kowalski looked at him crossly. "Well of course I am, John! What made you think I wasn't? You think I want to end up like Mikey?"

When backup second baseman Mike Reilly had been let go earlier in the season, someone asked him what he was going to do now.

"I never had a job," he'd said, blinking back tears. "All's I ever did is play baseball."

Amos stared at Kowalski and tried to hide the astonishment on his face. This kid was the hottest thing in professional sports—he'd be worth *millions* negotiating for next season—and had kept himself so isolated from the media and the world in general that he didn't seem to have a clue about what was really going on.

Which still didn't explain . . . "You told her you were going to college and she dumped you?"

Kowalski nodded. "She wasn't really smart, she was just smart about how to look smart. Thing is, she didn't want *me*; she wanted a baseball player. A superstar. Any superstar."

"So why did you stick with her?"

Kowalski smiled an embarrassed smile. "With her skills she didn't need brains. And I didn't care if she thought I was Napoleon. At least not at first."

Amos grunted knowingly. "So basically you used each other." He shot his hands up, palms out. "Not saying that's a bad thing, two willing adults and all. But she thought she was boffing a superstar and you were getting your ashes hauled, and now you're upset because this nuclear physicist didn't really like you for yourself all along?" He let his hands drop and shook his head disapprovingly. "You're smarter than that, Marvin."

"I'm smart enough to know you can't treat affairs of the heart like calculus problems. She was my first, John!"

"She was trash, Marvin!" Amos said before he could stop himself.

Kowalski grinned. "Not a very Christian attitude there, Deacon."

"Yeah, well, I'm only human, not Jesus Christ. Anyway, now you had a taste, I hope you find out real soon how good it can be with someone you truly love. What do you plan to study, anyway?"

"What?"

"In college. You said you were going to college."

"Oh yeah. Physics, what else? Been reading like crazy every chance I get, so I can jump a few courses as soon as I hit campus."

Amos nodded his approval. "Me, I read the Bible."

"How many times can you read the same book over and over?"

"Every time I read it, it's different." He pointed to the storefront behind him. "You ever had a Rumplemeyer's banana split?"

Kowalski turned at a familiar sound, the clip-clopping of horse's hooves. "Not much hungry, John. Kinda like to get to the ballpark."

Amos followed Kowalski's gaze to a policeman mounted on an enormous chestnut mare slowly cruising toward them. "Game's not until tomorrow."

"I know." Kowalski held up his watch. "I want to see it in the light we'll be playing in."

They stared at the cop, who touched his baton to his cap as he pulled alongside. "Say, how do we get to Yankee Stadium?" Amos asked him.

"Practice, buddy," the cop answered as the horse strode by without stopping. "Practice."

THEY STOOD AT HOME PLATE in the deserted ballpark.

Sal Spinale was there, too, and he told Kowalski about the field, about how the distances from home to the fences had changed over the years, shrinking from 500 feet in "Death Valley," deepest left center, in 1923 to its present 399 feet. Spinale told him that in 1930 a ball hitting the foul pole above the fence was in play, not an automatic home run as it was today, and that the bleachers in right center were called Ruthville and Gehrigville, and he told him about the monuments out in the field, Lou Gehrig on the left, Miller Huggins in the middle, Babe Ruth on the right.

"Funny, the things you remember a guy for," he said. "Everybody thinks of Gehrig as the Iron Man who played in over two thousand games without missing a single one, but he was a great all-around player aside from that. Ruth was a helluva pitcher at one time, too, not just a home-run guy."

"Tell him about Clyde, Sal," Amos said.

"Clyde Sukeforth." Spinale smiled to himself. "Died recently. Brooklyn Dodgers scout, coach and manager . . . he was the guy who introduced Jackie Robinson to Branch Rickey."

"Not a bad thing to be remembered for," Kowalski said.

Spinale laughed. " 'Cept that's not it. In the bottom of the ninth inning of the last Dodgers-Giants playoff game in '51, Clyde's the guy who answered the Polo Grounds bullpen phone and said Carl Erskine shouldn't pitch to Bobby Thomson."

Gears clicked in Kowalski's head and he turned to Spinale. "You're telling me *he's* the guy who recommended Ralph Branca?" Thomson hit a home run off Branca that gave the Giants their improbable pennant that year, and it was forever after referred to in baseball legend as the "Shot Heard 'Round the World," one of the most memorable moments in all of sports.

"One and the same. Course, it turns out the Giants were stealing signs all along anyway, so Bobby knew 'zackly what pitch Ralph was gonna throw."

Kowalski grinned and shook his head, then grew thoughtful as he examined the field more closely.

"What're you lookin' at, kid?" Spinale asked.

Kowalski walked a few steps, then stopped and squatted down. "Looks like there's dirt built up along the infield foul line. Except—" he stood up and waved to his right,"—I don't think anybody's played on the field since the grounds crew fixed it up."

Amos came over and verified the observation. "What else?"

Kowalski slowly walked back to home plate, pointing at the ground in front of it. "This is loose sand, not dirt. I don't remember that from the last time we played here."

Amos and Spinale bent to look.

"And the infield grass looks a little long. Do they change how they maintain the field later in the season?"

Spinale turned toward left field. "Pile a little extra dirt on the foul lines . . ." he said, letting his voice trail off as he tried to figure it out.

"World-class bunters like Fredo find their little taps funneled into foul territory," Amos guessed, receiving a nod in agreement from Spinale. "And this loose sand here in front of home plate?"

"Good solid chop from power guys like Cavvy and Salvanella," Spinale mused out loud, "they get changed into limp grounders because they don't get a bounce off this stuff."

"Huh. So what about the long grass on the infield?"

"Make those grounders slow up even more," Kowalski chimed in. "Huge advantage for the Yankees because Mars Lee throws a mean sinker and can pretty much force ground balls whenever he feels like it."

There was nothing unusual in any of this, and it was mild in comparison to some other tricks of the trade. In 1940, in an effort to help Ted Williams hit more home runs, the Boston Red Sox reduced the distance to the fence by 23 feet by adding the right field bullpen, still known as "Williamsburg."

Kowalski could hardly believe it. "You're telling me—"

"Same kinda shit we'da done in our own park," Spinale said with undisguised admiration, "we'da been clever enough."

"What I'm guessing," Amos added, "just before game time they'll water down the base paths, too. Make it harder for Bueno to steal."

Kowalski shook his head in wonder, then looked out toward the Gehrig monument. "So how come it's supposed to be so hard to play left field in this place?"

"Simple, kid," Spinale explained. "It's on account of it gets late early here."

Eighteen

Des Moines—October 16

THERE ARE TURNING POINTS in one's life, mere moments after which everything is forever changed. Very often these moments are explosive, but sometimes they pass by fleetingly and are only recognized as momentous with the advantage of hindsight.

"Last time you and me were in a bar . . ." Johansen began with a sly grin, hoping to defuse some of the awkwardness in the air by bringing up the painful subject in an offhand and humorous way. He looked around at the faux-marine interior of the seafood restaurant at the corner of Third and Locust, across from the Civic Center in downtown Des Moines and 990 miles from the closest ocean. Sal Spinale, world-class detester of fast food in all its forms, had found the place, which FedEx'd in fresh seafood from Key Largo, Boston, Seattle or San Diego on a daily basis. Johansen would have preferred the more muted Library Lounge of the Des Moines Club just on the other side of the river, his second most comfortable venue after the ballpark clubhouse (in which, as Reggie Jackson had put it, "you don't have to grow up") but feared that bringing the likes of Henry Schmidt there might jeopardize his membership.

Actually, that was a bit unfair. Schmidt could clean up pretty good when he wanted to. This morning he'd apparently figured it wasn't worth it, as he'd misbuttoned his shirt and the left side of his collar was riding up about two inches above the right. "You guys've come a long way, Zuke."

Johansen, uneasy but not sure why, turned away and looked up above the bar.

"It was incredible enough when the Majestyks won the first game of this amazing League Championship Series," Skeeter Phalango was saying on the overhead television, "and won it right in the Yankees' home park, no less." The positive fallout of the team's Cinderella season had affected more than its players and fans. For one thing, heretofore obscure characters like Phalango, of KDSM-Des Moines, were starting to get some national visibility: The television over the bar was tuned to ESPN, and there he was. "Heck, it's incredible enough that they're even *in* it!"

"People are going to remember the RBI double Donny Marshall hit off Yankees pitching star Mars Lee for a long time," reporter Natty Dolan opined.

"I think they're going to remember Lee getting pulled in the fifth even more," Phalango threw back. "Not something you see too often. He'd been doing great all game long, but there's no question he was starting to lose it."

Following that completely surprising first-game win, the Majestyks went on to lose Game 2 at Yankee Stadium and 3 in the Shit Hole, but Game 4 was a different story. Lee pitched absolutely brilliantly, allowing only four hits and one run in a complete game, but his offense let him down and the Majestyks took it 1-0 in Des Moines. They also won the fifth game there, then lost the sixth back in the Bronx.

"So it's all tied up at 3-3 going into the seventh and deciding game tomorrow," Dolan said into the camera, addressing his listeners directly. "And once more the Majestyks are going to be up against

Mars Lee. I'd say the boys from Des Moines are acutely aware that he's not just out to win, he's out for blood this time."

Johansen turned away and brought his attention back to the table. "Hard to believe so many people are still interested in this game."

Schmidt studied an imposing 275-pound blue marlin mounted on the wall, then the 11-foot Mako shark that dwarfed it. "You want to understand America, understand baseball."

"You think that's still true, Henry?"

"You don't walk away from a hunnerd and fifty years of national pastime overnight. Baseball in America is like snow in Antarctica. It's everywhere and it gives the place its character. Hell, it's even in our language, so deep we don't even realize it."

"You're getting a little dotty in your old age."

"Am I?" Henry leaned back on his chair. "Ever get to first base with a girl? If not, then you struck out. Ever have an idea that came out of left field?"

He gestured toward the bar. "Those yuppified dandies over there . . . you figure the boss ever asked for a ballpark figure or told one of 'em to swing for the fences, play hardball with the competition and hit one out of the park, or made sure he didn't drop the ball, but touched all the bases so he could hit a home run, maybe even a grand slam? Unless, of course, I'm way off base here. Come to think of it, how did tennis and golf wind up with grand slams? Stole 'em from baseball. Screw up too often and you've got two strikes against you. Three strikes on a convicted felon and he's out. Ever throw somebody a curve, or call him a screwball, or pitch a movie or an idea to someone? When it's your turn you're at bat, and if you're the guy who makes sure everything gets wrapped up right, you're batting cleanup. Ever get caught looking or go down swinging or face a full count? Ever hope for something by the grace of God and a fast infield, or go into extra innings or put a fastball right over the plate? What do you think . . . did I cover all the bases?"

Johansen smiled at the truth of Schmidt's observation.

Schmidt didn't return the smile. He didn't do anything, just sat there staring, spent after his diatribe, which Johansen was starting to realize was just a diversion.

"Henry?" Johansen peered closely at the ex-scout, who hadn't responded at all to his name. "Oh my God, Henry, don't you even *think* about telling me that . . ."

Schmidt sighed heavily and held up his hand. "Relax, Zuke. No more favors. Only . . ."

Johansen felt himself go pale even as his stomach imploded into a small, knotted ball. "Only what?"

Schmidt hitched himself up and took a deep breath. "I'm in some trouble."

This time it was Johansen's turn to stare silently. It was the eve of one of the biggest games of his career and here was Henry Schmidt telling him he was in trouble. Which meant it couldn't wait. Which meant . . .

"Like I said, I'm not asking you for anything, Zuke."

"Then why're we talking."

"Couple things I gotta tell you."

"Now? Tonight?" Schmidt nodded miserably. "Tell me you bet against the Majestyks and I'll choke you to death right here."

"I would never bet against you. I don't even have a bet down on the pennant."

"But you do need something."

"No, Zuke." Schmidt took a sip of his drink. "You do."

Johansen dropped back against his chair. "Henry, you got something to say, then say it. I got things I gotta do and playing games with you ain't one of 'em."

"I owe some money, Zuke."

"Well there's a big surprise."

"A lot of money. There are these guys, and they bet on the Majestyks . . . ?"

"Dumb bet. We're underdogs by like six to one."

"They know that. What they also know, you'd have a good chance, it wasn't for Mars Lee."

Johansen froze. He had to, because if he moved he might set the room to spinning and not be able to think straight. For the next ten seconds he replayed every pitch of every inning Lee had been on the mound. "You scouted Lee," he said in a strained voice. "Just like you did me, right out of high school." Little jolts of electricity started flashing around in his brain. "You telling me he owed you one too?"

"Matter'a fact, no. But that's beside the point, Zuke. Point is . . ." Schmidt's voice trailed off.

"Point is what?"

Schmidt sighed again. "Lee grooved his last pitch to Marshall."

"Bullshit."

"Not bullshit. Marshall been any kind of hitter he could've put it outta the park. So he got a double anyway, drove in the winning run . . ." Schmidt raised his hands and let them drop back on his lap.

"You're telling me we got handed Game 1?" It wasn't possible. He could prove it. "They pulled Lee out of that game in the fifth!"

"And why do you think they did that?"

"Because he refused to walk Kowalski, that's why! He kept throwing him fastballs, daring him to try to really hit one, and Kowalski kept popping them foul, just like he always does!"

"He was trying to wear himself out, Zuke."

The first hint of nausea began to well up in Johansen's belly. "What?"

"Trying to wear down his arm so it could never recover in time for the next game. If he got benched with a sore wing, it wouldn't be his fault and the hard guys would have no reason to go after him. But the front office phoned down and ordered him benched, and told him afterwards that if he disobeyed his manager again, they'd invoke the insubordination clause in his contract and toss him out on his billion-dollar ass."

Johansen went back over the games in his mind once more. Lee had been stunning in Game 4, throwing every pitch like it was the bottom of the ninth in the seventh game of the World Series and he was playing to save the entire solar system from intergalactic extinction.

And the whole time, his team had been down by one run. Had that changed, Lee could have shifted gears in a heartbeat and thrown the game. He simply never had to because his offense had done so poorly.

Schmidt nodded. "Game 4, too."

"And 5? Lee didn't pitch that one."

"Congratulations. You won that on your own."

Despite some neural tickle that told him what he was hearing was true, Johansen was having trouble swallowing it. "Mars Lee makes more money than a Colombian drug lord. There's no way your friends could have paid him enough to tank a game."

"They didn't pay him anything."

"Then—"

"They had something on him. Something Mars didn't want to come out."

"What—"

"It doesn't matter, Zuke! Goddamnit, what I'm telling you, what you need to know—"

"Lee's gonna dump tomorrow's game." The thought sickened him, and did so literally. Johansen started looking around for a place to go in case he had to throw up.

The dilemma was plain to him. There was no way he could walk into a game knowing a player on the other side was going to deliberately throw it. On the other hand, to expose the scam would let the world know that two of his own team's wins had been bogus, that his boys really weren't good enough to be in the playoffs and would never have gotten there without the gimmick of Marvin Kowalski.

Johansen knew better. He knew that his players had developed and matured and acquired the fire in the belly to rise to a championship level. But he also knew that few people on earth would believe that once all of this business came out.

He smiled bitterly to himself. The last time he'd done the right thing, stood up for what he knew was the proper course of action, it had cost him his career and almost his life. Now it would cost the dreams of a group of decent and committed men who'd placed their faith in him and would watch all their hopes disintegrate into powder.

Or, he could just forget that this situation existed. Yeah! Just walk out of the bar and into the night and onto a ball field and make history!

Except that, if it ever got out, he'd be ruined, as would his ball club. Dozens of people had seen him talking to Schmidt, huddled in muffled conversation that would later be described by witnesses as secretive, furtive and nakedly suspicious. Damnit, if only Schmidt had kept this to himself! What the hell was the point of—

Wait a minute. "Henry . . . ?"

"Yeah, Zuke?"

"Why are you telling me this?"

"Why?"

"Yeah, why? You said I needed to know, but I didn't need to know *shit* for your scam to work. Something's not right and—you haven't gotten to the meat of it yet, have you?"

Schmidt looked away.

"Haven't yet told me *why* I need to know."

Schmidt shifted uncomfortably.

"I *will* kill you, Henry. I will kill you ten times over."

The beleaguered agent started to turn back, but stopped as people yelled, "Quiet! Quiet! *Quiet!*" at the bar. Schmidt looked up at the television, long enough to see a "Breaking News" logo on ESPN and hear some presumably ominous lead-in music.

"American League playoffs" replaced the logo and Schmidt jerked a thumb toward the television. "This is why, Zuke."

"Bad news for you Big Apple baseball fans tonight," the announcer was saying. "Mars Lee, scheduled to pitch the seventh and final game of the playoffs tomorrow, has reportedly injured his throwing hand and will not play. Details about exactly what happened are sketchy but ESPN has confirmed that Lee will not be pitching, and may not even suit up for the game. Manuel Brisco is live at the hospital and has this special report. Manuel?"

As the on-site reporter started five breathless minutes of essentially saying that he didn't know anything more than the in-studio announcer did but at least he was on the scene, Johansen grabbed Schmidt by the collar with one hand and pulled him in close. "What the hell happened!"

"Cut his hand. On a kitchen knife."

"What the hell was he doing handling a knife the night before a big game?"

"He was cutting his hand, Zuke."

"Don't be a fucking wiseguy, Henry!"

"I'm not. He was cutting his hand. It was either that or cut his throat if he had to show up and throw another game. I'm guessing here—" He pulled free of Johansen's suddenly limp hand "—but I'm guessing it's a pretty good guess."

"Ah, Jesus," Johansen breathed as he slumped back on his chair.

"Hey, good news for you, Zuke!" some drunken fan at the bar yelled in their direction.

"Don't even turn around!" Schmidt commanded when he sensed the bile rising in Johansen's throat. "Pretend you didn't hear!"

Johansen choked back his anger and disgust as he complied. Remembered pain flooded back to him, his career ending in one brief flash of a four-inch piece of metal, and he tried to conjure up the depth of torment that it must have taken Mars Lee to do something like that to himself. Lee was wild, unpredictable and uncontrollable, but he loved baseball more than life itself, respected the game's history like few other players, and never threw a pitch without at least a few cells in his body connecting up with the gloried past of his profession, the past he would have had to betray had he not taken himself out of the game. "How bad?"

"Don't know. If he didn't hit a tendon . . ."

Schmidt let it go at that, and Johansen prayed that Lee had been smart enough to make a cut just deep enough to put him on the disabled list for a few weeks but nothing more.

He looked at his watch. Johansen had a firm policy of never violating the "suggested" curfews he gave his players. "Getting late, Henry. I still don't know why we're talking."

"You have to win, Zuke."

"Gee, glad you filled me in there, Mr. Schmidt. On account of I was thinking maybe we'd have a few beers before the game and just kind of, you know, see what happens."

"Don't joke around, goddamnit . . . this is serious!"

"Of *course* it's serious, you dumb sonofabitch! It's the goddamned game for the goddamned pennant, so just what in the holy hell do you think I plan to do other than win it!"

"You *have* to win it! If you don't, I'm a dead man. These guys lose their dough, they're gonna blame *me* for Lee slicing his hand, just because they don't have anybody else to blame!"

Johansen didn't even know where to begin to convey to Schmidt the full measure of his outrage. The fat piece of shit went and got himself into trouble again, after already ruining one good career, and now he was putting the burden on *again*?

Schmidt pushed on, unaware of the anger building in Johansen. "My father used to say to me—he came here in '37, did I ever tell you that?—he used to say to me that in a democracy the highest rank is citizen." He shook his head bitterly. "But these guys, these mob bastards, these *dictators*, they make that a joke. Once they get their hooks into you . . ."

"Don't go blaming the mob, Henry."

"What?"

"Nobody forced you to bet. No wiseguy ever walked up to you and said lay down a grand on Cincinnati or we'll break your legs. The only reason the hard guys even exist is because people want drugs and whores and quick loans and gambling. If nobody wanted to buy what they were selling, they'd be back to stealing apples out of pushcarts. Where do you think they got the dough to lay off your bets . . . from elves? You think maybe they stole it?" Johansen sat back and regarded Schmidt, wondering if the man was actually listening or just biding his time so he could drag the conversation back to where he needed it to be. "They got it from people like you, who willingly handed it over because they were weak."

"You don't know what you're—"

"They're not the problem, Henry. *You* are. So don't come whining to me that bad men have you in a tight spot. All you had to do was turn around and walk away but you didn't, and now you want to drag me back into it."

"I'm not dragging you into anything. I want you to *win*, not lose!"

Johansen gritted his teeth and forced his voice to calmness. "There's nothing anybody can do to make me try any harder to win this game than I'm gonna. So tell me again why we're talking?"

"I'm giving you some advice."

"Hah!" Johansen looked around to see if anybody had noticed his loud exclamation. He determined that just about everybody had, and leaned in close. "You're giving me advice?"

"You gotta throw away the rules, Zuke. You gotta—hey, where you—Zuke!"

Johansen had stood up and was reaching into his pocket for some bills. "This conversation's over, Henry. Never shoulda goddamned started in the first place."

"Zuke, gimme five freakin' minutes! What the hell can it possibly cost you?"

"Every time I see you it costs me!"

"Zuke!" Schmidt said it loudly then looked around to make sure people were noticing. "I'm begging you!"

Johansen winced at the sudden attention and pumped a hand toward Schmidt. "Okay, okay . . . just for Chrissakes pipe down, will ya?"

When they were seated again and had thrown enough glares to stop people from staring, Schmidt said, "No heroes, Zuke. Nobody gets to be queen for a day. Only thing that counts is winning the damned thing, no matter how you do it."

"Useful pep talk there, Henry."

"You gotta relief the whole game."

"You're nuts."

"Listen'a me! You put a fresh pitcher in, you keep him there two innings, less if he fucks up, then you yank him and put the next guy in. Every one'a their batters sees a guy who's rested and hungry and scratching at the walls to be let loose and has half an hour to tell the world who he is."

"You want me to run through the whole goddamned rotation?"

"What the hell're you saving 'em for . . . a cricket match in November? It's the last game of the season, so shoot 'em off like machine-gun bullets!"

"Who gets credited with the win?"

"Credited with—Who gives a shit! The *team* gets credited, that's who. *You* get credited, and for being a genius to boot. Throw the rule book away, Zuke, and you'll get credited with making history!"

Johansen thought about it, then he blinked suddenly and stood up. "I'm taking pointers from a degenerate casino rat who can't even manage his own wallet."

"Zuke . . ." Genuine pain crossed Schmidt's face, as if Johansen had been his last lifeline and he was now being cast adrift on a dark and frightening sea. "Zuke, please . . ."

"Forget it, Henry. You're worse than malaria, you are. Both keep coming back but you get worse every goddamned time."

"Nobody swings for the fences." As miserable as he was, Schmidt still needed to drive his message home. "You put men on base, you move them around slowly, you score some runs. The Yanks won't know what's hitting them. They'll have murder in their eyes, and they'll try to take it out on your guys, but the more you keep your cool the more they'll trip over their own dicks. It'll be the most boring goddamned game in playoff history, the Ali Rope-a-Dope, *but you'll win!*"

"Good-bye, Henry."

Schmidt gave up and hung his head. "You gotta win, Zuke," he muttered one last time. "You lose this game, you'll never see me again."

"I don't ever *want* to see you again!"

"You don't mean that."

"Henry—listen'a me, 'cuz I mean it—however it goes, this is the last damned time you and I ever occupy the same air space together, you get me?" He stood up and fished around in his pocket.

"Do what I tell you, Zuke!"

"Do what *I* tell *you*, Henry."

"What's that?"

Johansen threw some bills down on the table. "Go fuck yourself."

Nineteen

G AME 7 MAY NOT HAVE been the strangest baseball game ever played, but an awful lot of pretty strange things happened in it.

For one thing, it was being played in Des Moines, which would have been impossible under normal circumstances because Game 1 had been played in New York. Since the standard procedure was to play two games in one park, three in the other one, then head back to the first for the final two games, they should have been back in New York. But the "standard procedure" had never contemplated the highly unlikely simultaneous occurrence of a crippling airline pilots' strike, the failure of one of only two century-old water mains feeding New York City, and a West Nile fever outbreak in the Bronx. While the last of the three calamities was eventually determined to have been nothing more than several dozen cases of mild food-poisoning traced back to a neighborhood barbecue on East 168th Street, the scare had been sufficient to prod the two ball clubs, with the blessing of the league office, into crafting a quickie plan to scramble the schedule without sparking an armed insurrection by ticket-holding fans in either city. That plan called for the final game, if necessary, to be played in Des Moines.

Another thing contributing to the overall weirdness of Game 7 was that Yankee manager Augie Crandall had made the shocking decision to start rookie pitcher Abel Ganz in place of the injured Mars Lee. Ganz had only been brought up six weeks before, smack on baseball's August 31 deadline for submitting postseason rosters, when the Yankees had been leading their division by such a wide margin that they could afford to test their latest phenom. Always thinking ahead, the front office was already planning for next year and wanted their *Wunderkind* to get some big-league experience before the start of the next season. They'd used him as a short reliever in three games in which they'd held huge leads, then as a middle and long reliever in two others, and the twenty-three-year-old had been nothing short of dazzling. He was immensely talented, preternaturally mature and, most of all, he was hungry. All Crandall wanted out of him in exchange for the taste of real big-league glory was four or five strong innings. All Ganz wanted was to make history.

Zuke Johansen had thought seriously about Schmidt's suggestion to use his entire pitching rotation. Schmidt knew a lot about the game and its mechanics.

But he knew nothing about its heart. Johansen visualized the likely effect on his players of yet another gimmick, and knew that it might deflate them into a destructive depression. *You don't think we can win this the right way,* their eyes would say, and they'd be right.

Of course, they didn't know that Mars Lee had handed them one of their three wins. And they all knew the third one had been a squeaker, aided by a Yankee error in the fourth inning and a questionable call at second base that went their way in the seventh. It had been Schmidt's judgment that, even with the gimmick called Kowalski, the Majestyks couldn't win a legitimate game on their own without more tricks or some big breaks.

Maybe he was right. But Johansen was willing to bet Schmidt's life that he was wrong.

. . .

SPINALE LOOKED UP at the home town crowd, which was already cheering and yelling lustily. Scattered throughout the stands were New York fans who'd flown in for the final game and could be spotted waving banners with their team's venerable symbol, a superimposed "N" and "Y." "Rootin' for the Yanks is like rootin' for Microsoft," Spinale muttered contemptuously.

"Who's workin' the plate?" Cogburn asked him.

"Krupke."

Cogburn, nervous but still looking for more ways to drive himself completely nuts, gritted his teeth and made a choked, grunting sound. "I hate that fuckin' guy!"

"He's the best umpire in the league," Marvin Kowalski said.

Cogburn, ready for somebody to take his tension out on, turned on him. "The best! Whadda you, fuckin' kidding me? This guy's behind the plate, I gotta damned near groove a pitch smack in the middle to get him to call a strike!"

"No you don't, Wade," Kowalski said with irritating confidence and patience.

"Now listen, you—"

"The reason you don't like him is because he calls them the way they come over the plate, and you're used to them being called the way they end up."

"What the hell're you talkin' about!"

"Like if you throw a pitch that dives at the end." Kowalski made a swooping motion with his arm. "If the catcher grabs it with his glove touching the ground, the ump's going to call it a ball, right?"

"Obviously."

"But what if it was still in the strike zone when it came in over the plate, before it dropped? Most umps won't see that, but Krupke does. Most guys, they see a curveball heading outside, they're calling it before it even arrives." He pointed to home plate. "You hit the corners with breaking balls and he's going to give you strikes."

"What makes you so damned sure?"

Kowalski turned toward the field and watched as the meticulous Krupke measured the batter's boxes with the tape measure he always carried. "Because he sees like me."

THE TONE OF THE GAME was set in the very first inning, the crowd so juiced that outfielder Vince Salvanella got a standing ovation just for picking up a hot-dog wrapper that had blown onto the field.

Yankees second baseman Rudy Malinowski swung on a 3-and-0 pitch. With three balls and no strikes, he knew it was going to be a fastball down the middle, and he also knew he'd be thumbing his nose at a sacred cow of baseball—*Never swing at a 3-and-0 "cripple pitch"*—but this one had HIT ME written all over it and so he did, lining it past Cogburn toward the hole between first and second. Los Parados was off his feet like a cat, diving to his left parallel to the ground, fully stretched out. The ball hit the dirt at the same time los Parados did, then leaped right into his glove. The agile second baseman rolled once and sprang to his feet, his momentum carrying him down the base path. As Malinowski sprinted for first, los Parados reached into his glove to retrieve the ball and toss it to Federico Guittierez for an easy out.

But the ball wouldn't budge. Somehow, it had gotten stuck in the webbing between the thumb and forefinger.

Los Parados tugged hard, but it only made his glove start to slip off his hand. Still running at top speed and with Malinowski only a second away from touching the bag for a base hit, los Parados pulled the glove off and flipped it underhand to Guittierez, who caught it with both hands and stepped off the bag before getting run over.

The first base umpire stood without moving. Guittierez held out the glove and spread the fingers apart, showing the ball still buried within. Without missing another beat, the umpire jerked a thumb over his shoulder and shouted "*Out!*" to the uproarious merriment of the Majestyks fans.

Guittierez led off in the bottom of the inning, hitting a sweet little fly into the gap between short and left for a single, except he tried to turn it into a double and was put out at second base. John Amos sent a solid grounder into right field and made it to first. Vince Salvanella struck out, Donny Marshall walked, and with two men on and two outs, Chi Chi los Parados came up to bat and on the first pitch to him Amos stole third. Normally, the man on first would have gone to second at the same time, but Amos hadn't gotten the go-ahead to steal—he just saw an opportunity and took it—so Marshall wasn't able to pick up on it in time.

Now with one eye on Marshall, Ganz threw a vicious curve that fooled los Parados completely; the part of the bat closest to the ball when he swung was almost a foot away. Los Parados held up on the next pitch, a fastball just inside the outside right corner, but Marshall had blasted off from first as soon as he'd surmised that Ganz was fully committed to the throw. Unfortunately, Marshall had underestimated the catcher's skill and, despite a well-executed slide, was put out at second, ending the inning.

Cogburn held the Yankees scoreless, mowing down all three batters with a strikeout and two easily caught popped flies, and as the bottom of the inning began, los Parados was still up. He hadn't finished his at-bat in the first inning turn when Marshall had tried unsuccessfully to steal second.

The count started afresh at no balls and no strikes, though, and on the first pitch Ganz fooled los Parados once again with a terrific curveball. The next pitch was a sinker, again swung on and missed. Ganz aimed the third pitch directly at los Parados, who flinched and couldn't recover in time to take a swing at the ball, which arced hard to his right and dead into the center of the strike zone as it crossed the plate. It was a thing of beauty, and los Parados didn't need the ump to tell him he'd just struck out. He did what batters who struck out always did as they left the plate: examined the bat to find the hole in it, then looked at the pitcher, as if to say, "How the hell did that guy ever get me out!"

Los Parados' disgust with himself as he reentered the dugout was bad enough, and wasn't helped at all when Marvin Kowalski asked of no one in particular, "Hey . . . did Chi Chi just get five strikes?"

"Fock you talkin' about?" los Parados growled.

"I think you had five strikes in one at-bat."

"What're you, son' kinda—"

"He's right," Spinale said.

Los Parados whirled on him. "Are you *complatemente chiflado* here? How the hell does a guy get five strikes in one—"

"You had two when Donny Einstein over there tried to steal second," Spinale said, evoking a scowl from Marshall. "When you came up to bat in the next inning, you go back to zero strikes but it still only counts as one at-bat. So you had five strikes altogether."

"Thass a load'a . . . Hey, skipper, is he shittin' me here or what?"

Johansen shrugged helplessly. "Way it is, amigo." He might have added that it wouldn't be scored that way in the official record—his first at-bat would simply be ignored—but that would have spoiled all the fun.

"Hey, I made you famous, man!" Marshall yelled out cheerfully.

"Hey, I make you *dead*, azzhole!—"

Johansen hoped the television cameras didn't get any footage of half a dozen laughing ballplayers pulling Marshall and los Parados apart.

WADE COGBURN HAD NEVER LOOKED BETTER on the mound. By the fifth inning, he'd given up only three hits, two walks and not a single run.

Abel Ganz had allowed two hits, four walks and no runs. All the walks were given up to Marvin Kowalski and Juan-Tanamera Aires.

The Yankees were up. Cogburn threw and Willard Fenoke swung, a glancing blow that sent the ball awkwardly down the third base line, which it would cross before reaching the base for a foul.

Except that it hit something hard in the sand and skewed to the right, hitting third base too late for Darryl Bombeck, who'd been doing nothing because he'd expected the ball to go foul, to make a play on it. By the time he picked it up Fenoke was safe at first. Cogburn threw Bombeck a dirty look but it was purely perfunctory; Cogburn himself had turned his back on the certain foul and therefore couldn't have expected Bombeck to have anticipated it any better.

The Yankees' designated hitter, Sammy Velasquez, was up next in place of Ganz. The right-hander swung on the very first pitch and connected solidly, a line drive into center field. John Amos was off like a top-fuel dragster chasing it, knowing without having to look that Fenoke, a catcher and therefore not much of a runner, was hesitating off first base in anticipation of the ball being caught. Amos also noticed that Velasquez, seeing Fenoke still standing there, had slowed down on his way to the base.

With milliseconds to make up his mind, Amos also slowed down, and deliberately let the ball hit the ground in front of him rather than catch it. As soon as it did, Fenoke had no choice and sprinted for second base.

Amos scooped up the ball and used his momentum to get off a quick toss to Chi Chi los Parados, who already had his foot on second base. Los Parados got rid of the ball in a flash, twisting toward first and throwing in a single fluid motion. The throw was perfect and Guittierez was able to keep his foot on first as he snared it. It was close, but the first base ump, after only a minor hesitation, jerked a thumb over his back and toward the crowd, which roared its approval at the call.

Cogburn made a fist and pumped it in front of his chest as he jogged off the field following the perfectly executed double play that ended the inning.

"Wouldn't have worked back in the old days," Amos said as he jogged into the dugout. Kowalski got the impression that Amos, somewhat uncomfortable, was trying to deflect some of the praise being heaped upon him for his brilliant play and lightning fast judgment.

"What wouldn't have worked?" Donny Marshall asked.

"Letting the ball drop like that. Time was, you caught it on one bounce and it was an out."

"True," Spinale confirmed. "That was back before gloves."

"When was that?" Marshall asked.

"Eighteen sixty-four," Kowalski chimed in. "First glove ever in a game was a first baseman named Charlie Waitt. And it wasn't a *glove* glove, it was like what you'd wear to the opera."

"Come on!"

"He's right," Johansen said. "Wasn't until 1920 that a pitcher named Richard Doak sewed an extra piece of leather in between the thumb and forefinger. And speaking of an extra piece of leather . . ."

Equipment manager Geoffrey Slagenbach shuffled sideways into the dugout, looking as if he expected someone to hit him any second. "Mr. Johansen?"

"Yeah?"

"Sorry to bother you. I know how busy you—"

"What is it?"

"Well, like I said, didn't mean to—"

"Sal, get me one'a those bats over there!"

Slagenbach threw up his hands in horror. "No! No, I just meant, I didn't, uh, didn't mean to—"

"Here, I'll do it," Spinale said, raising the bat over his head in preparation for ending the equipment manager's life on the spot.

"There's a guy to see you!" Slagenbach fairly screeched as he tried to withdraw his head into his shoulder blades.

"Who?" Johansen demanded harshly.

"That same guy . . . from that time . . . when Marvin first got here?"

Henry Schmidt. "Where?"

Slagenbach pointed to a spot outside the dugout. Johansen leaned across the steps and looked up to see a frantic and near-psychotic Henry Schmidt being held back by a security guard.

"Hell's *he* want?" Spinale asked.

What indeed? Johansen stepped out and walked around the side of the dugout, clapping the security guard lightly on the shoulder. "It's okay, Elroy."

" 'Bout ready to clobber 'im, Mr. Johansen," the guard said as he stepped away.

"Stick around," Johansen responded. "May let you yet."

Schmidt, ignoring the insult, reached down and grabbed the fabric on the shoulder of Johansen's uniform. "Why the hell're you still pitching Cogburn!"

"None'a your goddamned business," Johansen spat back, yanking Schmidt's hand away.

"I told you what you needed to do to win this thing!"

"And I told you to go fuck yourself!"

"Cogburn can't go the distance! He almost gave up a hit there! You gotta—"

"I don't *gotta* do a damned thing!"

"But—"

"Elroy!" Johansen motioned to the guard, who had been waiting close by and came hurrying up. "If this sonofabitch crashes the field boxes again, call your supervisor and have him arrested." Johansen spun on his heel and walked away even as the guard smiled his willingness to comply.

ABEL GANZ STRUCK OUT all three Majestyks batters to end the sixth inning.

Wade Cogburn started the seventh by walking Orlando Perpado. He then struck out Willard Fenoke on four pitches and Sammy Velasquez came up to bat. He took Cogburn's first pitch and sent it rocketing nearly straight up in the air. Somewhere over second base it radioed in for reentry instructions and began to come back down. Los Parados ran backwards toward the outfield to position himself under it, and Amos ran in to back him up. Perpado stayed on first, anticipating the easy catch and knowing los Parados could fire it to first base with blinding speed once it was caught.

But los Parados had misjudged the sky-high pop-up. At the last possible second he leaped and stretched out his arm, but he wasn't able to snag the ball. It hit the leading edge of his glove and bounced back into the air.

Perpado shot out of the blocks like an Olympic sprinter and headed for second.

Amos, still running in from right field, smoothly shifted gears and caught the ball off los Parados' glove before it hit the ground. Velasquez was out, but Amos saw the speedy Perpado rounding second on his way to third without slowing down, which is when he realized that Perpado hadn't seen him catch the ball after los Parados missed it. As a result, he hadn't tagged up at first before taking off.

Grinning, Amos casually tossed the ball to los Parados, who stepped on second base, thereby putting out Perpado, who thought he was now safely ensconced on third. Amos high-fived los Parados and the two of them began jogging toward the dugout, as did Federico Guittierez on first, Aires in left field and Donny Marshall at short.

Perpado, brow furrowed in confusion, still didn't know what had happened. But Darryl Bombeck had seen it and didn't appear to be coming in from third base, nor was Cogburn leaving the mound. Cavvy Papazian was standing at the plate, hands on his hips, also apparently not realizing the inning was over.

Amos looked at los Parados: *Didn't these guys see me catch the ball?*

Now they saw that the home-plate umpire was waving them back into the outfield. Coming abreast of Cogburn on the mound, los Parados said, "Wodda hell . . . ?"

"Wodda hell what?" Cogburn said. "Why didn't you throw to third, John!"

"What the heck for!" Amos shot back. "The guy never tagged up at first, so it was a force at second!"

"He didn't have to tag up . . . he was standing on the goddamned bag!"

Amos looked around; hadn't anybody else seen what had happened? "It bounced off Chi Chi's glove and Perpado took off before I caught it!"

Now Cogburn realized the source of the confusion. "He's allowed to start running as soon as the ball is touched, John."

It would have been hard to say which sound was loudest, the hissing coming from the Majestyks fans, the lusty jeering from their Yankees counterparts, or the noise of rushing blood pounding in Amos' ears as he realized that he and los Parados had to turn and begin their eighty-mile walk back to their positions as God-only-knew how many millions of television viewers followed their every step.

"At least you got me *one* out," Cogburn said, using that phraseology peculiar to pitchers who felt that everybody else on the team was there solely to support the man on the mound, the only player who ever got official credit for wins and losses.

Yankees third baseman Jimmy Jacobson was up next. Over at third Perpado saw the sign from the coach that told Jacobson to bunt toward first, so as soon as Cogburn let the ball go Perpado took off for home.

Jacobson did exactly as he'd been told. Federico Guittierez came off the bag and charged it, but there was nobody on first to take the throw and he was too far to make the play himself. He'd figured all of that out before he reached the slow-moving ball, so in one smooth motion he snatched it up and threw it to catcher Cavvy Papazian, but it was too late: Perpado had already slid into home.

Although the cloud of dust raised by his slide obscured his vision of the ump, Perpado didn't need any official confirmation that he'd come home safely. He leaped to his feet, threw his arms into the air and then began dusting himself off. Behind him, Papazian coughed and wiped sand away from his eyes.

Krupke the umpire stood there, stock still.

Having used his extraordinary speed to score and tie the game, Perpado turned and waved happily to Jacobson, who was safe at first. Jacobson waved back and clapped his hands.

Krupke didn't move.

Jacobson doffed his batting helmet toward the crowd and then began peeling off his gloves. Perpado was on his way to the dugout, where his joyful team waited, hands already high in the air waiting to slap palms with their heroic left fielder.

Krupke pursed his lips but otherwise made no move.

Suddenly, Papazian whirled and ran, catching up with Perpado just as he was stepping into the dugout. The Majestyks catcher turned so the umpire could see, then banged the ball on Perpado's shoulder.

As if a remote-control switch had been flipped on somewhere, Krupke came to life. He spun, pounded the air with his fist, and shouted "Out!"

After a moment of truly profound stillness, Augie Crandall came out of the Yankees dugout as though he'd been fired from a cannon. How anyone could possibly work themselves up to that level of agitation in less time than it took to draw a single breath was a miracle of physiology, but Crandall was an old master at it.

As the Yankees manager emoted his way to an Oscar-caliber performance, down in the Majestyks dugout Johansen headed for the stairs. "What the hell happened?" Grover DuBois asked Kowalski. "How come Krupke just stood there like that?"

"Perpado never touched the plate," Kowalski theorized. "And Papazian never tagged him out."

"So . . . ?"

"The ump was just waiting for the play to end."

Perpado, who couldn't even see the ump because of the dust he'd kicked up, assumed he was safe and had started celebrating, ignoring what was still going on at the plate. But Papazian sensed that something was wrong and realized it could mean only one thing: The play was still in progress because Perpado hadn't touched the plate.

Had Perpado realized it as well, he might have gone back and gotten a foot on the plate, saving his run while Papazian was still puzzling it out. Instead, Papazian had figured it out first and tagged him with the ball. Perpado was out, no run scored and as the music began for the seventh-inning stretch, the score was still 0-0.

It stayed that way as the Majestyks failed to score in the bottom half of the inning.

DOWN IN THE DUGOUT Johansen was starting to digest his stomach lining. Warning bells were going off in his brain, telling him that his pitcher might be getting stretched too far. At the same time, the thought of capitulating even slightly to Henry Schmidt's judgment filled him with loathing. He tried to focus solely on the task at hand, winning this game, without letting his personal feelings get in the way, but it was like trying to separate water from wetness and it wasn't working. He needed some objective, level-headed help.

He called over pitching coach Lefty Peterson and then asked Cogburn how he was feeling.

"Feel great, skip."

Johansen might as well have asked Cogburn if he loved his mother. He turned to Peterson and lifted an eyebrow.

"Still throwin' great stuff," the pitching coach confirmed, then turned to Cogburn. "But you've thrown a lotta hard pitches, Wade."

Johansen could feel Schmidt's eyes boring in on him right through the dugout walls. There was a whole bullpen full of fresh, eager, talented pitchers raring to get in the game and shut the Yankees down.

Peterson saw the wheels turning in his manager's head and knew he was looking for some evidentiary scraps to tell him what he should do. Maybe what was needed was some sign that the pitcher was thinking about the team more than himself.

Peterson put his hands on Cogburn's right shoulder and rubbed briskly. "You'll let us know in plenny'a time, your stuff starts to go, right, Wade?"

"Count on it, coach."

But Peterson wasn't the one with the final decision, and Cogburn stared anxiously at the only man who could make it.

Johansen tried to drive Schmidt's face from his mind. He tried to think rationally, replaying in his head Cogburn's last batch of pitches, his equanimity, his command of the situation. He tried to apply a near-mathematical analysis of the man's strengths and weaknesses and not let his personal feelings about his own history and the nature of the game and what made ballplayers tick and what was at stake here get in the way of completely objective, straightforward thinking.

Cogburn slammed a ball into his glove with a loud smacking sound that snapped Johansen out of his reverie. "Christ A'mighty, Zuke! You think I'munna fuck wit' you with the pennant on the line?"

All the cobwebs disappeared from Johansen's brain and were replaced by a single thought: *Personal feelings is why they pay you. Any schmuck can add up numbers.*

He nodded at his pitcher, and could almost see fresh reserves of power pouring into the man as he whirled away, shot up the steps and sprinted onto the field.

"Kelly's up," Peterson called out after him, smiling. "Only thing that guy can hit is a mistake, so don't make any!"

Cogburn waved his understanding without turning around.

Pitching to Yankees center fielder Sticks Kelly, Cogburn threw low, sinking balls that teased the bottom edge of the strike zone, so that if Kelly did manage to connect he'd top the ball and send it into the ground rather than the air. Cogburn knew he was risking a bunch of balls getting called but on the 3-2 pitch the strategy paid off. Kelly sent a pathetic grounder to shortstop Donny Marshall.

Cogburn's sense of satisfaction was short-lived, though. Just as Marshall knelt to scoop up the ball for an easy out, it hit a small mound of dirt, popped up and hit him on the chin. By the time he scrambled around and managed to pick it up, Kelly was safe on first.

In the dugout, Johansen pressed his lips together and looked down at the floor. Such was the nature of this game, that you could make the right decision about one thing, but there was always something else waiting in the wings to keep you humble.

He looked up to see how Cogburn was reacting. The pitcher was nodding his understanding at Marshall—*Could've happened to anybody*—who in turn pointed at the mound—*These guys are toast . . . trust me.* Cogburn put it out of his mind and turned his attention to the next batter.

Rudy Malinowski, .317 for the regular season and .343 in the playoffs, was up next. He'd already been put out at first when los Parados had thrown his glove there, then struck out two innings later, and had worked himself up to some serious rage, taking a vicious swipe at Cogburn's very first pitch and sending it over los Parados' head. The second baseman leaped into the air and got his glove onto it, but only a piece. The ball bounced off and blooped onto the ground behind him. As he spun to go after it, shortstop Donny Marshall moved over to cover second.

"*I got it!*" John Amos screamed, chugging in like a freight train. He'd come in to back los Parados up and still had a full head of steam. Los Parados stepped away just as Amos scooped up the ball and snapped his arm forward. The ball shot out of the glove and toward Marshall, who caught it while still off the bag and dropped his arm quickly to touch the base just as Kelly slid in amid a great cloud of swirling dust and sand.

The players watched as the second base umpire dropped his upper body, spread his arms wide and shouted "*Out!*"

Marshall blinked, then straightened up and cocked his head in puzzlement. Los Parados, who'd fallen to the side to get out of Amos' way, stared at the ump and said, "Huh?"

Kelly, not bothering to wipe any dirt off his uniform, looked around to see if anyone else had heard the ump yell "Out!" even as he'd made the sign to signify that he was, in fact, safe.

"F'Chrissakes, ump!" Amos barked with uncharacteristic irreligiosity. "What is he!"

The umpire stood up slowly and looked around. "Well, you four guys heard me call him out." He waved a hand toward the stands. "Forty thousand people saw the sign for safe." He shrugged, helpless in the face of a decision that had obviously made itself. "Man's safe."

"*Mother*fucker!" Amos spat as he kicked at the dirt and spun on his heel to head back to center field.

Darryl Bombeck came jogging in from third. "Hey, you can't do that!" he said to the umpire.

The ump, already thoroughly infused with an entire season's worth of all the guff he was willing to absorb from disrespectful players, regarded Bombeck with a practiced eye. "Undoubtedly," he said slowly and deliberately, "we will reap the benefit of your wisdom in the fullness of time, but in the meantime"—he extended an arm and pointed to his left "—would you be so kind as to haul your bony ass back to third base!"

As Bombeck's bony ass obeyed, Kelly finally stood up and smiled, cocking his head toward Amos, who was still on his way back out to center- field. "Pretty harsh language comin' from the Deacon," he said to Marshall as he started brushing himself off.

"Eat me, you pussy," the shortstop said.

Two pitches later the pussy stole third.

Yankees outfielder Gerrold Greenstein was up next. He let two strikes go by and then swung on the 0-2 pitch, catching the upper part of the ball and sending it hard along the ground straight for Cogburn, who flinched and turned his head but stuck his glove into the path of the ball anyway, hoping to at least stop it even if he couldn't catch it.

He waited for the impact but it never came, and he opened his eyes to see the ball unaccountably bouncing away from him and heading for somewhere between home and third.

Papazian had already thrown his mask and was racing after the ball, leaving home plate open even as Kelly was tear-assing right for it. Papazian slowed and waited for the ball to come to him, hoping against hope that, if he didn't put himself too far out of position by chasing the ball down, he could scoop it up and swing around fast enough to tag Kelly before he scored.

Cogburn saw it developing and scrambled toward home to try to cover if Papazian could get the ball to him, but it was becoming pretty clear that it was a lost cause, as was Papazian's notion of making the tag himself.

Neither Cogburn nor Papazian saw Marvin Kowalski come shooting out of the dugout, and neither was aware of him as he crossed the fungo circle near the third base line until they heard a near-hysterical screech erupt from somewhere high in his chest.

"*Let it go, Cavvy!*"

Papazian hesitated for a barely perceptible nanosecond, but kept his glove down waiting for the ball.

"*Don't touch that fucking ball!*"

For reasons he'd be unable to explain later owing to his inability to coherently sort out two competing instincts, Papazian pulled his hand back and let the ball go, watching in horror as it dribbled over the third base line and Kelly stepped neatly over it on his way to a stand-up landing on home plate. That was bad enough, but then he became aware of Perpado rounding second and heading for third while nobody was doing anything about the ball. The next thing to impinge on his consciousness was the cheering from the crowd that seemed to be liberally laced with . . . mocking laughter.

Papazian finally looked up at Kowalski, murder and primordial savagery in his eyes. Kowalski, for his part, simply pointed at Krupke, the home plate ump.

"Foul ball," Krupke yelled above the clamor from the crowd. "Kelly, go back to third and, while you're at it, send Greenstein back here. He's still up, and it's still 0-and-2."

Papazian jerked his head around and looked at Kowalski. "Ball hit the rubber," Kowalski said, pointing to the 24-by-6-inch strip on the mound which had to remain in contact with the pitcher's foot at the start of his delivery. Papazian had missed it while tearing off his mask and thought the ball had bounced off Cogburn, who'd had his eyes closed and also hadn't seen what happened. A ball bouncing off the rubber and into foul territory was considered foul, one of the more obscure rules in the sport, but had Papazian stopped it before it crossed the third base line, it would have been judged fair and Kelly would have scored.

Having let it go, the net effect of the play was exactly zero. Sticks Kelly trudged back to third, Greenstein was still up at bat, Marvin Kowalski was the moment's hero.

On the next pitch Greenstein hit a sacrifice fly and scored Kelly anyway.

The Yankees were up 1-0, and it stayed that way through the eighth and right to the bottom of the ninth.

ABEL GANZ' DEBUT WAS BECOMING the stuff of legend, and it wasn't just for his blazing speed and tight control. It was that Ganz was playing with the canniness of a seasoned veteran. He wanted the win, not the stats, and everyone—in the Shit Hole, watching at home or listening in their cars—who understood the game knew it.

He wasn't afraid to give up grounders rather than obsess about strikeouts, and he'd intentionally walked Kowalski and pitched around Juan-Tanamera a total of six times, saving his arm to get the hitters on either side of them out. He'd listened to his catcher, too, shaking him off only when he'd doubted his ability to accurately deliver the requested pitch.

And he had all the strength and resilience of youth, his arm having been looked after by the best coaches in the league, men who knew how to strike a balance between experience and overuse, trainers who knew every therapeutic technique in the book and exactly when to use them.

Here in the bottom of the ninth he'd started off strong by striking out Vince Salvanella, putting the Yankees within two outs of their four millionth trip to the World Series. But then Donny Marshall got on base when the shortstop bobbled a line drive, and now Ganz faced a formidable challenge. Next up was Chi Chi los Parados, followed by Juan-Tanamera Aires and then Marvin Kowalski. If he let los Parados get to first, and then let Aires do the same, the bases would be loaded, with only one out when Kowalski and his certain walk came up to bat. Hell or high water Ganz had to get either los Parados or Aires out. Then he could let Kowalski on and only have to worry about Cavvy Papazian, who was 0-for-3 tonight.

Los Parados came to the plate with his usual swagger and contemptuous smirk, albeit ratcheted down a notch, which led Ganz to believe that he was all business. The first pitch looked like it was cannonballing right down the middle, so los Parados swung, but misread the slider and blew his opportunity to send it into the stands for a dramatic, game-winning homer.

Ganz threw again, the exact same pitch, and again suckered los Parados into swinging uselessly. Any fatigue the pitcher might have been feeling was swept away by the impossibly loud, jet-engine roar of the riveted crowd. This time he went for the outside corner with a fastball and just missed it, los Parados correctly anticipating the 0-and-2 pitch and wisely declining to swing.

Ganz lined his index and middle fingers across two seams and threw the next one down and away. Los Parados, apparently totally unfazed by the two strikes he already had against him, never flinched and it was ball two.

Fenoke signaled for serious heat and Ganz launched again, hoping someone would have a radar gun on him so they'd know how a real stud threw fastballs in the bottom of the ninth of a complete game, but knew as soon as the ball left his fingertips that he'd jumped the gun by a fraction of a second and released too soon. The ball sailed above the strike zone and again los Parados betrayed not a moment's hesitation in letting it go. The smirk that had temporarily left his face following the opening two strikes returned in all its grating glory. The count was 3-and-2 and no way was Ganz, who now understood what lightning reflexes meant in a batter such as the mighty los Parados, no way was he going to fiddle with the corners and think he could get away with it.

Augie Crandall called for time and trotted out to the mound, his pitching coach in tow. The first baseman joined the conference as well.

Johansen, chewing on a knuckle, watched the goings on, paying particular attention to Ganz's posture. When he saw the extraordinary rookie's shoulders droop ever so subtly, he pulled his hand from his mouth and blurted out, "They're gonna walk Chi Chi!"

"Bullshit!" Spinale spat back. "Put the winning run on base?"

But as he watched he saw Crandall turn and head back toward the dugout. When the manager was about ten feet from the mound he pointed at first base, and that's when Spinale's eyes opened wide.

Los Parados saw it too, and grinned openly now, immensely gratified that the opposition was so afraid of him that they were willing break a cardinal rule of baseball: *Never* put the winning run on base.

As soon as he took his base the Majestyks would have men on first and second, one out, and Juan-Tanamera and Kowalski the next men up at bat. Ganz would have to get Juan-Tanamera out, let Kowalski onto first, and then put Cavvy Papazian out in order to close out the inning and give the pennant to the Yankees. And that's if neither Donny Marshall nor los Parados stole a base out from under him in the meantime.

"Never mind the pitcher," Spinale said in amazement. "The freakin' *manager's* losin' it!"

Behind the plate Fenoke stood up and held his arm out well to the right, calling for the last ball to intentionally walk los Parados, who let the bat rest easily on his shoulder as Ganz brought his arm back to throw.

Down in the Majestyks dugout, Johansen was huddled with Spinale, Aires and batting coach Lefty Peterson discussing strategy. They were dissecting Bueno's upcoming turn at bat, how Ganz was likely to pitch to him and what his options were. They also discussed what kind of signs to send in to Marshall, depending on how things progressed. Should they let him attempt a steal? They discussed a lot of things, and weren't paying any attention to what was happening on the field.

So none of them saw Ganz rear back lackadaisically, and they didn't see los Parados standing nonchalantly at the plate, and they didn't see Ganz snap forward like a human missile launcher and fling a three-inch-in-diameter buzz bomb smack down the middle of the strike zone until they heard it slam into Fenoke's glove. And it was only then that they finally turned at the strange sound and saw los Parados standing at the plate looking like somebody had just encased him in a block of dry ice, and even in the highest row of the highest section of the highest deck in Mahoney Fertilizer Stadium a fan could hear the umpire, once he himself had caught on to the brutal and fiendishly brilliant deception, excitedly announce "Strike three!" against los Parados. They could hear it because, in a heartbeat, forty thousand voices had just gone deafeningly silent.

WHEN GANZ FACED BUENO AIRES for the fourth time in the game, it truly was a mere formality. Catcher Willard Fenoke stood and pointed to his right, and Ganz threw the ball wide, then did it again, on the way to intentionally walking the frustrated superstar.

Aires seemed to take the dire consequences of the hideous gaffe—and they couldn't blame it all on los Parados because there truly was collective responsibility for the lapse—personally. "Pitch to me, you foggin' ferry!" Aires shouted in wrenching exasperation as the third pitch wafted past him. He smacked the plate with the bat and pointed it toward the mound, taunting Ganz to come and get him, but the imperturbable pitcher might as well have been blind. He listened to his teammates and his coaches and his manager, not the opposition: What kind of an idiot did this bolo-spinning cowboy think he was dealing with?

With maddening calm, Ganz threw another forty-mile-an-hour piece of junk wide, and some alert but heretofore quiescent monitoring circuit in Aires' brain suddenly tripped, sizing up the trajectory and the speed and sending an urgent message to the rest of the integrated system called World-Class Athlete.

"*Wasshout!*" Aires called in fair warning to the catcher, whose arrogant insouciance about the deliberate walk could get him killed if he wasn't careful in the next half-second.

Were Bueno to step out of the batter's box he'd automatically be called out, but Ganz's understandable inattention about precisely locating these useless pitches had let one get a little too close to the plate. Aires stepped as far right as the rules allowed, noting that the newly aware catcher had moved smartly backward just as the bat started coming around. It couldn't connect solidly, because Aires

was still too far out of position, but out of all the power this her-
culean slugger could generate there was plenty left even if only half
got to the ball.

Which it did, and the ball took off toward a totally unprepared
defense that tried to rouse itself into action even as Aires began his
jet-powered flight to first, where he politely declined to safely land
after he saw the shortstop throw his body at the ball and manage to
slow it down just enough for it to dribble into the outfield, where
neither the shortstop nor the center fielder could make the play in
time to tag Aires as he slid into second.

Or Donny Marshall as he held up safely on third.

Back at home plate Yankee catcher Willard Fenoke was in a homi-
cidal fury, screaming at the ump that Aires had illegally stepped out
of the batter's box. Augie Crandall came storming out of the dugout
to take over the fray, buoyed by the righteous indignation streaming
down from the stands full of piss-and-vinegar Yankees fans who
were not afraid of the locals who outnumbered them because, if it
came down to it, the dumb hicks would probably fight fair which,
when tangling with a native New Yorker, would be like bringing a
letter opener to a gunfight.

Wisely, Johansen stayed in his dugout and didn't join in. Let the
Yankees shout themselves hoarse trying to change an umpire's judgment call. What did they think Krupke would do absent an instant
replay, which wasn't used in baseball . . . decide he'd seen it wrong,
based on all that yelling, and reverse himself? Johansen called
Kowalski in off the on-deck circle just in case blunt objects got
hurled around before it was all over.

Crandall, near-apoplectic and kicking dirt onto Krupke's shoes,
was trying to get himself thrown out of the game to inspire his players, but the ump wasn't buying it and waited for the manager to tire
himself out, which he quickly did. Order was soon restored.

"Gotta tell you, skipper:" The normally affectless Kowalski
turned to Johansen, smiled, and said something remarkable for him
and incredibly stupid for anyone to say to a manager minutes away

from ecstasy or catastrophe. "Whether we win or lose, I can't imagine it ever gets better than this."

As breaths were held in the dugout awaiting the reaction, Johansen looked at him and said, "You mean baseball?"

Kowalski shook his head. "I mean my life," he replied, heading for the dugout stairs. "Or anybody's."

Johansen turned back toward the field and watched as the kid headed for the batter's box. "I know exactly what you mean," he said quietly, to no one in particular.

YANKEE MANAGER AUGIE CRANDALL, tuckered out but not calmed down, signaled Fenoke to call for time, "spoke" to him briefly using hand signals from the dugout steps, then watched as the catcher tucked his glove under his arm and trotted out to the mound, where first baseman Brian McGowan had already joined Ganz. Crandall couldn't go himself because he'd already made one trip out there this inning; the rules said the next one could only be to pull the pitcher. (The same rule also said that Crandall's little tête-à-tête with his catcher was an attempt to circumvent the rules, and therefore should count as a visit, but such was the discretion of umpires that Krupke made no issue of it. Perhaps he decided that trying to defend the proposition that Crandall's semaphoric transmission constituted an actual conversation was simply not worth the trouble. More likely he didn't think about it at all, but let his instincts be his guide.) It was just as well that Crandall couldn't go to the mound, though, because it was a player kind of discussion.

They could barely hear themselves over the noise raining down from the stands, and huddled close.

"Soon's Kowalski takes his base," McGowan said as Fenoke reached the mound, "they got three guys on, then Papazian's up. Could be a little dicey."

"Why?" Fenoke asked. "Papazian's *ofer*—" meaning oh-for-three "—and Abel here is lookin' stronger'n when he started."

"He's pissed off, Papazian is," McGowan answered. "He's looking to nail Abel and sail one onto the interstate."

"Just 'cuz he's lookin' to don't mean he can. What was he lookin' to do his last three at-bats . . . strike out?"

Seeing that he was winning McGowan over, Fenoke went in for the close. "Abel here, he ain't gonna give him dick to hit. Guy won't be able'a run up his own asshole, right Abel?" He tapped the pitcher on the shoulder. "Abel?"

Ganz looked up slowly, then twisted his shoulder back and forth a few times, feeling it out. Fenoke's practiced eye saw that the arm was loose and strong. McGowan smiled as Ganz, in his zone and blissfully unconcerned, tossed the ball up and down, his fingers closing around it lazily.

"Let me burn this piece'a shit joke of a ballplayer," he said at last, referring to Kowalski.

It took a moment for Fenoke to process the suggestion. He'd been so fixated on what they were going to do after Kowalski walked that it had never occurred to him that there was an alternative. "Kid's never *been* burned, Abel."

"Just wreck your arm tryin'," McGowan agreed.

Ganz tossed the ball once more and then held it, cocking his wrist repeatedly. "Feel like I could throw this thing right through a god-damned brick wall, Willie, and still sting your glove comin' out t'other side. Guy's never been burned on account'a evvabody give up early in the season." He glared at Kowalski. "Throw some mutha-fuckin' speed, wear *his* arm out, not mine."

"I don't know . . ." Fenoke muttered.

"Hells'a problem with tryin', Will?" McGowan said. "Abel gets tired, he walks the sumbitch just like usual, and we're right back where we started."

"Except, like you said, Abel's tired."

"I got plenty left," Ganz insisted. "If I stop way before it gets even a little bad, McG's right: We're back to square zero, and you can tell Augie t'relieve me."

McGowan looked back toward where Kowalski was loosening up, and a nasty grin creased his mouth. "Love to see the skinny prick go down, I would."

Fenoke waved his glove toward the stands. "Whole goddamned *world* like to see that, Brian. Put a nice capper on this boring piece'a shit game."

McGowan rubbed his chin and thought it over. "Would at that, by God."

Ganz tossed the ball one last time, then looked at it as it snuggled comfortably against his hand. The anxious murmur in the crowd became an impatient buzz.

Fenoke looked over toward the dugout, found Crandall and pointed to Kowalski with a slight lift of his chin: *Abel wants him.*

The wily manager eyed him carefully for another second, assessing the strength of his conviction, then nodded and turned away: *Then let Abel have him.*

"What the hell, Abel," Fenoke said as he turned back to Ganz. "We got two out already, so let's go after him." He clapped his hands together and took his glove from under his arm. "Throw him a couple three bullets, see what you can do. We can always go after Papazian, it don't work out, so what's to lose, right? Only—"

"Yeah, I know," Ganz said happily as he stepped back. "I'll quit with plenty left. Now go on back and watch a man do his stuff."

The three of them slapped each other's backs and then Ganz was alone again, sixty feet, six inches away from the nearest human comfort, standing solo but aware that around the country fifty million pairs of eyes were fastened onto him, none knowing where tragedy and triumph would be perched when the dust finally cleared. If he got Kowalski out, he'd be almost as big a hero as if he'd pitched a perfect game. Okay, maybe not that big, but it would really be something anyway.

One out away from taking it all, Ganz wasn't worried about whether he was going to win the game; he was just wondering exactly *how* it would happen.

• • •

KOWALSKI TRIED TO LOOK as calm as he could. He knew it would be maddening for the pitcher, that it would look to him like a base on balls was so inevitable there was no sense getting excited about it. Maybe he could goad Ganz into being stupid, trying to actually strike him out or get him to pop one fair and end this game as a hero, but in reality only weakening his arm for when he had to face Papazian . . .

Kowalski dashed that thought as quickly as he'd conjured it up. It made no sense. Augie Crandall was one of the best managers in baseball and he didn't do things that made no sense.

Of course, Ganz was already a hero, at least to people who truly understood the game and realized that he'd put on an epic demonstration of strength, control and finesse. Kowalski truly didn't know how this was going to turn out—that was going to be up to Papazian, who'd have the bases loaded when he came up to bat. Maybe Marshall would try to steal home? Nah, stupid move with two outs. Then again . . .

"Play!" the ump yelled, and Kowalski shook his head to drive those thoughts out of his mind. He had a job to do, and never had it been more important to do it right. Let Johansen worry about strategy. As Sal Spinale was fond of telling overly analytical players, "Quit thinking; you're hurting the club."

He took one last practice swing and stepped to the plate, then swung lightly twice more and got himself set, staying alert in case Ganz decided to hit him rather than just walk him with wide pitches.

Pitching from the stretch without wasting any time, Ganz curled his right upper lip and threw.

How he managed to keep his arm in its socket was anybody's guess. Fenoke grunted painfully as the ball rocketed into his glove so fast the impact could be heard, unamplified, high in nosebleed heaven near the upper-deck lights.

Kowalski blinked and gulped as Fenoke, caught unawares, turned and looked at the equally startled ump, who got hold of himself and shot his arm to the side, choking out *"Straaggh!"* as if something were biting his testicles. A surprised sound exploded from the crowd, and behind that sound Kowalski could hear clapping and cheers from the Yankees dugout. He'd let strikes go by before—at least the ump had thought they were strikes although Kowalski knew better—but this one was no judgment call. This one was a laser-guided smart bomb of a pitch so dead center in the zone a plumb bob couldn't have found a flaw. And it had happened so fast Kowalski hadn't been able to get a bat on it.

No problem, he thought. *No problem. Just thought he was going to pitch around me and I wasn't ready. I got complacent, is what I got. But no more . . .*

He took a few more practice swings and got back into position. Ganz stood stock still and stared at him, which was disconcerting, so Kowalski just stared right back, one prizefighter giving it back to another.

Ganz took a brief windup, curled his lip again and threw. This time Kowalski had his radar flicked on to full alert. He homed in on the ball and, despite his amazement at its speed and accuracy, managed to swing the bat around just in time to get some wood on the horsehide.

Barely. The sound of the impact was a sickening kind of slap and the ball sprang up and back into the safety screen behind home plate.

Spinale immediately jumped to his feet. "No way he could do that on purpose!"

"No shit," Johansen mumbled softly. He'd been standing since Kowalski let a solid strike go by on the first pitch, and now he'd seen him mis-hit the ball. Johansen had thought he could sit this at-bat out and review his strategy for Papazian while Kowalski made his way to first base, but something was clearly wrong now and he wanted to do something about it, except he didn't know what to do because he didn't know exactly what it was that was wrong.

Ganz threw a curve, the spinning ball looking as if a cyclone had pushed it sideways. Kowalski let it go for a ball, the first, and the count was 1-and-2 as Fenoke barely managed to get his glove on it.

Kowalski slapped a sinker away, then another curve. Ganz, with no need to worry about anybody stealing since the only possible target was home plate, wound up big, curled his lip and let fly another chunk of molten metal. Kowalski, alerted by the pitcher's facial expression, hit it a bit more solidly this time and sent it foul down the third base line.

More curves, two sliders and another sinker. Kowalski batted them all away crisply and let one go for another ball: 2-and-2. Ganz wound up with his lip curled again and launched another screaming cruise missile, Kowalski once again barely getting the bat on it for another pop-up back into the screen.

Now Kowalski was scared. This hadn't happened to him all season. It had never happened to him in his *life*. He had no experience with it and wasn't sure what to do. He was quaking from so many epicenters of nervousness that the tremors were canceling each other out when they met, and he actually looked calm even while his insides were shrieking in protest.

Ganz threw another fastball, and Kowalski swung at it tentatively. He managed to foul it, but this admission to himself that he was in trouble only heightened his anxiety. He was tempted to look toward the dugout and plead with Johansen for some help, but he had at least enough sense left to know that there wasn't a damned thing anybody could do but call time and give him a reprieve, but he also knew that all he'd do in that time was work himself into a full-blown psychosis, so he kept his eyes on the mound and gritted his teeth. *This was the Bigs, goddamnit,* and everybody else got into situations like this and dealt with them and so would he.

Another lip curl and another monster fastball. Kowalski swatted it away again, and swore he could see ruby-red slivers of light shooting out of Ganz's eyes. It had to be costing the pitcher something, all the stuff he'd been pulling out of his bag, all the rockets he'd been throwing. He had to be tiring, his arm had to be hurting. He couldn't keep this up.

An outside-in breaking pitch, and Kowalski thought it would be his third ball, but then realized he'd been crowding the plate so he took a half-step back to keep from getting hit and swatted the ball foul at the same time.

Ganz threw a sinker but it dropped too fast and Kowalski let it smack into the dirt in front of Fenoke. Full count, 3-and-2. One more strike and the game—and the Majestyks' season—was over. One more ball and Kowalski was on first base with Aires on second, Marshall on third and Papazian up to bat.

The noise from the crowd at that point was probably waking up hibernating polar bears at the North Pole, but it looked to Kowalski like the single-minded Ganz wasn't even hearing it as he contemplated his next pitch. A sudden thought slammed into Kowalski's consciousness, the dreadful realization that this wasn't fun anymore, that he simply didn't want to be here, but as Ganz started into his windup, he once again forced a potentially destructive idea from his mind.

Ganz leaned way back, so far back it was hard to see how he kept his balance, and Kowalski steeled himself to receive what was undoubtedly going to be the fastest fastball ever launched in the entire history of the game. He watched Ganz's feet, the arch of his back, his throwing hand, and then he looked at his face.

Ganz's lips were set in a straight line. There was not the faintest hint of an upturn at the corner of his mouth.

No lip curl.

What the fuck is he doing! Kowalski wondered frantically and in uncharacteristically profane terms.

He figured it out in the subsequent millisecond, as Ganz brought his left foot down, uncoiling easily, letting his body run out of momentum and whipping his arm forward.

Except this time he didn't backspin the ball with one final snap of his fingers, but "squeezed" it out of his hand instead.

A change-up. Looked like a fastball but was really just a gentle lob. This one was straight for the center of the strike zone.

To Kowalski it was like watching a pearl drop through a jar of molasses in a Siberian winter. He felt like he could have gone out for a cheeseburger and gotten back in time to be there when it crossed the plate.

The ball heading his way didn't look to Kowalski like its thrower had been suffering any ill effects from all the missiles he'd been heaving for nine innings. Even this soft trick shot was elegant in its precision, every slow turn of the stitches exactly what Ganz had intended.

There was nothing cogent and sequential about Kowalski's decision-making process. It wasn't a reasoned conclusion following carefully considered propositions. It was far too powerful for that, far too *right*.

He brought his left leg up slightly as he took the bat back a few degrees, just like Bueno had shown him. Then he thrust his hips forward, building up potential energy to be used to swing his upper body around in synchrony with his arms as they extended. Every cell of every muscle in his body reacted in unison to focus energy down into the bat. He swung, and by the time the leading edge of the bat came perpendicular to the path of the ball and his eyes had squeezed into slits with the effort, his contribution to the swing was at an end and the bat was on its own, consigned irretrievably to the path Kowalski had chosen for it, and he prayed for the stinging shock in his hands that would let him know he'd connected.

UP IN SECTION F, Louie Scaluzzo, still groggy from the whiskey-drenched flight from New York, awoke with a start from the light snooze he'd entered into as soon as Marvin Kowalski had come to bat. It wasn't the crack of a struck ball that had woken him. It was something else, and as he sniffled and snorted his way awake, he realized that it wasn't noise that had roused him but, rather, the lack of it.

"Christ A'mighty," his buddy Ralphie Wiener was saying. "Fuggin' idjit hit it fair!"

"Who-wah?" Louie asked, wondering why the stadium had suddenly gone quiet. "Who hit what fair?"

"Kowalski," Ralphie answered, pointing to where a tiny white dot was rising against the robin's-egg sky.

"Kowalski?" Louie sat up straight and blinked several times. "Gedadda here!"

•   •   •

"YOU DUMB SONOFABITCH!" Spinale was screaming as he tried to climb out of the dugout so he could strangle Marvin Kowalski in front of fifty million witnesses. Only Zuke Johansen and Cavvy Papazian hanging from his back managed to stop him from making it to the field.

When he was sure Papazian had good hold of Spinale, Johansen stepped forward and held up a hand to shield his eyes from the sun burning away above the upper deck. Sure enough, Kowalski had taken a full swing and only now was the ball reaching its apex and starting to succumb to gravity. It looked from this angle like it was headed directly to the foul pole in the stands beyond third base, but it wasn't clear what it was going to do once it got there.

Kowalski was frozen at home plate, watching just like everybody else. Even Bueno on second base was rooted to the spot, not even bothering to try to figure out what he ought to be doing right about now.

In fact the only person in the entire stadium—and, as a practical matter, in the entire country—who was keeping his head and taking decisive action was Yankees left fielder Orlando Perpado, who had been thinking about what to order at Sardi's later that evening back in New York until he saw Kowalski swing. Once he realized what was happening, he'd lit out for the foul pole, losing his hat as he tilted his head up to follow the ball.

Perpado felt the warning track under his feet and took a quick look over his right shoulder to make sure he wasn't going to slam into the wall, then positioned himself just at the base of the foul pole, ready to make any required midcourse corrections as he continued to judge the ball, but there were none to be made. Now, he could only wait and watch.

"GET READY, RALPHIE!" screamed Louie Scaluzzo, now fully awake.

"I'm there, baby! Come to Papa!"

Louie and Ralphie were seated in foul territory, where this ball was headed, and they were ready to execute The Plan, the one where Ralphie, the better catcher of the two, would snag the ball while Louie "t'rew a good beatin'" to any would-be contenders who thought they had as much right to it as they did.

Ralphie had his hands up—the ball was headed right for him—and Louie tore his eyes away so he could concentrate on threat assessment, but they'd badly misjudged the trajectory, because the ball hadn't been struck perfectly clean and was carrying a high rate of spin.

"Whu'happened?" Ralphie asked, befuddled.

What happened was that the purely ballistic component that had initially sent the ball on a straight path was beginning to give way to aerodynamics as the stitches on the leather cover started biting into the air. The ball, as though having made an en route decision, began drifting to the right.

Louie looked up just in time to spot it well away from where it should have been. "Ah, shit," he said dejectedly, not even bothering to watch it as it floated uselessly away.

ORLANDO PERPADO, WHO'D AT FIRST positioned himself well outside the left field foul line, began to shift slightly as his brain quickly calculated the ball's change in trajectory. He took a step, then another, then several more. Then he stepped over the white line painted on the ground.

And found himself in fair territory.

Suddenly it wasn't about turning a foul ball into an out; it was about making sure that it wasn't a base hit.

The ball picked up speed as it plummeted downward, and Perpado saw that it was headed right for the wall above his head. At the last possible second he jumped up as high as he could, reaching with his glove hand, seeing that the ball was a few inches further back than he'd projected, bending his wrist so that his hand extended over the upper lip of the wall.

He felt the ball strike his glove just as he ran out of upward momentum and started back down. He flexed his knees to absorb the shock of landing, then reached in with his free hand, grabbed the ball and held it up in the air, dancing as he celebrated the final out and yet another pennant win for the venerable Yankees.

At least that was the plan. But when he reached into his glove there was no ball there, and as he stared at his hands, confused and disoriented, a sound erupted out of the stands the likes of which hadn't been heard since lions had been let loose in the Roman Colosseum some two thousand years earlier.

It took a few seconds for the enormity of it to set in, because Perpado's benumbed mind couldn't figure out what was worse: That he'd missed the catch . . .

. . . or that Marvin Kowalski (*Marvin Kowalski!*) had hit a home run . . .

. . . or that the Majestyks had just won the pennant and everybody was going to blame *him*.

While that last bit was going through Perpado's head, it was also going on in Ganz's, the pitcher paralyzed into catatonia even as the Majestyks were emptying out of their dugout to begin an on-field celebration not seen since the one the Miracle Mets of 1969 had at Shea Stadium that had resulted in five hospitalizations. Delirious fans were already throwing themselves over the wall to get onto the field and the security force, mostly local Iowans whose only experience with civil insurrection was what they'd seen on CNN, were seriously questioning whether minimum wage comprised a moral obligation to put one's life in danger on behalf of baseball players who were making nine hundred times that amount.

Down on the field, Kowalski had recovered enough to motion frantically to his teammates and then hold his palms parallel as he repeatedly pumped his hands toward first base. Chi Chi los Parados caught on right away, and waved two dozen scurrying security guards into formation behind him, leading them to the edge of the playing field and then sending them forward.

By that time Johansen and Spinale had joined up as well, and Johansen yelled, "Get him around the goddamned bases!"

Nodding their understanding, the guards quickly formed a flying wedge in front of Kowalski and aimed it toward first. Kowalski fell in step behind them and began his trip around the bases, the guards running interference against the mob that was rapidly filling up the field.

The fans caught on right away, and began yelling and waving at one another to stay back. By the time Kowalski rounded first, they'd begun linking arms to form a gauntlet on either side of the base line as the surging mass of bodies pressed inward on them. The line held, and the people standing twenty- and thirty-deep on either side of it stopped shoving and started applauding. They clapped, they screamed as loudly as they could, they whistled and blew air horns and jumped up and down and generally did anything they could think of to let the full glory of their delirium rain down onto the skinny kid who was trying to make sure to touch every base lest some nit-picking umpire decided to make a case that, while it probably wouldn't stick, would likely get that ump an instant face-to-face with whatever deity he called his own.

Massed at home plate were the remaining Des Moines Majestyks, manic with jubilation, wild in their dancing and gyrating. That it had been only a few inches that stood between this tumultuous celebration of a home run versus an on-field lynching for Kowalski's unauthorized swat at the ball seemed hopelessly irrelevant at the moment, the ecstatic ballplayers quivering with the anticipation of jumping on the kid and mashing him into the ground before tossing him as high into the sky as they could. Impossibly, unbelievably, the rocket-engine roar from the crowd nearly doubled as Kowalski stepped on home plate and was immediately swept up into the arms of his teammates.

"Ah, piss," Ralphie in Section F said as he kicked disconsolately at the seat in front of him. "I really wanted that freakin' ball."

Twenty

JOY IN MUDVILLE!" screamed the banner headline in the *Des Moines Register*.

"Slumlord Gets Probation" was the front-page story in the *New York Daily News*.

The tone of the headlines carried over into the detailed stories as well. Dailies throughout Iowa and neighboring states variously described Kowalski as having ripped, smashed, launched, clobbered, slugged, drilled or blasted the ball over the fence.

The *New York Post* said that hometown pitcher Abel Ganz "had given up a grand slam in the ninth."

"Holy cow!" Marvin Kowalski yelped as he looked at his watch.

"S'matter?" Juan-Tanamera Aires asked him.

Kowalski rubbed at his eyes and sat up, trying to get his bearings. Looking around, he was momentarily surprised to find himself in the Majestyks locker room at Mahoney Fertilizer Stadium, then remembered that he'd gone there the night before to try to escape from Ocheyedan. The little town in Osceola County had more reporters in it than permanent population, and fighting them off was like fighting off a cold in the middle of an Arctic snowstorm.

As for the other players sprawled around the room, they'd also sought some respite from the nonstop celebrating that had overtaken not only the city of Des Moines but the entire state of Iowa.

"Supposed to meet somebody for breakfast," Kowalski replied as he got to his feet and headed for the shower.

When he came out he found Aires, Papazian, Amos and Spinale huddled in muted conversation, which stopped as soon as he reentered the locker room. "What's going on? How come everybody's looking so glum?"

"We open the Series in a National League park," Amos said.

"Yeah, so?"

"So," Papazian picked up, "you won't be playing in the first two games."

"Or the last two," Spinale added. "Assumin' we need 'em."

The World Series alternated yearly between starting in the American League team's home field and the National League's, and it was two games there, the next three in the other ballpark, then back for two more, depending on how many games were actually needed for one team to win four in the best-of-seven contest. This year the first two games would be in the National League park, where the designated hitter rule wouldn't apply.

Kowalski turned to fetch a clean shirt out of his locker. "So what's the big deal?" he said as casually as he could, knowing full well what the big deal was. He heard some loudly exhaled breaths followed by more muttering. He paused for a second, then got the shirt and shrugged it on. He reached in for his pants, then turned and walked toward where his teammates were rousing themselves to sitting positions.

"Be real, kid," Papazian said. "This isn't some pissant team from Palookaville we're talkin' here. These guys won the National League pennant, f'Chrissakes!"

"Lot damn tougher than ours was," Spinale pointed out.

"And you're thinking, what?" Kowalski asked as he began pulling on his pants. "You can't beat them?"

"No, I think we can beat 'em," Papazian said, then pointed to Kowalski and made a circle encompassing everybody. "*We* can beat 'em, but that includes you."

"And joo not playin' in a copple games," Aires threw in.

Kowalski tried to act normally as he fiddled with his belt, but soon gave up the pretense and sat down on a bench facing the others. "That's why you're all so gloomy? Because I'm not going to be playing?"

"Well, shit," Spinale said. "You think we need a better reason?"

Kowalski shook his head. "You don't need anything else, Sal. And you don't need me."

"Yeah," Spinale *harumphed* noisily. "I ain't one to get sloppy sentimental, kid, but we weren' azactly settin' the league on fire before you got here."

"But you are now," Kowalski countered.

"Proves my point."

"No it doesn't."

"Listen—"

"Sal, whatever it was I might have contributed, that's all there is. And you've got it all."

"What're you talking about, Marvin?" Amos asked, perplexed. "What you do at bat, how do you figure you can't do that anymore?"

"Didn't say that, John. What I'm saying is, you don't *need* me to do it anymore. You guys can win on your own."

"Marvin—"

"I'm just a gimmick, don't you get it? Maybe I was able to get a few things moving here and there—"

"You showed us how to read pitchers," Papazian said.

"Even umpires," Amos concurred.

"You figured out what was wrong with Zacky's knuckleball," Spinale threw in. "And a lotta other stuff."

"Okay," Kowalski said, hands in the air. "So what are you telling me now, Sal, that as soon as I'm off the field you're going to forget it all?"

There was some squirming, until Aires reminded them of something. "You still da guy gets to first ever' time, Marvin. You still dat guy."

"Yeah, well, there's that," Kowalski said, grinning sheepishly, and drawing smirks from the others. "But what I'm trying to tell you is, you don't need that. You haven't needed it for a while."

Kowalski looked at his watch again and stood up to finish buckling his belt. "You guys won thirty-eight of your last fifty games."

"*We* won 'em," Papazian reminded him. "Including you."

"And of those," Kowalski continued, as though he hadn't been interrupted, "*you* won eighty percent by more than two runs." He stopped, assuming that the conclusion would be obvious, but got only blank stares.

"And somehow this explains everything to us," Spinale finally said with considerable sarcasm.

Kowalski spread his hands in front of him. "In most of those games, the number of runs that I had something to do with was *less* than the margin of victory."

"Ah, I get it now," Spinale said.

"Joo do?" Aires exclaimed.

"Nope," Spinale affirmed.

"What I'm trying to tell you," Kowalski said, "in all of those games, if you take away the runs I helped to get, you had enough extra to have won anyway. And who's to say you wouldn't have also gotten the runs I *was* in on?"

His analysis was greeted with some skepticism, which he interpreted as reluctance to concede the point, so he pressed it. "We also won most of the interleague games we played in National League parks. I didn't play in any of those."

Kowalski furrowed his brow, as if in amazement that these guys didn't get it. What could be simpler?

"For a guy without a contract for next season," Spinale said at last, "you sure are makin' a helluva argument for somethin' less than billions."

Kowalski turned and walked rapidly back to his locker. "I really gotta go. Late already."

Spinale watched him leave. "Swear to God," he said, shaking his head in amazement, "I can still see a piece'a wheat hangin' outta that hick's mouth."

ZUKE JOHANSEN AND MARVIN KOWALSKI sat in the Metropolitan Grill of the Des Moines Club, one of the few places in the United States where they could be assured of not being disturbed.

"Lot of pressure coming down from the front office," Johansen said after the waiter had taken their breakfast order, "and you need to give some serious thought to the future."

Kowalski looked at him, a trace of puzzlement evident in his features. "Zuke, I—"

"Problem with baseball, it doesn't have this college draft business like football and basketball. We've got guys barely made it through high school, and the thing is, if they don't get called up they're worse off than if they'd never gotten signed at all, because they don't have the sheepskin to fall back on, see? That's why a good agent, he tries to get new guys an ironclad deal way up front, just in case."

Kowalski looked away, clearly uncomfortable with where his manager was steering the conversation.

"You want to end up working as a bed buddy at the Garden of Eden?"

"What?" Kowalski jerked his head back. He couldn't have heard that right. "What'd you say?"

"You ever hear of a ballplayer named Anton Stuyvesant?"

"No."

"Played for the Marshalltown Riots, farm team of ours. Arguably the hottest prospect in baseball three years ago until he tore a rotator cuff five weeks before signing one of the richest contracts ever. Know what he's doing now?"

"You said, um, something about the Garden of Eden?"

"Of *Feedin'*. Stuyvesant's a bed buddy, Marvin. Sleeps with four or five dogs a night at a super-ritzy kennel called the Garden of Feedin' Pet Hotel. They take care of rich people's pets, kind who're used to sleeping in bed with their owners who can afford to pay for other people to do it for them when they're away on vacation or what-the-hell-ever."

Kowalski smiled. "That's a good one, Zuke."

"I'm not kidding. One of the potentially greatest players in baseball is providing warmth and comfort to Binky, Muffin and Snookums for seven bucks an hour because he waited too long before signing a long-term contract which, even though he would've gotten injured anyway, at least would have protected him financially."

He could see that he had made an impact, so he moved in. "We're going into the World Series in a couple of days and neither you nor I know what's going to happen. You could be worth a fortune in two weeks or you could wind up being—"

"Zuke, I'm not playing in the Series."

Some instinctive defense mechanism that had been present in the species since it first crept up out of the swamps kicked in deep within Johansen's brain, preventing him from fully processing Kowalski's entire sentence but still allowing a sense of danger to seep through. "I . . . did you . . . what?"

"I'm not playing in the Series. Hey, are you okay? Zuke?"

THE WAITER BROUGHT A GLASS OF orange juice with ice. Johansen managed to refocus after a few deep gulps.

"I *can't* play, Zuke. College started weeks ago, and if I don't get there right away I'll blow the whole semester."

Johansen set the glass down carefully. "You were serious about this going to college business?"

"Why do you think I've been reading all those physics books?" Kowalski grimaced and looked away, then back again. "But if you could learn that stuff just from books, I wouldn't need to go to MIT, would I? So I'm really behind and I can't wait any longer."

He could easily read the competing emotions on the manager's face. On the one hand, he wouldn't feel right trying to talk somebody out of getting an education. On the other, college sure seemed trivial compared to the World Series. What was the right counsel here? To whom—and to what—did Johansen owe greater loyalty?

But Kowalski knew there was no need for him to feel so conflicted, because there was really nothing for him to decide. "We're not negotiating, Zuke. I'm just telling you some news, is all."

That sounded harsher than he'd intended, but he didn't want to soften it and risk inadvertently stringing Johansen along, so he changed subjects. "So how much did you end up paying Jannine?"

The non sequitur threw Johansen completely. "Who?"

"The girl who went to the police in New York. What'd you pay her?"

Johansen scrambled to recover. "You mean to drop the charges?"

Kowalski smiled. "I mean, to set me up. And what did the cops get out of it?"

Johansen blinked several times and scratched his nose, fighting for time to think. "What are you talking about?"

"I'm talking about how you got her to fake an assault charge and got the cops to go along and scare the living bejesus out of me."

There was no sense pretending it was otherwise. "When'd you figure it out?"

"When I had a chance to calm down and think after I was through being the biggest jerk on the planet. Wondering why some girl just happens to have a gun in her handbag and just happens to have this perfect scam for a celebrity she had no way to know she was going to meet, after Chi Chi just happened to maneuver me right to her. Why the cops backed off so fast, and how you even found her in the first place."

"How'd you know she didn't just drop the charges after we paid her off?"

Kowalski laughed. "That's something you only hear in movies, Zuke. She can't 'drop the charges,' she can only withdraw a complaint and refuse to testify, but the cops don't need her to move ahead and charge me."

"What if she refuses to cooperate?"

"Supposedly, she'd already provided all the evidence they needed. That's what she told me she was going to do, and they could have nailed her for filing a false complaint if she backed away. None of it made sense."

Johansen, busted, looked away.

"What made you finally decide to do something?"

"Your parents called. Saw you on television and knew something wasn't right." He could sense Kowalski wincing at that. "Weren't you mad?"

"Mad?" Kowalski leaned forward, forcing Johansen to look at him. "It's why I stayed as long as I did, Zuke. That you guys would go to that kind of trouble for me?"

Johansen shifted uncomfortably in his seat. "Yeah, well, don't get the impression we did it because anybody liked you. Just needed you to play."

"Got it." Kowalski picked up a piece of toast, turned it around a few times and put it back. "So what else did they say?"

"Who?"

"My folks. They want to know if I was going to church?"

"Never came up. But your pop said you once asked him why they didn't walk the Mighty Casey."

Kowalski smiled, whether at the memory or out of relief that an uncomfortable stretch of the conversation had passed, Johansen couldn't tell. "The Mudville nine were down by two runs in the bottom of the ninth," Kowalski said.

"Cooney and Barrows both went down at bat," Johansen continued. "Two outs, with Flynn and Blake up before Casey would get his turn, and those two guys were awful hitters."

" 'But Flynn let drive a single, to the wonderment of all, and Blake, the much despised, tore the cover off the ball.' "

" 'There was Jimmy safe on second and Flynn a-huggin' third.' Blake got a double. Men on second and third."

"First base was open."

"So you wanted to know why they didn't just walk Casey, the most feared slugger in the league, and set up an easy force at any base. How come you never asked me?"

"Didn't have to; you told me anyway."

"I did?"

Kowalski nodded. "July 16. We were playing Oakland, Donny pitching. Bottom of the ninth, us up by two, they had two outs and guys on second and third, with Benny Green coming up to bat."

"I remember. Green was hitting .333 at the time."

"Right. We could have walked him and pitched to Alonzo Peete, but we didn't. I asked you why not and you said—"

"Because you never put the winning run on base."

"So Donny played Green straight up and got him out on a grounder." Kowalski held up his hands and let them drop. "Which is why they didn't walk the Mighty Casey."

Johansen shook his head in wonder. "Never occurred to me we were playing a poem." He grinned wryly. "Guess you must'a thought I was pretty smart, eh?"

Kowalski shrugged. "I did for a minute. Then the Deacon said something . . ."

The grin left Johansen's face. "Whud he say?"

"He said, 'The success of a rain dance is entirely dependent on timing.'"

"He—" Johansen's jaw fell open. "That sonofabitch!"

They laughed together, but soon the pleasant moment passed and an awkward silence set in. "Look," Kowalski finally said, "the most games I could play in anyway is three."

"That plus one more wins us the Series," Johansen shot back. "You want to let your teammates down?" He almost added "again," but it wasn't necessary.

"You don't need me, Zuke. The guys can win it legitimately. Just look at the stats the last half of the season. You always said baseball is about numbers, right?"

Johansen already knew the numbers. "But you're forgetting something, Marvin."

"Am I?"

Johansen nodded. "You're forgetting the spark-plug factor."

Kowalski smiled skeptically. "More baseball history?"

Johansen took another sip of orange juice. "Look, you're the one who told the Deacon you can't treat affairs of the heart like calculus problems."

"Which has what to do with the price of eggs in Hungary?"

"You can't ignore the effect you had on the team, that's what. They had some talent, but what they needed was some extra motivation after Canfield blew the player budget." He held his hand out, fingertips pointing toward Kowalski. "You supplied that. You gave them something to rally around. You got them reading pitchers, reading *umpires*, for Pete's sake." He put his hand down and sat back on his chair. "What you did, Marvin, you got them not only believing but *thinking*."

"Maybe. But these are grown men, and assuming they needed me in the first place, they don't need me anymore. They *know* they can win. They've already proved it."

"But—"

"And if I stay on for the Series and we win but I don't come back next year, they're going to spend the entire off-season worrying about if they can do it again, listening to reporters telling them they can't, starting to believe it themselves . . ."

Johansen saw the wisdom, but also knew that Kowalski's analysis was missing a crucial piece of information, that Mars Lee had tanked one of the pennant games the Majestyks had won. There was no way Johansen was going to mention that in this conversation.

But something else about this interaction was nagging at him. It just wasn't possible that this kid was throwing away an opportunity that a billion other people would kill for. "That explains the boys, but what about you?"

"Sorry?"

"You, Marvin. Tell me the real reason you can't just put MIT off for a year."

Kowalski lost his smile and his slightly condescending attitude along with it, and looked away. The tables in the near-empty Grill were set fancier than the last wedding he'd been to in Ocheyedan. "Because I'm a joke, Zuke, and I don't want to be a joke."

Johansen fingered his butter knife, turning it over and over in his hands. "What you do is legitimate, Marvin."

Kowalski shrugged but didn't turn toward his manager.

"It may be novel and unusual but it's legitimate, and it's completely within the spirit of the game. Look, the first time somebody figured out how to throw a knuckleball it was the same thing. A baseball that dances around like a drunken sailor, unpredictable and crazy and how the hell is anybody supposed to hit the damned thing? Now it's as routine as a double play. So who knows?" He dropped the knife with a clang, and Kowalski finally turned and looked at him. "Maybe in a few years there's gonna be a dozen guys in the league who can't hit worth a shit, but they can read pitchers and they're coordinated enough to hit foul balls all day. Maybe they'll even call 'em Kowalskis, who the hell knows?"

Kowalski laughed, despite his sudden feeling of dejection. "Maybe. But you know that won't happen, for a few reasons, the first being that nobody in his right mind would take the time to cultivate a ridiculous skill like that. Second, it wouldn't be worth it, and you know why."

Johansen did know why. It was because very few managers would waste the precious DH spot on batters who couldn't hit doubles, sacrifices, the occasional home run, and who couldn't run like the wind once they got on base, stealing once in a while and grabbing extra bases if they saw even the slightest window of opportunity. Marvin Kowalski really was a one-trick pony, and maybe his contribution did have more to do with his effect on the team rather than his perfect on-base percentage.

But there was no discounting that effect. "Is there anything at all I can say or—"

Kowalski shook his head. "It's been the greatest experience I ever had, and will probably ever have. But I know deep down that if I stick around, it'll all go sour, and then nobody will remember how great it was, only how it ended. You know what DiMaggio said when somebody asked him why he was retiring when he still had some years left?"

Johansen nodded, knowing this non-negotiation really was over: *Because I want them to remember me as I am, not as I was.*

He caught the waiter's eye and made a writing motion in the air, indicating he was ready for the check. He picked the napkin out of his lap and threw it onto the table, then said to Kowalski, "So what are your plans for next summer vacation?"

Epilogue

October 21—Game 1 of the World Series

FREDO GUITTIEREZ COULDN'T DRIVE the butterflies out of his stomach, and was sorry he hadn't taken a ten-mile jog that morning. Adrenaline might be just the thing for a linebacker or a marathon runner or a speed skater, but for golfers and baseball players it could be deadly. There is no harder feat in sports than hitting a big-league pitch, and nervous chemicals whizzing around your system did not make for a calm eye and a steady hand.

Guittierez jumped up and down in place several times and drew a few deep breaths. The pitcher threw one last warm-up pitch and nodded at his catcher. The umpire pulled his mask down and pointed to Guittierez. "Play!" he said, unable to keep a slight but clearly excited smile off his face, and Guittierez dropped two of the three bats he'd been swinging and headed to the plate, the already deafening noise from the crowd growing even louder.

•   •   •

IN THE VISITORS' DUGOUT Zuke Johansen had run out of finger-nails and was getting ready to start chewing skin as the last strains of the national anthem drifted off into the early evening sky. He could picture the news guys up in their little glassed-in aerie chortling over how the Majestyks, the beleaguered leaguers, had managed to worm their way into the Series. Many thought they'd done it on the coattails of Marvin Kowalski, the player they'd dubbed "The Kid Who Batted a Thousand." Because walks didn't count in computing batting averages, Kowalski had only had one of-ficial at-bat all season. He'd hit a home run and was therefore one for one, and that translated to a batting average of 1.000.

It was just a joke, of course, because you needed a minimum num-ber of at-bats to actually get an official percentage. The league might even change the rules to prevent the recurrence of the situation, just like, as Kowalski's father had told Johansen, the New York City school system had outlawed the dunk in high school basketball in order to stop a human redwood named Lew Alcindor from making a mockery of every game he played.

But Kowalski had left them with more than a dubious legacy and a pennant win, and Johansen had gotten over his trepidation that the wheels would come off again now that the kid was gone. He watched as Guittierez took his warm-up swings, tossed away the extra bats and strode purposefully to the plate. Sure, Fredo was nervous as hell. Joe DiMaggio had been nervous as hell, and Ted Williams and Babe Ruth and Mario Andretti and Luciano Pavarotti and Jack Nicklaus and anybody else who'd ever taken the spotlight in major events.

Guittierez was nervous but he wasn't *scared*. Johansen could see that in his confidently squared shoulders and his chin held high and the casual dip of his head to the catcher as he came from behind him and took up his position next to the plate. Nobody on the team de-luded themselves that they were going to walk off with the champi-onship in four games, nor did many of them hold out a lot of hope that they'd win at all, but they were fairly sure they'd at least give these guys and the fans a run for their money.

• • •

GUITTIEREZ TOOK A FEW MORE SWINGS as the pitcher checked to make sure his teammates were in place and alert. The pitcher then assessed Guittierez's stance—how close he was standing to the plate, was he holding the bat loose or with a death grip, were his elbows high or low and was he swaying with anticipation or locked into a tight posture—then he turned to the matter of getting a sign from the catcher and nodded his agreement to the very first one.

Guittierez picked the bat up off his shoulder and wiggled the tip to make sure he knew where his wrists were. He saw the pitcher breathe in deeply and then lean back as he lifted his left leg and brought his right arm back up over his shoulder. Guittierez kept his eyes locked onto his face and just as the big man started to bring his leg back down, saw both his eyebrows rise up in unison and the corner of his tongue flick upward over his lip . . .

Guittierez felt serenity beginning to radiate outward from his chest as he waited patiently for the outside slider to arrive.

Afterword

IN ELEMENTARY SCHOOL some forty years ago, I heard about a baseball book written for children in which a rookie ballplayer could hit any pitch foul and walked every time he came to bat. In the years since, I'd never forgotten that simple story line, but all my efforts to locate a copy were of no avail, and I always regretted that such a wonderful story might be forever lost to obscurity.

Last year when Doubleday asked me to write a book about baseball, my instincts drove me clearly in one direction, which was to take that basic premise and write a story for adults. Only after I turned in the manuscript did a remarkable coincidence come to light: Doubleday itself had published the original, in 1951. It was entitled *The Kid Who Batted 1.000*, by Bob Allison and Frank Ernest Hill, and I was finally able to obtain an original copy and read it.

My version has little in common with the original other than its very simple, very wonderful premise.

Acknowledgments

OPINIONS EXPRESSED in this book are those of Joe Adcock, Atilla, Bob Babbitt, Red Barber, Jacques Barzun, Yogi Berra, Yogi Berra, Yogi Berra, Jim Bouton, Lefty Gomez, Sandy Koufax, Bowie Kuhn, Reggie Jackson, Pete LaCock, Sam MacDowell, Machiavelli, Willy Mays, Hizzoner Robert Morrill, Jim Murray, Satchel Paige, Rick Reilly, Vin Scully, James Thurber, Joe Torre, Ted Williams, Rick Wise, *et pluribus al*, and not necessarily those of the author, who takes no responsibility whatsoever. The author also wishes to observe that any errors are solely the fault of others who, if they had any real stones, would assume complete liability for all of them, including any consequential damages arising therefrom.

The author is particularly indebted to Morgan "Shortcake" Brenner, a true lover of baseball and a walking treasure trove of information about the game, even if it is usually delivered accompanied by some of the most atrocious puns in the history of the language.